IN BONDS OF THE EARTH

First published in 2016 by Sinful Press.
www.sinfulpress.co.uk
Copyright © 2016 Janine Ashbless
Cover design by Deranged Doctor Design
The right of Janine Ashbless to be identified as the author of this work has been asserted in accordance with the Copyright, Designs and Patents Act, 1988.
All rights reserved. No part of this publication may be reproduced or transmitted in any form or by any means, electronic or mechanical, including photocopy, recording or any information storage and retrieval system, without permission in writing from the publisher.

A CIP catalogue record for this book is available from the British Library

ISBN-13: 978-1-910908-08-2
This book is a work of fiction. Names, characters, businesses, organisations, places and events are either the product of the author's imagination or are used fictitiously. Any resemblance to actual persons, living or dead, events or locales is entirely coincidental.

NB: All Bible quotes are from the King James Version. All quotes from The Book of Enoch are from the R. H. Charles translation (1917).

Wishing you heavenly fun!
xxxx Janine

JANINE ASHBLESS
IN BONDS OF THE EARTH

BOOK OF THE WATCHERS:
PART TWO

SINFUL PRESS

"An absolute must read. In this, *In Bonds of the Earth*, Janine Ashbless' impressive knowledge of primeval Christianity and her passion for plot-brimming storytelling renders yet another gripping fantasy that ravishes readers, all while on a journey to the ancient rock-cut churches of Lalibela, Ethiopia. I must confess…I would follow Ashbless' *Milja* and her exquisitely rebellious *Azazel* anywhere. My heart quickens for book three."

—

Rose Caraway, writer, audiobook narrator, and editor of The Sexy Librarian series

"No one weaves together sizzling erotica and ace storytelling better than Janine Ashbless. Her books are always a pleasure to read."

—

K D Grace, author of The Tutor & The Initiation of Ms Holly

"Janine Ashbless creates pure magic with words—her stories are darkly erotic and enticing, powerful and wickedly strange, yet at their very core, romantic. Poetry for dark angels and a tale that will literally hold readers enthralled…hold them, and not lightly set them free."

—

Kate Douglas, bestselling author of Wolf Tales, Spirit Wild, and Intimate Relations

Dedicated to the amazing and beautiful land of Ethiopia and especially to our guide, Gebre.

And from henceforth you shall not ascend into heaven unto all eternity, and in bonds of the earth the decree has gone forth, to bind you for all the days of the world. And previously you shall have seen the destruction of your beloved sons, and ye shall have no pleasure in them, but they shall fall before you by the sword. And your petition on their behalf shall not be granted, nor yet on your own: even though you weep and pray
  - The Book of Enoch 14: 5-6

Contents

Prologue

Chapter one
Professional Misconduct 1

Chapter two
Egrigoroi 15

Chapter three
Roshana 37

Chapter four
Let's be Friends 53

Chapter five
The Seed of Angels 66

Chapter six
Penemuel 82

Chapter seven
There Were Giants on the Earth in Those Days 107

Chapter eight
Lalibela 124

Chapter nine
Empty, Swept, and Garnished 145

Chapter ten
Blessed are Those who Die in the Lord 163

Chapter eleven
Delivered Them Into Chains 182

Chapter twelve
A Complication We Don't Need 197

Chapter thirteen
Fever 214

Chapter fourteen
From Out of the Strong Came Forth Sweetness 231

Chapter fifteen
Sympathy for the Devil 245

Chapter sixteen
Colors of the Fall 265

Chapter seventeen
Only Blood is Forever 283

About the Author 304

PROLOGUE

In the beginning God created the heavens and the earth...

That's how we're used to hearing it, and yes—that's how Azazel would tell it. I think. Bear in mind that he's not exactly forthcoming with explanations. He's got more urgent things on his mind when he pays me a visit. I'm piecing the story together from fragments he's dropped in the limited moments he's both present and not busy nailing me, as well as from things told to me by other angels. I'm flat-out guessing at bits, I admit.

God created the earth and He wanted someone else to appreciate what He'd done, so He made angels. I think this was shortly before the appearance of life on the planet, so... about four billion years ago. Yeah, that whole six days thing is just not literally true, I'm afraid. Don't blame me if that upsets you. And if that does get you riled you might prefer not to read any further, because you are in for some serious offence, believe me. The story as I know it isn't told from the point of view of the guys in the white hats. Azazel is one of the damned.

Which means, I guess, that I am too.

It's not my choice, but I don't see any alternative.

God created life, and life evolved, and the angels watched and applauded. That was their job, after all. Eventually primitive humans appeared on the scene. Was that part of the Divine Plan? I honestly don't know. Azazel is vague on the details. But humans multiplied and filled the earth.

Then something happened. Azazel calls it the Ash Winter. I'm taking a guess that it was to do with the eruption of the Toba super-volcano, about seventy-five thousand years ago. The atmosphere was blanketed with dust and the earth was plunged into an environmental catastrophe. The Stone Age human population crashed as cold and hunger came within an inch of wiping us all out. Paleontologists reckon there were maybe as few as a couple of thousand humans left on the planet, a pocket population clinging to life amidst the dead forests and the half-frozen sludge-filled marshes.

That's when God stepped in to save us. Maybe he saw something in humanity that he hadn't seen in all the millions of species that had gone extinct over the eons. Maybe there really is a Divine Plan. The Archangel Uriel certainly claims that there is, but I'd trust that supercilious bastard about as far as I can spit a rat.

Uriel, after all, is…but I'm getting into really murky waters here. Uriel, as Azazel pointed out, is *not my friend*. I'm going to leave it there.

The point is, the angels were given instructions to keep the human race alive. They were appointed as Watchers, shepherds to us sheep. They took material form in order to guide or drive us to places of safety, to clean water and sources of food; as animals at first, as far as I can make out, giant cave bears and shaggy aurochs and such. They protected us from mundane wild beasts and called down fire from Heaven to stop us freezing to death. They nurtured that tiny human gene-pool and cared for it like gardeners tending fragile hothouse plants. They taught us to cook our meat, to make tools, and to look to the heavens in wonder and worship.

And to do those things, they later had to take human form, at least on a temporary basis. Beautiful, charismatic, insanely powerful men.

Yeah, I'm pretty sure it was always men, not women. So much easier to get people to do what they're told that way.

Between seventy and fifty thousand years ago, so far as archaeologists can tell, the human race underwent a vast and fundamental change. *All* human culture stems from that time of population collapse, when we teetered on the brink. We discovered cooking and fishing and started crafting musical instruments. We started making art. We started wearing clothes and jewelry. We started burying our dead with reverence. We started believing in some sort of higher power, and using ritual to invoke it. That makes sense, because after all, the gods walked visibly in our midst.

The angels changed us.

But we changed them too. Again, I'm going off something Uriel let slip: taking material form seems to involve buying into the biology too. Things like hormones. Natural appetites. Pain and pleasure, both. A perspective from below instead of on high.

Above all, I imagine, a sense of one's self as an individual. No longer a living manifestation of the Divine Will, but a finite, bounded, needful entity. Something entirely different to the Creator. With an ego of one's own.

Can you or I imagine what it must have been like for a being whose natural element was spirit? How unsettling? How deliriously overwhelming? For the first time, they must have understood in themselves the true significance and lure of a shy smile, a full breast and a hard nipple. Or the soft skin at the small of someone's back, the flare of hips and ass from a slender waist and the bewitching tick-tock of a woman's walk.

What more dangerous attribute could you possibly inflict

upon a being of vast power than testosterone?

"They saw the daughters of men, that they were fair."

Their downfall should have been predictable. Two hundred of the Watchers, a third of the Host of Heaven according to *The Book of Enoch*, decided that they shouldn't deny themselves the sex their new bodies craved.

"They took to them wives of all that they chose."

It's there in Genesis. Just before the story of Noah's flood. The Sons of God interbred with human women, and those women gave birth to half-human babies.

"There were giants on the earth in those days."

I've seen a couple of Azazel's children. Not in the flesh, sure—I was shown a cosmic flashback to the Bronze Age, right at the end of the age of the Watchers. Those two sweet little boys hadn't looked like giants or monsters. But it was the existence of those half-breed children, the Nephilim, which caused the loyal angelic troops of the Almighty to launch an all-out attack on their fallen brethren. And those two boys died bloody deaths for the sins of their father.

It was Raphael who fought Azazel and took him down after a devastating battle. Then the four archangels imprisoned him under the earth, tethered to the raw rocks with the guts of his slaughtered children. Starving, blinded by centuries of dust and darkness, racked with physical and mental agony, there he was to remain until the Day of Judgment when God would finalize his damnation by casting him into Hell forever.

Azazel was the first, but the same fate descended on all the Watchers. One by one the Fallen were captured and imprisoned, and their children butchered. Then humans were set to watch over them, the emotional drip-feed of their care and devotion keeping the prisoners alive. And now, in secret corners all over the world, in vaults under temples and in crypts behind walls of stone, the Watchers still remain in torment awaiting the end of the world.

Azazel's prison was located in the mountains of Montenegro, deep in the Balkan region of Europe. For five thousand years he remained there, cursing his enemies and raging against God. Guarded by my family.

Until I fell in love with him.

Until I set him free.

Now all hell is about to break loose.

One

PROFESSIONAL MISCONDUCT

I'm giving a presentation on my proposal for a commemorative footbridge to the Senior Design Team at Ansha Engineering, when Azazel strolls up to the glass wall of the office and smiles in at me.

It isn't a reassuring smile. His never are. My heart meets my stomach with a big gloopy splash. This really isn't the best moment for him to drop in.

Don't get me wrong—a part of me is always delighted to see my boyfriend, if that's the right word for him. No prizes for guessing *which* part of me is always delighted. Let's just say that my clothes suddenly get too tight and I can feel a wet blush erupt all the way up from my panties to my face. Azazel is so ridiculously hot that just the sight of him melts me.

But I'm at *work*. The wrenching sensation as I tip from my professional headspace is far from comfortable. And that's before I even begin to factor in the fear.

What does he want?

No normal boyfriend should ever come in and interrupt a

girl at work—especially when she's just switched jobs and city because he got her sacked from her last position, and she's pretty sure her extended family will do something awful to her if she stays in Boston, and she's desperate to make a good impression at her new place of employment. Especially when she's showcasing her first design project. Most of all when she has the Senior Design Team watching her. It would just be incredibly intrusive and undermining to pay her a visit under those circumstances.

He lifts a hand to the door and I could swear I hear thunder in the distance.

See; that's the thing about Azazel. He's not a normal boyfriend; I've a nasty feeling 'master' would be closer to an accurate term. He's made it very clear that he *owns* me. And yes, he loves me in his own primitive way. And he needs me: my eagerness to open my legs for him is more important than oxygen as far as he is concerned. Literally. But. But.

Not normal at all.

He's not human, remember.

He's one of the Fallen.

He pushes open the office door and strolls in like he owns the place. The misters Ellis and Singh and Constanzo and Mackenzie, who are sitting either side down the long table and have all been wondering why I'm staring slack-faced and flushed past their heads, all turn to look at him and frown. He's not wearing an office suit. Not even any shoes, in fact; he never wears shoes. Just faded black jeans and a white long-sleeved T-shirt in some soft material that makes me want to press my face to it and feel the hard wall of his chest beneath. His dark hair is long and unkempt, his jaw scruffy with black stubble, his eyes slits of wicked anticipation. As an employee, he wouldn't get away with that sort of appearance even down in the bowels of the drafting department where they hide the techies.

But he doesn't look like an engineer. Broad at the shoulders and lean at the hips, six foot-and-then-something of ropey muscle, he looks like a Spartan god who got lost in a thrift store. He moves like ink through water. And his eyes, when you get a good look at them, are silver. Not gray. Silver. You might take their inhuman shine for fancy contact lenses. You'd be wrong.

"Milja," he greets me, his smile wolfish. "Come out and play."

"Aziz," I say weakly, trying not to use his real name, "you shouldn't be here."

"Last time I heard that I ended up imprisoned for eternity."

He makes jokes about it sometimes. Brittle, jagged jokes, like snarls of rusty old barbed wire. Jokes that hurt him more than anyone. It's best to ignore them.

"Excuse me—do you know this man?" Mr. Singh demands.

"She's my leman," he says, managing to sound helpful and yet not being helpful in any way whatsoever.

"Go away!" I beseech him.

"What's the magic word?"

"Please!"

"Oh, I love it when you beg for me."

He's as old as the earth, and he's prickly with rebellion, and he has *no boundaries* when it comes to sex. No social shame at all. That's not a good thing.

"What's he doing here, Ms. Petak?" asks Mr. Ellis, stabbing his notepad with his ballpoint pen in irritation.

"I want her," he purrs. "Now."

Excuse my language, but Azazel will screw me anywhere. In front of anyone. He'll turn up without warning, wanting action, and he'll fuck me breathless and then vanish into empty air leaving me in a puddle of exhaustion and bliss and shock. And in these months since I released him from his underground prison, I don't think he's managed to really wrap his head around the concept of 'consent' at all. I am, after all, his mortal pet. I'm a powerless, infinitesimally ignorant, transient blip in the annals of eternity. How could I possibly argue with him?

"Please, I'm working, this is important—just wait till I've finished?" I try.

"Important?" He comes up beside me and glances at my little audience. "More important than me?" he wonders as he runs his fingers through my hair. I've tied it back in a ponytail but the whole lot comes loose at a touch, allowing him to knot his fingers there. The gesture, as always, fills me with a wet heat.

"Of course not," I stutter, "but…"

That's when he kisses me. Hot, hungry, just this side of threatening. His mouth steals away my breath, and his hands in my hair and on my flank steal away my free will. One thumb presses into the soft flesh inside my hip, probing the pressure point there that makes me go weak.

"Milja," I hear Mr. Constanzo growl; "this is most inappropriate."

I tear my lips free with a gasp. "I'm sorry!"

"No she's not," says Azazel. His free hand drifts to the buttons at the front of my blouse. "She loves this."

"Azazel!" I whimper, squirming with shame as his fingers flick open the first button, but unable to escape his grip in my hair. "Don't!"

"Shush," he admonishes, stooping so that his lips brush my ear. "I want you. You want me. These men want to watch. See?"

He turns me back to face them, sliding behind me. 'These men' are wide-eyed and open-mouthed by now. But oddly they voice no objection as he pulls aside my bra cup and pops my right breast out for all to see.

Oh God, they're all looking at me.

My panties are soaked and my legs are actually trembling. Azazel knows me only too well. I get off on being claimed by him in public. I was always the girl no one noticed. But I can't be ignored now. He's right that I love it. Even when I hate it. Even when I'm crimson with shame. He wipes away all my common sense with a flick of a finger, the press of a palm, the first hint of a lecherous, knowing smile. I'm watching my career go down the can *again*, and all I can think of is how hot this is making me.

The other thing is that, if he were human, I'd at least have some sort of choice about walking away from it all. As it is… I'm not so sure.

So when Azazel lovingly touches my breast, when the dusky point of my nipple rises stiff and swollen under the play of his fingers as he sighs in my ear, I don't fight him. Even when he pushes my bra-straps all the way down my shoulders to bare me and cups both my orbs, soft and quivering in the rough heft of his hands, to present me to my audience, my only protest is the squirm of my hips and the press of my ass against his body. My face is averted, my lips soft with submission.

"She has beautiful breasts, hasn't she?" Azazel asks. I can hear the sounds of throats being cleared, of uncomfortable shifting in chairs. But no one answers or stands up to my defense. It's all been so fast they've gone into shock.

"You know, I hate these ugly clothes she wears," he muses. He means my white lacy bra, my button-down blouse, my respectable A-line skirt. "I would have her naked, all day, so that I might see her beauty any time I choose. But she persists in defying me."

He abandons my breasts to unhook the catch at the back of my skirt and draw down the zipper. My skirt slithers down my thighs and hits the floor at my feet, baring my legs. Suddenly the rest of me is on display too—my white thong panties, my narrow hips, my vulnerable thighs, creamy in contrast to the fabric. I know the dark shadow of my fleece is visible through the white lace. All four men are staring at me. I lift my gaze and see, through the glass beyond, that fellow-workers in the office have started to notice. Some have stopped in their tracks.

"Forward over the table, Milja," Azazel orders.

I obey. My bare breasts squash against the varnished wood as I press my forehead to the hard surface, surrendering the right to see my audience for the moment. I sneak my hands back and grip the edge of the table by my hips, holding tight.

Azazel slaps my ass cheeks, right then left, once each. His hand is heavy, yet I know he's not doing this to admonish me, but merely for the pleasure of seeing my ass bounce. It's sharp enough to make me gasp out loud, nonetheless. Then, as if in compensation, the sting and burn is followed at once by the stroke of fingers along the edge of my panties. A broad strip of lace runs down the cleft between my cheeks and he explores this, his fingertip playing with the sensitive dimple of my ass. I didn't think I could feel any more shame than already burns my veins—but now I do, and my skin glosses suddenly with sweat.

Azazel chuckles. Then his fingers slip lower, teasing the pip of my clit, pressing the narrow gusset of my panties. "These are soaked," he observes. "Are you so wanton, Milja?"

He's got an odd turn of phrase sometimes. I mean, English isn't my own mother-tongue either, so I can't criticize, and it's been five thousand years since the last time he was free so I guess the subtler points of modern American can be forgiven him. Especially in comparison to his next move, which is to take the lace of my shameful garment between two hands, first over one hip and then the other, and snap it.

He's really strong. I've learned not to get too fond of my items of underwear.

"Here," he says, dragging the ruined piece of clothing deliciously over my pubis and my pussy and up the valley of my ass before drawing it out from between my cheeks. "Sodden. Am I right?" He tosses the scrap of lace straight at Mr. Ellis, who manages to catch it before it slaps him in the face.

Ellis doesn't throw the garment from him in disgust. He just sort of holds it. His middle-aged face is beet-red.

"Soaked, isn't it?" says Azazel.

Ellis nods. His pupils are dilated.

My sight mists. If I could cry with shame I would, but the ability to cry is one of the things Azazel took from me when I freed him. I only sob and quiver as my lover fingers me.

"Divest yourselves of any concern that Milja is not enjoying this, gentlemen. She is wetter than you could possibly imagine." I hear the rasp of his zipper. "But you will have to take my word for that, I think."

Oh Jesus, he's going to shaft me in front of them all.

I brace myself. But there is no steeling oneself against the descent of a Son of God. And besides, he's right: I'm so wet and so turned on that I'm practically a gravity-well drawing him into me. I ache with needing him to fill me. I burn for his fire.

The first huge thrust is enough to make me cry out: enough to push me over into orgasm.

Enough to wake me up.

☙

Crap crap crap crap!

I jerked awake in my own bed, wrapped in twisted sweaty sheets and twitching with the contracting spasms of my climax.

Just a dream. Another dirty dream. The relief was almost as great as the disappointment. Open-mouthed, I flopped back onto my hot pillows. I'd been stressing about that presentation to the Senior Design Team way too much.

I was alone. Azazel hadn't been to see me in over a week, which was a long time for him. I didn't know where he was, and to be honest I was getting fretful. I had zero idea where he went or what he did when he wasn't with me, slaking his ravenous carnal appetite. He just turned up when he wanted, banged me senseless, and then vanished into the dark without explanation.

And he visited me in my dreams.

Like I said, it wasn't the most modern or egalitarian of relationships. Look, I'm not stupid. I knew that this relationship wasn't healthy by any normal human standards. But here's the thing: he wasn't human. How could it make sense to judge him by our standards, any more than I ought to be able to pronounce on the morality of monkeys?

That night the hot humid summer still had Chicago in its grip, despite the October date on the calendar. I staggered through to my shower cubicle, ran cool water down my back, and pressed myself to the damp tiles as I fingered myself again and again. I missed him. I wanted him. I ached inside and out for his ungentle touch.

For decades I'd watched over him, dreamed of him, longed for him, wept for him. Now he was mine…kind of.

Well, I was his. Whenever he chose to indulge himself. His bit of human tail. His concubine. His sex-toy.

His food.

You're letting yourself get too negative, Milja. You know that the moment he shows up, it'll be all sunshine and bluebirds and valentines. You want him just as much as he wants you.

༻✦༺

Less than eight hours later, I was giving my long-dreaded presentation on the anniversary footbridge to Misters Ellis, Singh, Constanzo and Mackenzie…when Azazel walked in.

Oh hell.

"Excuse me, gentlemen," I said loudly, lurching around from behind my desk, grabbing Azazel's arm and spinning him back to face the door. "Not here, come on, please," I implored through clenched teeth.

If there was one thing I'd learned by then, it was to not ignore warning dreams. If I'd paid them more attention from the start, things between me and Egan might have gone very differently back in Montenegro…

No, better not to think of Egan, not when Azazel was around. One guy at a time was quite enough to wrap my head around. Especially this guy.

He humored me though, this time, letting me pull him out of the meeting room and through the open plan office without resistance. We attracted a lot of stares, but there was nothing I could do about that except hold my head high.

"Where are we going?" he asked.

"Out. Anywhere."

"You're so impetuous."

I didn't need to glance up at his wicked smirk. I could feel it burning its way into my breast.

Bryce, the beardy guy in my new team who'd shown me the ropes of the job and seemed just a tiny bit too eager to talk every morning, stood up from his cubicle to intercept us. "Milja, is everything okay?"

"It's just fine," I rasped, towing Azazel faster.

"She's insatiable," my demon lover confided with a helpless shrug to my colleague as we swept past.

Bryce stared, mouth open.

"Goddamnit," I muttered, and Azazel chuckled.

Sometimes it was hard to remember that he'd risked everything to save me.

We reached the doors at the end of the room and I pushed through, past the lobby with the elevators and into the concrete stairwell of the emergency stairs beyond. The only people who came here were smokers on their way to the roof, and it looked empty for now. My panicky momentum fizzled away and I swung to face him.

"What are you doing here?"

"What do you think?" he countered, taking my face in his hands.

"Azazel—" But he cut off my protests with his hungry kiss; a kiss that lanced through me all the way to my core. I gave up resisting, and speaking, and almost breathing, as his lust rolled over me in a hot wet wave. I slid my hands around his neck and tangled my fingers in his messy hair, pulling myself into his embrace. His body was hard as rock, his hands heavy on my waist and hips. The yearning for his touch that smoldered in my flesh day and night woke to a roaring heat.

I'd missed him. His skin, his smile, the peppery scent and salt taste of him. The sweetness of his lips and the harsh rasp of his stubbled chin. I'd missed him *so* much. Like an addict missing her hit.

I knew there was no point in resisting him, and there was no will in me for it either. When he plucked me from my feet and parked my bum on the angled curve of the handrail, pulling my thighs apart, he took from me all responsibility, and that was a huge relief. I didn't have to take care of my career, I didn't have to worry about the aborted presentation, I didn't have to stress about what my colleagues and superiors thought of me, about making a good impression, about being an adult in a cold corporate world. It was way too late for all that.

I was Azazel's alone.

"Oh," I whimpered as he pushed up my skirt and pulled down my panties, flicking them to the cold concrete. I knew his moods and right now it was *impatience*. His silver eyes glinted inches from my own, his breath hot and sweet on my lips as he worked the buttons of his fly.

This was going to be swift and fierce. Azazel was ravenous, and he intended to bolt his repast. As he pushed forward between my open thighs, he caught me tight around the waist and covered my mouth with his own, swallowing the reflex cry jerked from my lips as he entered me.

So big. So hard. So unbearably good.

I think I flailed in his grasp, but my own movements made little difference. He was taking what he wanted and my body could only yield, back arched, legs kicking for purchase around his thighs. I was tight and slippery-hot, and that was exactly what he needed. His urgency drove him on, impaling me.

My shoes fell off, clattering on the cement floor. My groans ran up and down the stairwell.

"Yes," he grunted, catching the lobe of my ear in his teeth.

I cried out, straining my thighs.

He knew what I liked. He knew that only too well. Knotting his hand at the nape of my neck, he pulled the neat plait of my long dark hair cruelly tight, drawing my head back and stretching my throat. I clawed at his back and flanks, all I could reach. The little pain made him thrust harder—faster—deeper.

"Bad girl," he growled into my throat.

Bad? Oh yes. That was the understatement of the century. I'd freed an angel from captivity, one—it had turned out—with absolutely no compunction about killing mere humans. I'd betrayed my family, my Serbian Orthodox faith and my God. I'd gotten Egan brutally tortured trying to keep my secrets, and almost fatally shot trying to defend me. I'd brought about my father's death at the hands of the Church. I'd been the occasion for other murders too, when Azazel took vengeance on those who tried to mistreat me and recapture him. How many men had died for my sake? I couldn't even be sure of the number.

Oh, I was bad alright—guilty as charged. Cast out. Damned for eternity.

And all for this—this lust; this aching need to be with him, to feel his mastery, to have him inside me. To feel the hot joy he took in my body and in my adoration. To know he was free. To see him, just for a moment, uncomplicatedly happy.

All for love.

A love that might yet bring about another war in Heaven, and destroy us all.

Bad girl. The guilt swelled within me, a slick black wave

that rose to a tsunami and then swept all before it, tumbling pride and propriety to ruins, making me cry out over and over, my voice echoing up the concrete stairwell from the basement depths to the heights. Orgasmic spasms racked my frame—and Azazel knew, Azazel felt it and heard it and joined his pleasure to mine, fire in my darkness.

"Oh. Oh. Oh," I whimpered as the tide receded in a sucking backwash from my soul, managing to choke back the *Oh God* that came automatically to my lips for my lover's sake. Such sexual blasphemy would be as crass and cruel in this situation as calling out the name of his Ex.

"Milja," he whispered, cradling my name on his tongue as he wrapped his arms about me. "Oh, my love."

My love, my dark god, my torment. I let my head droop against his neck, unable to tell the pounding of our entwined pulses apart. Into the space left by the roaring retreat of orgasm surged all the pent-up emotions I'd been struggling with for days.

"I have ached for you," he growled, tilting my face up so he could kiss me again, lips and throat. Something brushed my brow and I looked up into a whirling scarlet cloud.

Is it snowing? In a stairwell?

But no, it wasn't snow. It was petals, velvety red rose petals, tumbling down the central shaft, touching my upturned face like kisses, filling the gray space with glory.

He brought me flowers. A groan thrust its way out of my throat and became a sob.

"What?" He cupped my face, stroking his thumb across my cheek. There were no tears there, but he knew something was up. "What's wrong?"

"I… Uh." I couldn't meet his gaze. I pushed against his chest, creating space between us as he yielded. "Oh *crap*, you've gone and ruined it."

His black eyebrows shot up. "Ruined what?"

"My job. You've just lost me my job." It was the only pain I could put into words.

He huffed out air, then curled his lip. "So?"

He doesn't get it. Why should he?

"Oh for... Azazel, I needed this job! I have to *eat* when you're not around—remember?"

"Are you hu—"

"I'd only just started here! It pays really well and it's an amazing company and I've just ruined it all by walking out of a top meeting with my scuzzy boyfriend for a quickie in the public stairwell!"

"Scuzzy?" He almost never blinked, but he did then.

"You're not even wearing shoes!" I knew it sounded completely stupid but there was no way I could info-dump modern cultural standards onto someone who didn't even see the point of dressing. Or corporate authority. Or restraint of *any* kind.

And yes, he laughed. "I will fix your job problem. Come on."

"Where?" I asked, alarmed, as he stepped back and tidied his length back into his pants. I slid off the banister, my legs as wobbly as wet cardboard.

"I will take you out to dinner. That's what a boyfriend does, no? Even a scuzzy one?" He laid hands on my shoulders even as I stooped to smooth down my skirt and brush away the petals.

"Wait," I said. "Hold on, my—"

He pulled me with him as space tore open at his back and we fell through into the nothingness beyond.

Two
EGRIGOROI

"——Panties," I spluttered, as light burst around me and air filled my lungs once more. Then I glimpsed through streaming eyes where we were standing and I yelped "Aaaah!" and grabbed for Azazel's solid frame, gripping him so hard that I'd have left bruises on a lesser man.

We were outdoors. I knew that from the ruddy sunset light. We were high up, on a tower or something, pale stone beneath my bare feet and below that a terrifying drop to an arid building site, all foundation walls and rows of stone blocks. I tried to cram down the instantaneous vertigo, telling myself *You won't fall, he won't let you, ohmygodohmygod.*

He'd always had a preference for heights: rooftops, mountains, balconies. I used to think it was because he'd spent so many years imprisoned underground, but it had turned out that Uriel did it too, so maybe it's just an angel thing. I guess it's the way they're used to looking at the world.

I forced my eyes open. The sunset was pouring into a bowl of land between dusty hills. We were standing on a hilltop, a great knurl of rock, with a modern low-rise city spread at its feet. The air was warm and stank of the traffic fumes that spread an orange haze in the low light. I dared another glance down and realized that it wasn't a construction site below us—in fact, quite the opposite, more like a demolition site. The low walls were ruinous. This high wall on which we balanced was only a few feet wide, and seemed to be part of a huge rectangular lintel frame supported by fluted pillars.

I recognized it almost at once, though I'd never been there before. I knew it from pictures. Everyone did. I'd seen it depicted in my *Child's Encyclopedia*, years back.

"Athens?" I squeaked. "We're on top of the *Parthenon*?"

Casually, Azazel spun me in his arms until I was facing over the center of the building, my back to his chest, my toes actually sticking over the edge into the interior of the roofless enclosure. It was truly exhilarating, in a dizzying fear sort of way.

"What do you see?" he asked.

"The temple to Athena," I gasped. It was a stunning sight, and I was trying hard to empathize with his enthusiasm for human construction and creation, one of his more endearing traits—although I couldn't help feeling I'd appreciate it a whole lot more from ground level.

"No," he said flatly. "That's what you've been told it is. What do you *see*?"

I saw ancient blocks set aside for conservation and big yellow wheeled machinery for lifting them. I saw tourists wandering about, none of whom seemed to have spotted us yet, high over their heads. "I don't know what you mean."

"Close your eyes."

I obeyed, gratefully, in the hope that it would quell the

IN BONDS OF THE EARTH

flips going on in my stomach. Azazel slid a hand up to the nape of my neck—and slowly my senses bloomed. Not my sight, but my hearing—a bird flapping overhead, the tinny ululation of a distant radio, voices, footfalls on grit, a dog scratching its ear, something pattering in a burrow…then these too faded away and I heard something else beneath all the cacophony: breathing, slow and labored, but seeming resonant enough to fill the world. At the end of every inhalation came a tiny whimper. It was the sound of someone so exhausted by pain that they could not cry out.

The skin prickled up my spine. I knew what I was hearing. I'd heard it in my dreams all my childhood, when Azazel lay bound in darkness beneath our mountain home.

And the great stone pillars of the temple did not fade from my mind's eye. Behind my lids I saw them, sunset gold flipped to a blue-black negative. The vast bars seemed to descend into the earth forever.

"It's a cage," I whispered, opening my eyes. My heightened senses shrank back to normal.

"Oh yes," said Azazel softly, his lips to my ear. "Oh, that is good."

"What do you mean?"

Without answering, he stepped backward off the stone, taking me with him. It was a good thing I trusted his arms, or I might have screamed as we plummeted.

His feet thumped into the sandy earth and I jolted against his chest, the breath momentarily knocked from my lungs. The world spun around me.

"Azazel," I gasped, leaning against his breastbone. I was never sure in those moments whether I wanted to slap him or kiss him. "I can't get used to you doing that."

He grinned down at me, looking more triumphant than

he ought. "You are amazing."

"What?" Misgiving seized me. "What's going on? What did you just show me?"

"I showed you nothing. I can't *see* the cage. That was you—your insight. Could you make out anyone inside?"

I felt cold all of a sudden. "I heard…someone. Someone in pain. What's happening?"

"Come on." He took my hand like any ordinary boyfriend who hadn't just teleported us thousands of miles and then jumped forty-five feet down from the crown of one of the most iconic buildings in the world. He led me toward a cluster of lower buildings at what turned out to be the site exit. And I followed tamely, just like a tourist finished with the day's visit, not an escapee from an office who'd left her panties on the other side of the Atlantic after a torrid quickie on the stairs. My body was still thrumming with the pulse of our tryst, and the evidence of it was leaking onto my inner thighs.

I looked back once at the great ruined building on the hilltop. It was beautiful. But now all I could see was cage bars, not columns.

"Who was that?" I asked as we walked down the zig-zag path beneath pine and cypress trees. The pavement slabs were warm and smooth under my soles. "Who's under there?"

"My brother Batraal." He sounded grim. "The Hellenes remembered him as the Titan Pallas."

"You found one then? Another Watcher?" That was what he had promised outside my family chapel weeks ago—to free all his Fallen comrades and rise up against Heaven.

"I've not found anyone. All I can tell is the interior of the ruin is still consecrated after all these millennia—which seems wildly unlikely unless there's a reason, and an active guardian. I can't see any cage. I can't hear my brother cry out. But you can."

"Is that why you brought me here?" I swallowed hard. "Am I like your sniffer-dog?"

He didn't answer. His stride was long and I had to hurry to keep up, which hurt in bare feet. He seemed to know where he was going, even when we left the main path and cut downhill.

"Will you free Batraal now?"

"I can't, yet."

"Why not?"

Again, no answer.

"You could at least tell me what you're planning to do now, you know," I mumbled.

"Why? Are you aiming to help?"

I sucked in my cheeks. That was the big question, wasn't it? Was I really going to offer to go to war against the Heavenly Host? I'd been brought up in the Church, my father had been a priest, and until this year I'd had no quarrel with it. Until it all went pear-shaped, that is, thanks to my freeing Azazel, and I'd spent days chained in a monastery cellar, been staked out as bait, and finally suffered Father Velimir's attempt to murder me. That hostility felt pretty personal, even if I'd only been a pawn in the bigger game.

Whether I was ready to declare war on God Almighty was another matter entirely.

"What you're up to—it's really dangerous," I said, swallowing my tangle of fears and doubt. "What am I supposed to do if you just don't come back to me one day? What if they catch you again?"

That gave him pause. We came to a halt where the path emerged onto a small road lined with shops. He studied my face. "I've no desire to endanger you," he said at last.

"Too late for that!"

He nodded, abashed. Sometimes he could be almost human. "Yes. But would you help me save Batraal, if you could?"

My shoulders drooped. How could I say no? I'd lived my entire twenty-three years with the horror and the guilt of Azazel's incarceration. Did the others deserve my sympathy less?

"I guess," I admitted.

He smiled, brushing his fingertips to my cheek. "I have one ally then."

"For what that's worth," I muttered.

"More than the Hosts of Heaven." He stooped to kiss me, sweet and dark and hot as burning sugar, and as we broke for breath I could tell from the glow in his eyes that desire was on the verge of distracting him again. His hand on my waist could so easily pull me against him if he chose, and then… "This way," he murmured, regretfully.

I was so surprised that I let him tow me across the road without even looking at the traffic.

We stopped outside a bank. "Here."

"What?"

He waved a hand at the ATM in the wall. "This is where you get money from, yes?"

"Yeah, but…"

He put one hand on the screen, one on my shoulder. "Tell it how much you want."

"I haven't got my bank cards with me!" After all I'd been through I'd vowed never to leave the house without plastic and a toothbrush—but Azazel's visit had taken me by surprise.

"We're going for supper. Just tell it."

I shook my head and tapped 100 onto the keypad, having

no idea how much food cost in Greece. The machine whirred and spat out multicolored euro notes, while Azazel took advantage of the moment and pressed up against my ass.

"Okay," I said doubtfully, taking the small wad and wriggling out of his embrace. "Whose account did this come out of?"

"Account? No one's. I told it you are a friend. It will tell the others."

"But the cash comes from somewhere."

"Yes. Inside this wall."

Yeah, but…? "Uh…that's theft, Azazel," I said, before belatedly reminding myself that this was someone who didn't balk at murder.

"You don't need your job now, do you? Take as much as you want, whenever you like."

My mouth fell open. I had no idea how to answer that. I should have gone with: *My job was more than a paycheck, Azazel. It was my career. Validation. Human interaction. My place in society. And I was so insanely lucky to get it after my screw-up in Boston! What do you think I should do with your free money—lie around all day in my perfumed boudoir, eating chocolate and waiting for you to come and pork me?*

Except that his answer to that would almost certainly be an unselfconscious *Yes.*

"Thank you," I mumbled, my numb lips fumbling the words. Because *money.* Free money. Not losing my apartment. Not starving.

He smiled, wholly satisfied.

Oh God. How do I…? It's like being in a relationship with a genius level caveman.

"Now you want to eat?"

"I…uh…yeah." My stomach was still doing flips, but I'd

unwisely missed breakfast that morning and I did need lunch. Even if it looked like supper, thanks to the time difference. "Coffee would also be good."

We set off down a side road lined with small shops selling *I ♥ Greece* T-shirts and plaster statues of satyrs with improbable phalluses. The lane opened out into a square lined with cafes, their menu placards carefully illustrated with photographs for us illiterate foreigners. Most of them looked far from full and I guessed that local people ate late, or elsewhere. In the open space vendors had set up ad-hoc stalls on plastic tarpaulins, selling bric-a-brac and fake designer handbags, and a quartet of musicians were playing folk instruments, a sound eerily reminiscent of the music of my own homeland. A man was amusing passers-by by blowing huge soap-bubbles and catching them in plastic frames to make intricate mathematical shapes; cubes within cubes and spheres within spheres. We headed at random for a restaurant under a trellis draped with grape-vines, where Azazel carefully pulled out a plastic chair for me. He'd clearly been studying up on manners.

Well, that was what I thought until he parked himself in a chair facing me and, leaning forward, slid a hand up the inside of my thigh, all the way to my damp sex.

I stiffened, arching my spine. "Azazel!" I gasped as his touch sent thrills cascading through my nerve-endings all over again.

"Hm?" It had suddenly gone so quiet that I could hear even that quietest of speculative murmurs as he pushed probing fingertips into the wet split of my sex and sought entry to my body. Blessedly, thankfully quiet. No voices, no music, and even the omnipresent hum of traffic was silenced; the world had stopped. I glanced around us and saw that the figures in the square were frozen in mid-motion, their eyes glazed. A dead leaf, just fallen from the vine, hovered motionless over his shoulder. Across the flagstones an iridescent soap bubble hung just beyond the tip of its plastic wand, defying the elements of air and gravity and fate. I wondered distractedly if it would burst if I touched it, or whether it would feel hard like crystal.

"We shouldn't do this!"

Azazel's fingers plunged into me, slick with our mingled juices, stretching me, making me buck in my seat. Wicked delight boiled in his eyes. "But you enjoy it so much, my sweet."

"Oh!" Blood rushed to my face. We might be the only actors in our secret play, but the audience were all around us, unblinking. I was being pumped in full public view, my skirt pushed up my thighs, my whimpers suddenly alarming in loudness.

"Do you deny it?"

I grabbed the arms of my chair. "No," I admitted, stammering.

"You like the idea of being watched. That handsome waiter there. Those nice old gentlemen playing chess. It makes you wet when I touch you in public. You want everyone to see."

"Please, no."

"They should see." He slid to his knees in front of my open thighs so that he could get a closer look at his hand working my wet sex. "You are so beautiful like this."

"Unh."

"Open your blouse," he ordered. "Show me your breasts."

I shook my head mutely, eyes widening.

He grinned, then pushed his fingers deeper, scissoring

them, curling them to caress me within. I heaved, unable to control my own reaction. Heat roared from my sex to my flushed face and seemed to set a fire in my breasts. I could feel dampness springing out on my skin beneath my too-constricting clothes.

"Show. Me." His thumb slithered over my clit, implacable.

I couldn't bear the heat in my flesh any longer. I fumbled the buttons of my blouse, pulled down the camisole top and the bra cups beneath. My nipples prickled in the unnaturally still air, my breasts quivering.

Jeez. Now I really was at his mercy. If he released his grip on the frozen moment I would be exposed for everyone to see —tits out, thighs squirming open, hips jerking, his hand buried in the molten heat of my pussy. Everyone would see me being finger-fucked.

Everyone would see me coming, like this.

Right now.

I nearly kicked him in my spasms, nearly bit my mouth trying not to squeal out loud. Not too loud, anyway. I couldn't actually keep silent.

Azazel watched hungrily, oh so hungrily, like he was gorging himself on the sight of my shame and lust. He ate me through his eyes and his hand, cupping the thud of my racing pulse in his palm, until I stopped twitching and managed to swallow and moisten my lips.

He withdrew gently; so gently that I wanted to beg him to put his hand back. Then he lounged back in his chair, the flimsy plastic bending alarmingly under his torso.

"Five," he said, his eyes glittering.

Five what? I was still breathless and half-witted with the shock of my climax.

"Four."

Oh crap! I scrabble desperately for my buttons, trying to restore my disarranged clothes. And I managed to pull my skirt desperately down to my knees just as he reached "One," and the day suddenly roared into surround-sound and motion again, like he'd pressed *Play* at last.

The young waiter swept up to take our order as I brushed my skirt down and tucked my hair back behind my ears. Maybe he wondered why I was blushing furiously and shimmering with perspiration.

Azazel sucked the tips of his fingers, savoring my surrender. Draping himself over the chair at an angle, he watched indulgently as I ordered a Greek salad, coffee and a small plate of baklava. He acquiesced only to a glass of ouzo and a bowl of mixed olives. He rarely ate much now, as I reminded myself, though I'd fed him stolen bread and goat's milk when he was a prisoner. I'd seen him drink alcohol though.

I'd seen him drunk. Not a memory I cherished.

I looked out across the square, trying to calm the thunder of my heart. I wondered how it was that people were carrying on with their ordinary lives instead of staring at us. If I'd been one of those people I'd have stared. To me, Azazel's long-limbed frame looked like a dark and ragged hole cut into the fabric of reality.

A calico restaurant cat limped out from under the table and wound itself ecstatically around Azazel's feet. Cats, of course, loved him—just as much as dogs found him terrifying. He picked it up into his lap and commenced stroking it, oblivious to its gummy eyes and ragged ears. The cat collapsed into his caress, purring.

I relaxed a little, at last.

"You're being watched," said Azazel casually.

"What?" I just about managed not to commit the movie-error of looking around me. "Who?"

"Not now. Back where you live. I've seen cars following you as you walk home."

I took a sip from my water glass and licked my lips nervously. "Is it my family? The Church?"

"I don't know."

"Didn't you…investigate?" *Though if so I'd probably have seen the police tape and the bloodstains*, I reasoned.

He snorted. "If you are ever in trouble, you only need call for me."

I blinked, remembering how well that had gone the last few times. "Father Velimir is dead," I said quietly. "It might be *Adzo* Josif." I didn't want to meet with my cousin or her husband, no—never again. They'd sworn vengeance on me for dishonoring the family by whoring about with a demon and—in their eyes—killing my father. It wasn't the sort of reunion I looked forward to, and I'd hoped I'd escaped it all by leaving Boston for Chicago.

"Shall I kill them for you?"

My eyes widened involuntarily. "No! They're family!"

Azazel shrugged, as casual as a hawk with a captured mouse. "Does that matter?"

"Yes it does!" I poured more water into my glass, clumsily. "To me it does, anyway. To most people."

"Fine." He wasn't much interested, I could see. The cat was getting most of his attention as his dark hand poured across its fur.

"Excuse me." The good-looking waiter reappeared at my elbow with a tray. My smile was unfeigned as I accepted the big bowl of cucumber, onion slices, beef tomatoes and feta.

The salt cheese was delicious. Azazel flipped a green olive into his mouth as if it were a bar peanut. But as I ate, thoughts of my estranged family and my late father, and all the sailors and monks Azazel had slaughtered, intruded again.

"What happens when we die?" I asked quietly. "Am I going to Hell, Azazel?"

Azazel's smile was like a wall. "You ask a lot of questions."

"Maybe if you answered some..."

"Why should I?"

"Because you know what's going on! Isn't that important? You've got the answers—you've seen God, you've seen Heaven. You know who's going to be saved. You know the truth about all the things we've been asking, for thousands of years."

His quicksilver eyes flicked over me, unreadable. "And you'd like to let everyone know the truth too, would you? You'd pass it on?"

"Yes!"

"Oh, that is exactly what your species needs—another prophet. Some new dogma to put your faith in." His mouth twisted. "Work it out for yourselves. You have all the tools you need."

I stared into my salad.

Then it all went unnaturally quiet once more.

Really, again? I looked up, alarmed, from my meal, but Azazel was frowning this time. He didn't appear lascivious, he appeared troubled.

"What?" I asked.

"When we made the great leap into this realm," he said, gesturing around us, "I was one who led the rebels. But not alone, you understand."

I froze momentarily, locking my gaze to his. Was he

actually volunteering information? This was almost unheard of. And it was clear he was trying to make sure we were not overheard.

"You asked me what I'm planning. You've read the *Book of Enoch*?"

"Mmm." I had read it repeatedly, online, though I'd found the centuries-old tome a dizzying mixture of contradiction, poetic vanity and psychedelic religious hallucination. It just happened to be the nearest thing out there to a first-hand account of the fall of the Watchers, that was all.

"You know then." He seemed hesitant, awkward. If there ever was a boyfriend who didn't like opening up about his past, it was Azazel. "Two hundred of us, fully one third of the Host. I was the greatest warrior amongst them. But it was not my idea." He smiled, a little ruefully. "All I wanted to do was lie with the human women."

"Okay," I muttered.

"It was sufficient reason for me." He wasn't in the least embarrassed, and of course did not register that I might find the subject uncomfortable. How could I possibly be upset by his behavior five thousand years before my birth, after all? *How unreasonable*, he would think, amused by how short-sighted I was. "But my brother Samyaza had vision. He wanted to advance your kind." He flicked a forefinger at me across the table. "He'd been at it for millennia before the Ash Winter, even. Back when you were only apes. He was the one who made you human in the first place. There is an echo of the story in Genesis, as in all your creation myths. The Serpent, they call him."

Oh right. The Garden of Eden. "Wasn't that Satan? It says it was Satan." *And Satan is...*

"No it doesn't." Azazel rolled his eyes. "Don't you even read your own holy texts? It says *the serpent*—that's all."

I turned a tomato slice over with my fork, confused and disappointed. "So we did Fall."

"You rose. The knowledge of good and evil, remember?" He stroked the cat under its dirty chin. "How could that make you *less*? Some animals have self-awareness, but only you know that you are not the center of your universe. That you are an individual, separate from all Creation. That all others live with the same sense of separation and hope and fear as you do, neither lesser nor greater than yourself. And that just as the world existed before you, so you will inevitably die and be forgotten." He smiled darkly. "That way lies empathy, and hence justice and all morality—and despair too. Such loneliness. You are no longer innocent."

"Cast out of Paradise."

He shrugged. "Cast out of Nature."

"That was Samyaza's thing then?" I wasn't sure how I should feel about that.

"Yes. He believed in what the human species could become. And he persuaded me to join him in his great project. I stood at his right hand, as my brother Penemuel stood at his left. We three led the others into this realm."

Samyaza's a good guy then, you're telling me? It's the story of Prometheus again.

Azazel drummed his fingers on the table, and I wondered what words he was rejecting as he sifted them behind his eyes. "I need Samyaza. I am one against four hundred, and I cannot fight them all if they turn on me again."

"But they haven't done that," I said nervously. "I remember you saying to U—"

"Don't use his name. He can hear you, remember?"

"I'm sorry." I could have slapped myself for such a beginner's error. Angels can hear you when you speak their name. And they can *all hear anything you say* if you do it on holy ground. Churches are dangerous. "You told him that if the Host were coming to get you, they would have done it already. Something is stopping them, isn't it?"

Azazel drummed his fingers again. "I don't know," he admitted. "They have largely tolerated my freedom this far, though they moved your Church against me. They left the dirty work up to men. Why they are holding back...I don't know. Perhaps it is fear of the destruction that will be wreaked." He pulled a face. "I think if I release Batraal and the others, if I find the two hundred lesser Egrigoroi and try to set them free one at a time...I fear that the divine patience will snap."

"So you have to keep your head down."

"No—I have to find Samyaza. He is the key. He will know what to do. Penemuel is smart, he knows the names and the signs, but Samyaza has the foresight. He sees the paths of the future."

Yeah, I'd already been told—somewhat cruelly—that Azazel was the muscle of the rebel leaders, not the brains. "Where is he being held, then?"

"That I don't know, either."

But you think I might be able to help. That's why you brought me here to look at Batraal's prison. I wonder why I can see things that you can't?

Pondering the question, I popped a piece of syrupy, crunchy baklava between my lips and chewed slowly, then licked my fingertips clean. I should have realized this would distract Azazel from more abstract concerns. As my awareness dawned of the renewed intensity of his gaze, he smiled.

"You've finished eating then?"

Subtle, babe. "Yeah. I mean, give me a moment."

The world shot back into focus, with its sounds and smells and motion. Oh, being around him made it all seem so unreal sometimes. Like a movie one could pause or set aside for later. You didn't really have to worry about other people, because you could always put them on hold or just walk away. There were no inescapable consequences. It was both exhilarating and disturbing.

"Where would you like to go, Milja?"

Oh, I was being indulged today. Dinner *and* a passionate night out of my choosing. I wasn't used to this. "Venice?" I said. "I'd love to see Venice."

He set the cat down gently on the ground, stood up and held his hand out to me. The animal trotted off with no sign of a limp.

"Um, if you don't mind, can I have a look at those handbags over there first?" I needed a new one. Preferably one with a designer label on it, albeit ever so fake. Americans noticed things like that, I'd found. It mattered in the office what you wore and what you carried. As a girl brought up in a dirt-poor mountain village without even a television, I had found that a steep learning curve.

"If you like."

We wandered off from the table, undoubtedly leaving the waiter very confused; from his point of view he'd only just served us and there I was abandoning empty plates and a generous overpayment within seconds. Azazel even tried to wait quietly in the background as I checked over the faux-Versace and -Prada and -D&G offered by a diffident Somalian youth wearing scuffed plastic sandals, though when Azazel squeezed my ass for the second time I had to slap him away, giggling.

"Get off! You're not helping!"

He blew a fake sigh of disappointment and wandered off.

The vendor was grinning at us when I looked back, but he stifled it. I made my purchase at last and turned, only to find my angel dropping to his haunches before the offerings on another of those makeshift stalls. I thought at first that the old lady in black was dealing in retro second-hand goods, and then I realized that the objects set out on the piece of carpet almost certainly represented the contents of her living room—everything from ash trays and photographs of bishops to an old CD player. I felt sad looking at this dingy collection. The global recession, as I recalled from the news, had hit Greece hard. A lot of people were struggling just to feed themselves.

But the old lady wasn't letting any distress show, at least for the moment. She rose from her stool and advanced on Azazel, grinning from ear to ear. He stood as she grabbed his arm and patted his shoulder, hooting appreciatively and talking loudly as she squeezed his muscles.

I knew bits of Greek from my father's vocation as a priest. Enough to make out the word 'god,' anyway. Then she swung around to me, laughing, and said "Ares, yes? Ares?"

I couldn't help smiling back at her. *You don't know how close you are*, I agreed inwardly. I wondered if Azazel would take offence, but he seemed only amused as she rubbed his six-pack through his shirt with her skinny little hand. He towered over her, but she seemed not the least bit intimidated. Old women just don't care.

"*Poios eínai aftós?*" he asked, pointing at a framed watercolor on her carpet. At least that distracted her momentarily from committing what would have been tantamount to sexual assault if she'd been a younger woman.

Not that I could really blame her—that body and that wickedly lupine face and those feathery black lashes were an irresistible combination in my opinion—but I was startled by her boldness.

She pointed to it and then to her own breast, chattering to him rapidly in Greek and sighing. He listened attentively, nodded, and then smiled and took her hands in his, drawing her into the center of the square. She followed his lead, giggling, and then as he started to move his feet she joined him, her movements a little tottery. They were dancing. The folk band noticed almost instantly and swung into an appropriate melody. Quite suddenly this little hunched old lady was the center of attention as her god of war spun and paced with her, accompanying her with simple and self-effacing grace. Her steps became more confident, her movements more fluid. She looked up into Azazel's face, her own expression alight with pleasure.

Onlookers joined in, clapping along to the rhythm.

Once I got past my initial surprise, I moved over to look at the picture, wondering what had provoked this strange exchange. The painting showed a young woman in a flowing skirt, dancing on the tips of her toes, her long dark hair swirling around her.

Is that her, I wondered, *painted in her youth?* I couldn't help, despite my shame, feeling the tiniest bit put out—Azazel had never danced with me, after all.

He was loving dancing with her.

"He's got quite a way with the ladies," said a man behind me.

"Yes," I said dryly, looking from the watercolor to the dancing couple and sparing only a glance for the stranger. His accent had sounded American, and even out of the corner of my eye his clothes confirmed that: blue denim shirt, big belt buckle, office-casual jacket.

Long hair.

That got my attention enough for a second glance, even though most of my mind was wondering what on earth Azazel was thinking of, flirting with an old woman like that. My second glance told me that the stranger wasn't just New World, he was First Nations, with the most beautiful waterfall of straight dark hair I'd ever seen on a man.

"He had great aptitude as a warrior. A shame he wasted it all." Then he blinked, deliberately, and for an instant his deep brown eyes flicked to pure gold without pupils.

My heart jumped up into my throat. I looked wildly to Azazel but he didn't see me, absorbed as he was in his dance and in his partner. I turned back to the stranger, my heart pounding.

He was gone.

An angel. That was another angel! Oh hell, what do I do? What did he want?

"Azazel," I breathed, looking all around me, as nervous as a mouse under the shadow of a hawk.

The music broke up into a few final phrases, and applause rang out across the little square from their audience. I hurried up to Azazel and grabbed at his arm, whilst still trying to watch all around us. "We should go now."

He laughed. "What's your hurry?" The old lady was still on his other elbow, wiping at the tears running down her radiant face. She seemed to be standing taller, her back less bent and her shoulders less crooked. He stooped to kiss her fingers tenderly.

"Please!"

Azazel arched an eyebrow at me. I practically had to drag

him away from his new girl and out of the crowd, and he blew a kiss at her as he left. "She was a dancer when she was young," he said happily as we passed into the shadow of the lane. "Inside her heart, she still dances."

"We have to get out of here."

"What?" He caught my shoulders and pushed me back against a wall. "Impatient, love? This will do. Right now." He cupped my breasts, his appetite boiling to the surface again.

"Azazel—No! I saw another angel!"

All the horny humor went out of his face. "Who?"

"I didn't recognize him. Long hair, really athletic looking." That didn't narrow it down much, I suspected. "He looked Native American."

The evening shadows ran inky as Azazel's mood bled into our surrounds. "He saw you?" he demanded.

"He *spoke* to me! Who is he?"

"Piece of shit." Azazel drew himself up taller, and the shadows thickened. "He wants me to know he's watching. He's got nothing better to do with his existence than dog my tracks."

"*Who?*"

The gloom was so dense now that his teeth seemed to gleam as he bared them. "Michael," he said, but the name was not addressed to me.

"Hello, Daughter of Earth," said the handsome man who stepped out from a lit doorway. His muscular arms were folded across his chest, and the thirty-watt bulb behind his head loaned him a halo of deep gold. "Don't listen to him—he's just a sore loser. Well, Azazel... Shall *we* dance?"

Azazel slapped his hand onto my breastbone and *pushed* me out of the way—out of the alley, out of Athens, and for a split second right out of the world.

JANINE ASHBLESS

I landed flat on my back with the wind knocked out of my lungs, on my bed, back in Chicago.

Three
ROSHANA

I went into the office first thing the next morning. I planned to clear my personal effects from my desk before anyone else from my team got in, but to my chagrin Bryce was already there, lolling back in his chair and drinking a *grande* coffee from a paper cup.

"Hey," he said, lifting an eyebrow.

"Hey," I mumbled, not meeting his gaze. I dumped my cardboard box on the desk top and opened the top drawer.

"You have to go up to the eighteenth floor."

"What?"

He pointed at the piece of paper taped up to hang over my monitor. I'd given it one glance and, assuming it was my marching orders, deliberately ignored it. "Roshana wants to see you. Right away."

"Roshana?" I struggled to recall if that was someone I should remember from Human Resources. Was there some sort of paperwork I had to collect to be formally fired?

"Roshana Veisi."

Still it didn't sink in. I stared at Bryce blankly.

"The chair of the board."

Whoa. That Roshana Veisi? The boss? The woman who owns this company?

I'd never met anyone that senior in the hierarchy of Ansha Engineering, of course. I didn't even know what she looked like. "Why does she want to see me?"

Bryce shrugged. "Like I know."

I pulled the piece of paper free and read the scanty lines typed there. I was required to report to Roshana Veisi's secretary as soon as possible, in person. There was no indication of any reason and the tone of the words was entirely neutral.

"Was that your boyfriend then?" Bryce asked, casually, as I stood frowning at the paper.

"Huh? Um, yeah."

"He…wasn't what I pictured."

I blinked, refocusing on his face. *What can I say to that?* I knew that Azazel and I made a mismatched couple. "I guess I got lucky," I said, not bothering to hide the bitterness in my words.

Bryce seemed to shrink back a little from me, then turned away studiously to his own monitor.

Well, orders were orders. I collected my few belongings as I'd planned and carried the box under my arm to the elevator. I felt a little nervous, but at this stage it wasn't as if I had anything to lose. I'd already thrown away my job, so what else could they do to me?

No, what mostly occupied my mind and churned my stomach was confusion. What on earth could Ms. Veisi want with an employee of my lowly station? *Ex-employee, even.* As I watched the LED numbers counting up to eighteen, I tried to recall what I'd heard about her, but it didn't amount to much. She was a keen local patron of the arts; that was about all. Many original paintings hung in the atrium downstairs and in the elevator areas on each floor, all of them too modern for my taste. Oh, and she owned a small gallery uptown that we were all granted an annual pass to as a perk of employment here.

I hadn't visited the gallery. Now I felt vaguely guilty.

The decor on the eighteenth floor was a revelation after the office areas I was used to. Lush carpeting muffled my footfalls, and soft concealed lighting made the foyer seem more like a spa lobby than anything to do with engineers. Only a gigantic oil painting behind the receptionist's desk, depicting one of our most prestigious bridges against a background of cyan sea, reminded visitors what it was we created in this building.

"I'm Milja Petak," I told the painfully pretty young woman at the desk. "I've been asked to come to Ms. Veisi's office." Privately I doubted anyone would want to see me at this early hour and I still suspected the summons was the result of an administrative error somewhere.

She looked me up on her screen. "Go right ahead down that corridor, Ms. Petak. Ms. Veisi's secretary is at the end."

Ms. Veisi's secretary turned out to be a young man with soft brown eyes somehow full of harsh appraisal. I was glad I'd worn a high-necked, even prim, blouse this morning to cover up the scattering of bruises that Azazel's fingertips had left across the upper slopes of my breasts.

"If you'd like to wait in here..." he told me, opening a door to an inner office.

No, it wasn't an office, at least not as I knew such things, I thought as he shut me in. There was a big mahogany desk, but it was conspicuously clear. There was no computer, just a wall-mounted screen currently playing silent footage of grasses blowing in a breeze. The thick carpet, the soft armchairs, the potted plants and the framed paintings—they all seemed to suggest an upmarket hotel bar.

I perched uneasily on the lip of a cushion, setting my box down on the floor. It was completely silent in here, despite the downtown cityscape outside the big windows. For the moment I had nothing to distract me from my own thoughts, and my worry for Azazel welled up again. He hadn't reappeared after sending me home so abruptly. It scared me to think of what sort of trouble he might be in.

But I'd checked the international news channels when I woke first thing, and there were no reports of inexplicable devastation in Athens or anywhere else, so I had to assume he'd not launched into a full-on fight with Michael. Azazel would not have gone down easily. With any luck it had just been a stand-off.

Where is he? Is he okay?

I hadn't dared call him this morning. I'd wanted to get my last trip to the office out of the way first. I'd whisper his name as soon as I got home, I promised myself.

And then he would come to me. Or not. As he chose.

I pictured him dancing with the old woman. His utter concentration, excluding even me for those moments, and his inexplicable tenderness. What had drawn him to her? His pleasure in the dance left me baffled and uncomfortable. I had to admit I didn't understand all his moods. Angry, yes. Horny, yes. But sometimes he took me by surprise.

You're not jealous, are you, Milja?

Twitchy, I rose to my feet and prowled around the room. A frantically baroque silver statue on a low table turned out to be a haloed and armored saint stabbing a dragon. I wondered just how much a thing of that size and antiquity was worth.

It's Michael casting Satan down into Hell.

Saint Michael, the warrior archangel. Patron saint of my own family line. If anyone could recapture Azazel, it would be Michael.

I jumped as Ms. Veisi's secretary re-entered, bearing a tray with a coffee pot and hot pastries. He didn't address me as he left them on the desk and departed. I looked at the tray, surprised. There were two cups. This wasn't the reception I'd been expecting. My lips felt dry, and I wondered if it would be considered rude to help myself, then decided I didn't dare.

I distracted myself with another turn around the room, looking at the paintings hung there. The first was a vivid panel depicting a crowd of androgynous figures in complex robes holding what looked to me like an iridescent beach ball. The second, rendered in a very different impressionistic style, showed a youth, shirtless but wearing a blue sarong, sitting with his arms about his knees and staring pensively into the distance. There was another painting beyond that, possibly by the same artist but this one much bigger—I had to study it to work out what it depicted in its chaos of blues and pinks and golds. A high mountain range, its snowy peaks lit by sunset. Occupying the foreground was a naked, prostrate figure whose neck was twisted at a terrible angle, possibly broken. He lay amidst a welter of golden peacock feathers, as if the fall had smashed his glorious wings.

Icarus? I wondered, but a cold worm of doubt and dread had crept up my spine.

"*Demon Downcast*," said the woman I'd not heard come into the room behind me. "By Mikhail Vrubel. I bought those two after the collapse of the USSR."

I spun around, swallowing hard. The woman smiled.

"Such a sad story, really—the artist became obsessed by the notion of a wicked angel who falls in love with a mortal. He painted the subject over and over again. The same demon every time. He couldn't stop. Even when this picture hung in the Moscow gallery, he would come in and repaint the face—until he had a breakdown and had to be taken away to an asylum. He died blind and insane."

The part of me that was listening to her story knew exactly what that felt like, what that meant. Vrubel, undoubtedly, had been in thrall to an imprisoned Watcher just as I had been obsessed by mine. The more aware part of me managed to respond, "Ms. Veisi?"

She was short. I mean—okay, *I'm* tall, I'm Montenegrin, and we're on a par with the Dutch. I guess she was average for an American. And while I'm tall and skinny, to put it bluntly, she was a doll-like package of womanly curves, and even in her business suit she carried them with pride.

"Roshana." She turned to the coffee pot on the desk and began to pour. "Call me Roshana, Milja. Have you eaten breakfast yet?"

"No."

"You should never skip breakfast. It's the most important meal of the day." She dropped a pastry into the saucer and presented the gift to me. She had black-lashed sloe eyes and her long hair was a blue-blonde like I'd never seen before, but I suspected entailed many expensive hours in the salon. When she smiled her mouth moved but her forehead stayed Botox-smooth. I guessed she was in her thirties, but it was hard to tell.

"Thank you," I said meekly, though I didn't like coffee with cream.

"Do you know why you're here?"

I had a presentiment, but I didn't want it to be true. "I assumed it was some sort of disciplinary hearing," I mumbled, even though that was stupid.

"Far from it. Milja, I want to offer you a new position. Personal attaché."

My mouth fell open.

"Flexible hours. Add a naught to your current salary. Take on any design project you find yourself interested in. I've seen your portfolio—you're clearly very imaginative. With a fine aesthetic eye." She gestured with a small remote at the screen on the wall and the soothing video was suddenly replaced with scans of my college designs, one after the other. "Some of them aren't practical of course, but that comes with experience and I'll assign you a mentoring advisor."

What. The. Actual. Hell.

The cold feeling had spread from my spine into my stomach. "That's very kind. Why?"

She perched her magnificent rear on the edge of the desk, taking her time as she sipped at her own coffee. "Did you notice a theme here?" She indicated the room around us with a flick of her dark eyes.

My throat was so dry I could hardly swallow. "Angels."

"Yes. It's a hobby of mine."

"I... What has that to do with me?"

"Oh, don't be disingenuous, Milja." She tilted her chin. "Let me see—does any of this sound familiar? You can't cry any more, not normal tears anyway, though in *extremis* you leak blood from your eyes. Cats adore you, but dogs are terrified. You have strange visions, and can sometimes see the dead. You create dreams so powerful, so real, that you can draw other sleepers into them, and sometimes those dreams seem to come true in real life. The lights are never against you when you want to cross the street, in fact you have the ability to force the hand of Chance in all sorts of little ways. Have you tried playing the lottery yet, by the way? I recommend you don't do it too often—you wouldn't want to draw attention to yourself."

I stared at her, speechless. Then I put my coffee cup down on a low table because it was rattling in my hand.

"When was the last time you had a cold, Milja?"

"I…don't know."

"You won't get ill anymore. You won't suffer from hangovers, or food poisoning. You won't be able to overdose, either, should you try it. Your body is changing under his influence. Optimizing. And if you are relying on hormonal contraception, you need to be aware it won't work. You will become super-fertile."

Oh no! I can't have his children! I think my eyes flashed wide at that point because I saw a glint of amusement in hers. Angels could be bound, among other things, by fetters made of the flesh and blood of their own progeny. Any child of Azazel's was a weapon that could be used by archangels, or men, to bind him again in the darkness. Just as his Bronze Age sons had been used before now.

"Don't worry, you have control over your body, if you wish. You can make sure his seed does not take root—but you do need to *pay attention*."

I drew myself up. "I have no idea what you are talking about," I rasped.

"Valiant try, Milja. But I've done my homework, very thoroughly. The Scapegoat Azazel himself has taken you for his paramour. And exposure to his essence changes you. You're becoming what Enoch called a siren."

A witch, Father Velimir had labelled me. "Are you with

the Church?" I asked through gritted teeth. It hadn't occurred to me that she could be Serbian Orthodox, not with a name like that—but Catholic maybe? One of Egan's lot?

"Hardly. I'm very much a private individual."

"How do you know all that stuff then?"

"I have a great personal interest in angels. And I would very much like, in return for the promotion I'm offering you and all the opportunities it affords, to meet your extremely handsome boyfriend."

An angel groupie?

"I'm not his pimp," I snapped—unwisely, as it turned out. Roshana lifted the remote again and the picture on the screen was replaced by video once more. Only this time it was footage from a security camera in the office stairwell.

"I can see that," she said smoothly, as onscreen Azazel fucked me against the banister. His face wasn't visible on the footage, but mine was. So were my spread thighs.

Heat flooded my face. "Stop that."

The merest twitch of her finger hid the shameful images, affording me temporary relief.

"I don't control him," I managed to say, mastering my words. "I can't make him come to see you."

She spread her hands. "I'm only requesting that you ask him. Nothing more."

"He might kill you."

"But that would make you feel very bad, wouldn't it, Milja? Because you still like to think of yourself a good person, despite the fact you're getting it on with one of the Fallen. Setting a vengeful angel on someone who's upset you would be pretty despicable, don't you think?"

I wanted to slap her, but she wasn't wrong. "What the hell do you intend to do to him?"

She looked as affronted as the Botox would allow. "I don't intend to do anything. I'd just like to meet him in the flesh. At a time and place of his choosing, if you wish. I'll come alone." She smiled. "Unarmed. What are you afraid of?"

I didn't know. "Who the hell do you think you are?"

"Me? I'm *jealous*, Milja. You've made love to a creature of the heavenly realms. Wouldn't any woman be jealous? You've had experiences I can only imagine…"

"He's not going to want to fuck you."

"Of course not. But it's rare enough to encounter one of the Host still walking this world. Lethally dangerous to seek out the imprisoned Watchers. Your Azazel, fallen but free… he's unique."

I knotted my fingers together, my palms sweaty.

She knew she'd won, at least for the moment. "Listen, take a few days to think it over. I'm making you a very generous offer and you'd be foolish not to consider it, at least. You've got a whole life ahead of you, Milja, and there's more to life than romance. Think about how you want to shape yours. Think about the support you'll need as you change physically and mentally—because it doesn't stop with street lights and scratchcards."

I shook my head, overwhelmed.

"I can help you. We can be good friends. Now, when you go outside, Mario will have a company credit card waiting for you. Buy yourself a nice new dress, some shoes, some ear-rings maybe. I've helped sponsor an exhibition at the Art Institute and the gala opening is on Saturday night. I'd like to see you there and I'm sure you'll enjoy it."

All I could think was that she'd given me leave to go. To get out from under those appraising black eyes. I grabbed my box and lurched toward the door. But a thought stopped me before I got there. I'd learned the hard way from Egan not to believe in coincidence.

"Is this why I got this job in the first place?" I asked, my voice shaking. "Have you been watching me all along?"

Roshana smiled like the cat with the cream. "I've been aware of your potential for a while, Milja. And it's an honor to offer you a hand up in life."

I sucked my lips in tight to stop the words that rushed to them escaping. Then I swept out.

Mario the secretary was waiting for me with a raised eyebrow and a purple credit card upraised between two fingers.

I don't need this, I thought. *I can manage on my own. I can play the lottery and steal cash from ATMs and keep moving...*

"You should buy a blue dress," he said. "It would work with your coloring. Try Hannah's on 131st."

I snatched the plastic from his hand and stalked off.

I went home.

And, remembering the murder and dismemberment of Azazel's sons, I spent a long time concentrating very hard on *not being pregnant*, because, dear God, that was absolutely the last thing I needed.

༄

Maybe I shouldn't have gone to the gala opening at the gallery. Maybe I should have just taken off and run for it. In theory I could have gone anywhere I liked, with Azazel's help.

Except that he hadn't reappeared and he wasn't answering my whispered pleas for attention. He wasn't what you might call reliable. So I was alone, in a new city, without any family on my side, without any friends to call on. My father was dead and I could never return to my homeland. Even my beloved cat, Senka, had been given over to my roomie when I left Boston, since I couldn't be sure that I'd be around to look after her. I was teetering on the edge of unemployment and the financial strategies at my disposal all put me on the wrong side of the law. Which, when you're an immigrant, is not a comfortable place to be.

And I hadn't the faintest doubt that Roshana, if she chose to be vindictive, could make sure that I never worked in the engineering field again. She had the contacts and the influence, and that security footage could pursue me forever. She'd made no overt threat, but I didn't think she needed to.

I was way out of my depth.

All she wanted was to meet Azazel. That's what she'd said, anyway. And he was big enough to look after himself, surely? I couldn't believe he'd find her much of a threat.

If he was still around. Maybe he was lying low to throw Michael off my scent.

If Michael hadn't somehow forced him to abandon me.

Crap crap crap. I paced my apartment for hours, trying to see through the fog of uncertainty. Wishing that there was someone there to hold my hand.

In the end I went shopping, as Roshana had suggested. I bought a dress and earrings and a necklace, and was persuaded into heels that I could barely walk upon. Because security is better than insecurity—or at any rate, easier. Even when you know they've not got your interests at heart.

Of course I did everything I could to find out about Roshana Veisi online. It wasn't that much, so I suspected money had bought her a measure of privacy. She owned a number of companies, was a patron of the arts and bred racehorses as a hobby. She was a wealthy second generation Syrian-American who had inherited a fortune from her mother. I couldn't find out if she had any religious affiliation, but assumed she was either Muslim or Syrian Orthodox. I'll admit that from a purely selfish point of view I hoped it was the latter, as the Syriac Church was a persecuted denomination with many more things to worry about than my relationship with Azazel.

Despite a long history of ethnic conflict between my people and Muslims, Islam was a mostly unknown quantity as far as I was concerned. An Abrahamic religion, of course, and they believed in angels too, even if they numbered and named them differently.

I arrived in a cab at the Art Institute of Chicago on the Saturday night. The gallery on Michigan Avenue turned out to be an arched stone building which I thought quite ugly, though I liked the green bronze lions standing guard over the steps outside. My fear that I had overdone my attire in my sparkly mid-thigh cocktail dress—copper colored, not blue—was allayed as soon as I saw the other guests in their sweeping gowns and their formal evening suits. A group of musicians in folk costume played whiny stringed instruments in the main foyer, completely at odds with our finery but looking a lot more relaxed than I felt. We handed in our coats and processed up broad staircases and through corridors and courtyards to where the *Treasures of Sheba* special exhibition was housed in the more modern Rice wing. Blown up photos on the walls here showed jagged mountain profiles, vast geometric steles and weathered buildings carved out of the living rock.

Everybody else in the crowd seemed very gracious and garrulous, but no one spoke to me except the waitresses bearing canapés and flutes of champagne. I felt completely at sea. Clinging to a glass as if it were a lifebelt, I looked around for Roshana Veisi, but I didn't spot her until several people mounted a small dais and the opening speeches began.

The antiquities on display here were mostly books and artworks on loan from collections in Ethiopia, and three slender men dressed in white wraps represented, it turned out, the Ethiopian Orthodox Church authorities who were responsible for the ecclesiastical treasures. They left most of the talking to a middle-aged American man who looked corpulent by contrast, and he introduced the various sponsors of the exhibition, including Roshana Veisi.

She wore the most beautiful gown I'd ever seen; a strapless black lace sheath over shimmering jade green that left her shoulders bare and clung to her curves all the way down to her ankles. She looked even more assured in her beauty here than she had done at the office. I stared at her as thanks were offered and applause rippled through the elegant crowd.

How do I even know someone like that? I grew up in a house with no electricity and no hot water. This is not my world.

As soon as the talking was over I buried my nose in the complimentary information leaflet. It told me that Ethiopia converted to Christianity in the fourth century, well ahead of the rest of the world including the Roman Empire. Its ecclesiastical language was Ge'ez, its calendar ran sixteen years behind the rest of the world and consisted of thirteen months, and even before conversion it had strong connections with Judaism, including the visit of its legendary Queen of Sheba three thousand years ago to the court of King Solomon. Menelik, her son by him, founded the Ethiopian royal line that continued into the twentieth century.

These dizzying claims were entirely new to me. I'd had no idea that there even was a pre-colonial Christian church in Africa, never mind one with such deep roots in history and myth. Roshana was right; my interest was piqued. Which was more than could be said of the other guests, who seemed more interested in talking to each other than in perusing the exhibits. I walked from one glass case to another, fascinated and uneasy.

The physical treasures were a little disappointing to be honest—copes and robes and stoles sewn with gold and gems, silverware croziers and censers in unfamiliar designs, their symbolism opaque but their significance only too familiar. I'd spent the first eighteen years of my life surrounded by ecclesiastical regalia so I found nothing very exotic here. It all only served to remind me of the father I'd lost, and I felt the weight of his absence in my breast.

At least I'd seen him again after his death, I told myself, and had the chance to ask forgiveness.

But the books were glorious. Codices and scrolls were covered in black Ge'ez calligraphy, enlivened by paintings of biblical stories and the lives of saints. I confess that to my eye, brought up on the grave and melancholic icons of my own faith, so painstakingly crafted, these pictures looked garishly technicolor and almost cartoonish, even though some were several hundred years old.

The subject matter wasn't always familiar either— Ethiopia had its own unique traditions so yes, some Bible stories I recognized straight away, but I was startled by a depiction of the Virgin Mary beating the infant Jesus with a knotted rope. And those saints! Their hagiographies were wildly unfamiliar. I goggled at pictures of a bearded saint climbing a cliff via the body of a gigantic python, of a nun who descended into Hell to ask the Devil to repent, and of a holy man who stood on one leg for so long that the limb fell off and he grew wings instead. Even the national patron Saint George, quite recognizable slaying a dragon, featured in a long and incredibly gruesome concertina of images in which he suffered three hundred separate tortures—flayed, boiled, impaled, roasted on a griddle—and was put to death and resurrected three times.

Eww.

I'd never seen anything like it. I shook my head in amazement and moved on to yet another room, another glass case. The books laid open in this showed various angels. Saint Raphael spearing a whale, for reasons the accompanying card description did not make clear. The Archangel Uriel stood holding a goblet in which he'd caught the blood of the crucified Christ.

I shivered. *Why would Uriel do that?* Knowing what I did of him, it suddenly seemed less an act of piety and more something deeply suspicious.

I moved hurriedly to the next open codex. The handwritten script was broken by two pictures: the first a winged angel holding a scroll and pen, surrounded by many smaller kneeling figures who seemed to be writing. The second picture showed the same angel, still clutching his pen or stylus, but lying down on a hillside beneath a building.

Something stirred in the back of my brain.

"Milja?"

Roshana? I spun so quickly on my new heels that I lost my balance and, toppling, clipped my glass against a display case. My champagne flute shattered at the stem. "Oh crap!" I yelped —and looked up into a face that wasn't Roshana's at all. The face of the man I least wanted to ever see again in all the world.

The least, and maybe the most.

It was Egan.

Four
LET'S BE FRIENDS

Egan Kansky. The man who'd saved me and betrayed me. The man who'd snatched me from under the noses of my Orthodox enemies and taught me to trust him, only to try to deliver me to his own masters.

Egan, who'd done his best to bury Azazel for an eternity of torment again, for the good of us all. I'd let him hold me as we slept together. He was the gentlest, most caring man I'd met apart from my own father—yet I'd seen him coldly shoot dead the thug who tortured me.

Egan: Irish-American, ex-military, now Vatican agent. He'd stepped in front of a bullet for me.

There were no words for the confusion of feelings in my breast right at that moment, seeing him there before me. His square face looked a little more lined than I remembered, but his sandy-blond hair still stuck out over his forehead and his eyes were still that blue strangely flecked with gold; eyes for staring at horizons. The formal evening jacket suited him; way more than it would Azazel, say.

"Egan?" *Go away, go away, I can't bear to see you*, I thought, but the words refused to rise to my lips. "What are you doing here?"

I was actually shaking.

He didn't answer. Instead he sank to his knees before me. It took a moment for me to realize what he was doing; picking up the pieces of my broken glass. Standing again, he dropped them deftly on the tray of the waiter who'd hurried over. "Thank you," he told the young man.

"I'm sorry," I gabbled to the waiter, "I'm not used to wearing heels."

"No problem, madam. May I get you another glass?"

"No… No, thanks."

The distraction reset our conversation. As we looked back at each other Egan smiled, tentatively. "Hello, Milja. How are you? You're looking…very well."

I blushed, wishing that the saleswoman hadn't persuaded me into a dress quite so short or so tight, wishing that my hands weren't trembling. "I'm good."

"I'm glad to hear it."

The depths of all that we dared not speak about yawned like the Grand Canyon. "You made it out then?"

"Yes. I walked." He gestured with open hands. "Then hitch-hiked."

I brushed my fingers over my face, wanting to hide.

"How's your hand?"

Of course. The last time he saw me I'd just had my finger broken. "It's fine. He fixed it." I didn't have to say Azazel's name.

Egan nodded, sucking his lips in. "Are you still with him?"

"You don't need me to tell you that, one way or another," I

said, finding some backbone at last. "Your people will have been keeping an eye on me, I assume."

He looked suddenly uncomfortable. I got the distinct impression he was winging it. "I've recused myself from that particular mission."

"Meaning what?"

"Sure, I told my superiors that I couldn't in good conscience accept their plans for you."

Imprisonment. Breeding. The murder of my children. "I bet that was a fun conversation."

He grimaced. "That it wasn't. But they accepted it. I'm not here on their behalf."

"You're not planning to kidnap me, then?"

He shook his head. "No. You won that round, Milja. You were right and I was wrong. You know how I feel about what happened."

"No." I shook my own, defiantly. *Let him spell it out.* "I've no goddamn clue."

"That it's not right to do a heinous evil for the sake of doing greater good later. I slipped into error while spending time with you, unacceptably so."

"What—*liking* me? That was an error?"

"No." His pale eyes narrowed with pain. "Betraying your trust. You were an innocent. I ask your forgiveness."

That was it: his apology. I stared at him mutely.

"Liking you…" He blinked and looked over my shoulder. "It wasn't what I planned. It messed things up, from the point of view of my superiors. But I don't regret it."

My eyes stung and my throat felt swollen, but I knew no tears would slip down my face. "Thank you for letting me choose," I said, my voice a wobbly whisper. "You did *let* me choose, didn't you?" *Between you and Azazel?*

"Yes."

"I chose him. Now go away. Please." I turned my back on him, staring blindly into the reflection of the glass case.

From behind, he put both hands on my waist. My world flipped upside down. His breath was on my hair, his warmth against my back. "Milja," he whispered, his lips soft against my ear, "that's not forever. You can change your mind."

If Azazel sees this, I don't know what will happen.

I shut my eyes, swaying, almost leaning back against him. I wanted him to slip his arms right around my waist. I wanted to turn within the circle of his arms and press my face to his chest, breathing in the warm sweet scent of him.

Here's the thing, the terrible stupid thing. Azazel loved me, Azazel was powerful as a thunderstorm, and he would protect me from men and angels even if he had to tear the world apart and drown it in blood to do that. But I never, ever felt safe with Azazel. I felt *safe* with Egan. Even with everything I knew and everything I guessed, even in moments of horror and rage, there was a part of me that instantly and instinctively fitted into the shield of his arm, that felt like *this is my home, I belong here.* I could think of no other way to articulate it to myself.

"Choose again," he whispered, sending shivers from the whorl of my ear down my neck and my spine, right inside me. "Please—come outside with me. We need to talk."

"Milja, you're not too busy, I hope?" Roshana's voice, clear as a bell, pierced the hot entanglement we were weaving together. Egan pulled away from me as I jumped guiltily, my eyes opening wide.

Roshana stood flanked by two men. Only their dour expressions and the security lapel badges on their impeccable evening dress revealed their status as muscle, not cash. "Do introduce me to your friend, Milja honey," she said with bright cold jollity.

"Egan Kansky," I mumbled. If there's one thing more shameful than your boss having pornographic footage of you fucking an angel, I suddenly discovered, it was your boss having pornographic footage of you fucking an angel *and finding you fooling around with another guy.* "He's not my…"

"Really?" Her smile was like a paper cut. "Mr. Kansky. I'm afraid I'm not familiar with your name. In fact…" she put a finger to her lip in mocking, coquettish innocence, "I don't think you're on our guest list at all."

Egan let his shoulders fall, visibly submitting as the two security men moved in to flank him. "Milja," he said to me quickly, "I've got my phone number back. If you ever need help, you can ring me. You know that."

"Thanks. I don't need any more help." No. People were more or less queuing up to offer me help these days, and not one of them was lacking an ulterior motive.

Roshana, triumphant, slipped her arm through mine and led me away as Egan was escorted from the room. I tried to follow him with my eyes, because it hurt me to see him go.

Oh Egan… Why do you do this?

Her skin was warm and silken, and though I didn't welcome the gesture, it didn't actually feel unpleasant. "You do like to play with fire, don't you?" she said.

"Me? No—That wasn't what you think…"

"Of course it was. It's hard to be owned, believe me. I don't blame you for trying to assert a little independence. Every tyrant's wife in history has had their bit on the side."

Was that all it was, the effect Egan had on me? I shook my head, wide-eyed.

"I admire your spirit, Milja, even if I don't appreciate the risks you take with my investment." She nodded pleasantly at other people as we strolled through the throng, greeting each by name but not letting anyone snare her in conversation.

"Investment?" Her perfume was subtle and not too sweet. She felt *soft*. I was only used to the male touch, that rough skin and the hardness of muscle beneath. My mother's embrace was so long gone that I could barely remember it.

"I'm investing in *you*, honey, of course. I do like the dress, by the way." She glanced down at my sparkly copper sequins. "You have the legs for it."

"Uh…"

She waved a hand at the exhibits. "Now these must remind you of home."

That threw me. "Why?"

"Your father was an Orthodox priest, wasn't he?"

"Serbian Orthodoxy and Ethiopian Orthodoxy aren't the same thing!" I protested, more wound up by the fact she'd been prying into my family background than by her parochialism.

"But they're similar, I assume?"

"I have *no* idea, honestly."

"Huh. Well, it's all priest stuff as far as I'm concerned. Your father was a priest, right? What about your mother, Milja? What did she do?"

"She died when I was a little girl. I don't…I don't remember her that well."

To my surprise Roshana shot me a swift dark frown of sympathy, almost understanding. For a moment she seemed on the edge of saying something, but then she visibly blinked her eyes clear and bright and cheerful. "Here, take a look at this." We'd stopped facing one of the display cases right at the far end of the exhibition. Under a row of silver sistrums, two huge old Bibles lay propped open. She released my arm to point at one. "Here he is."

Dense calligraphy crowded a picture I struggled to comprehend. A group of doe-eyed, androgynous men in white robes stood at the top of a hill. Down the slope a white goat galloped—or fell, or flew, it was hard to tell. And at the bottom of the picture waited a devil, gray-blue in color, horned and fanged and hairy.

"What does it mean?"

She spoke softly, below the conversational buzz of the room. "Leviticus 16: The Day of Atonement. *And Aaron shall cast lots upon the two goats; one lot for the LORD, and the other lot for Azazel. And Aaron shall bring the goat upon which the LORD's lot fell, and offer him for a sin offering. But the goat, on which the lot fell to be the scapegoat, shall be presented alive before the LORD, to make an atonement with him, and to let him go for a scapegoat into the wilderness, to Azazel.*" Her fingers danced over the glass, not touching. "That's him."

"That's not a very flattering likeness." It was all I could bring myself to say.

"He inspired so much fear. Hundreds, even thousands of years after he was imprisoned, people were still making propitiatory sacrifices to stop him devouring their souls."

I made an undignified snort, trying not to laugh. "If there's one thing I know for sure, it's that it's not my soul he's after."

She looked at me, her perfectly groomed eyebrows arched, and as she said nothing I blushed uncomfortably under that challenging gaze. I'm no good at cool and defiant.

"What? What have I said? You've seen *exactly* what it is he wants from me. He's not evil. And he doesn't care what I believe or how I pray. He doesn't collect souls; he just likes to…you know…*fuck*." I dropped my voice even lower for that last word, in case we could be overheard.

"I doubt Mikhail Vrubel would agree with you."

"Well." I straightened my shoulders. "I know what that's like. Before I freed Az… When I was at college, yes, he messed with my head. He was like a drowning man grabbing at anyone swimming nearby—you can't blame him for that. And if you're holding a pillow down on someone's face, you can't blame him for clawing at you! But Vrubel never let his angel out. That's why it killed him."

"You're saying your boyfriend's harmless?" She seemed genuinely surprised.

"No. I mean…not harmless." I blinked. "He's impatient. He doesn't see things from anyone else's point of view easily." I sniffed and amended; "At all, in fact. But he's not evil. Not really."

"And you're quite happy with him?"

I'm crazy-in-love with him. Oh God. "Oh yes." I let out a sigh. *Deliriously happy. When he's with me. And we're alone. And I'm not teetering over a hundred-foot drop.* "For, you know, whole minutes at a time."

"You're not what I expected, Milja."

"What did you expect—something from *The Exorcist*?"

She smiled.

"If you think he's evil, why do you want to meet him so much?"

Roshana's eyes narrowed. "Maybe I like bad boys."

"The world's full of those," I snapped. *Find your own,* I might have added.

"But your Fallen sweetheart isn't one of them? Out of interest, what would he do if he caught you and that good-looking Kansky guy together?"

I felt like she'd slapped me. "I, uh...I don't know." Oh there was a can of worms. Azazel's attitude to Egan seemed to be largely contemptuous, but sometimes amused, even encouraging—and sometimes a roiling mess of irritation. Egan meantime reciprocated with flat-out loathing.

"Would he hurt you?"

"No!" No, I didn't believe that for a moment. Did I?

"Would he hurt the unfortunate Mr. Kansky?"

"Maybe," I admitted.

"Then perhaps, for his sake, you should be more careful."

Now I wanted to slap *her*. For being right.

I think she saw that in my face, because she smiled. "Remember, you're still a good girl. He *isn't* corrupting your soul, you've said. Not yet."

"You're assuming that Egan's one of the good guys," I said stiffly. "You don't know what he's done."

"No, you're right, I don't know that. Like I don't know why he inveigled his way into this soiree to see you. Relax, honey—I'm not terribly concerned either. He's cute, but it's your other boyfriend that really interests me. Have we reached an agreement on that front? Will you introduce us?"

I didn't want to say *Yes*. I didn't want this strange cat-eyed beauty messing about with my lover. But she had information about things I needed to know too, if I was going to manage my precarious life. I had no one else to turn to. It wasn't as if I could rely on Azazel for support or advice. He hadn't even warned me not to fall pregnant. If he sensed the terrible danger in that direction, he hadn't thought to let me know.

"I can't guarantee he'll be interested."

"I know that. We work within our limitations. Just try."

"Okay, I can tell him you'd like to meet him," I agreed reluctantly. "But you have to answer my questions."

"Such as?"

"Such as, if I'm the first person to let a Watcher free, how do you know so much about the effects of sleeping with one?"

She batted her lashes. "Honey, you can fuck prisoners."

My stomach tried to rise into my throat. I think she saw the look in my eyes, but I know she didn't read it properly. Because beneath my revulsion the tiny voice of my conscience was stabbing me with the words: *And were you all that different as a teenager, Milja?*

"Oh, not me." Her carmine lips twisted. "But there are groups, you know. People with specialist interests. They've had a long time to network. Not very pleasant people, most of them. You're fortunate they never found your family."

I'd thought the Churches the great villains in this drama. The vision Roshana suggested, of people deliberately abusing the captive Egrigoroi—Occultists? Perverts? Oligarchs desperate for health and physical advantage?—made me recoil a half-step from her.

My decision was white-hot in its clarity: *Oh hell, yes, I will help Azazel free them all.*

"But you're not one of those people?" I spat the words out.

"Me? When it comes to meat, I'm strictly organic and free-range." She twinkled, daring me to take offence. "And I'm very glad we've come to an arrangement beneficial to all parties."

I fumbled vainly for words. I wanted another drink now, badly. I wanted Egan standing at my back, telling me everything was fine, that he'd look after me. I wanted Azazel to turn up and reduce this whole building to smoking rubble and make everyone *go away* and leave us alone.

No, no I didn't. Not that last one. I had to keep

reminding myself of that.

"Milja, honey." She reached out and squeezed my arm. "Take your time. Let's be calm and sensible about these things. We're not in a rush, are we?"

"I'm not."

"There you go. Let's be friends." She leaned in and kissed me on the cheek, filling my head with the scent of her perfume. "Now, enjoy the party. I have mingling to do." Waving her fingers merrily, she sashayed off into the well-heeled throng.

Leaving me alone.

I wanted, suddenly, to sit down. I wanted out of this scented, cosseted atmosphere. I wanted off these too-high heels. I wanted to splash my face with cold water and clear my head and turn over everything I'd been told until I found the little gold seed of certainty beneath. *Come outside with me*, Egan had asked, and I wished now that I'd agreed to the offer swiftly enough to escape Roshana.

But that thought reminded me of something she'd said too, something I'd not had time to dwell on mid-conversation: *I don't know why he inveigled his way into this soiree to see you.*

That was a really good question. It was such a good question that, midway to the exit of the gallery, I paused and leaned against a door jamb to consider it.

If Egan just wanted to talk to me, why did he put in the effort to gate-crash a society party where he'd be surrounded by witnesses? Why not find me at home, or on the street?

Why here? Why now?

He'd said he had recused himself from stalking me on behalf of his handlers. I believed him, sort of. He was a good Catholic and he didn't lie because that would be a sin. Or rather, he didn't tell *overt* lies. *Mental reservation*; that was what he'd called it. I'd looked it up. It means you're allowed to tell half-truths and lies of omission, even when you know you are leading someone into false expectations.

He'd misled me before. Deliberately. And oh so badly.

What are you doing here? I'd asked him, and he hadn't answered.

I stared back toward the gala crowd and the glass cases overtopping their wealthy heads. Egan had stepped up to speak to me just as I was looking at that display nearest the fire exit. When I'd turned my back on him and faced the case again—that was when he'd put his hands on my waist and got all personal.

A very effective distraction.

Biting my lip, I sidled back into the room. It took me only a few moments to re-find the right case and the right spot where I'd been standing. Oh yes—there it was. The picture of the angel lying down on the hillside.

A slight chill ran up my spine. The primitive picture lacked all perspective. It was easy to misinterpret. A kind of black blob surrounded the angel's form, which I hadn't even noticed last time.

Not lying on the hillside. Lying *under* the hill, eyes wide and staring in the dark.

This was an entombed angel. Imprisoned.

I looked at the interpretation card next to the manuscript, and even then it took a moment for my brain to click.

The Book of Enoch, Aksumite Period, Bet Giyorgis, Lalibela, it said, followed by a translated quote from the text. One which, so help me, I already knew because its astonishing lack of self-awareness had struck me as laugh-out-loud funny the first time I came across it: *And he instructed mankind in writing with ink and paper, and thereby many sinned from eternity to eternity and until this day. For men were not created for such a purpose, to give confirmation to their good faith with pen and ink.*

This was the actual *Book of Enoch*. Not the first 1821 translation into English by Laurence. Not a printout of R H Charles' 1917 version from the Internet, which is what I'd been cribbing off. *This* was how it looked in its original state, because only the Ethiopians regarded it as canonical and only in Ethiopia had the text been preserved since its first composition, copied and recopied and used by the Church there—for who knew how long? The Western Churches had lost Enoch's text for centuries, though they knew about its stories by reputation and from fragments in Greek and Latin. It was even quoted in the New Testament epistles from Peter and Jude: *God spared not the angels that sinned, but cast them down to hell, and delivered them into chains of darkness, to be reserved unto judgment.*

Here was a picture of a Watcher incarcerated beneath the earth.

And I knew exactly which one.

JANINE ASHBLESS

Five

THE SEED OF ANGELS

Azazel snatched me from my bed early on Sunday morning. I was still half-asleep as he scooped me in his arms and pulled me through a fold in space to…well, to somewhere else. Somewhere simultaneously soft and slightly prickly. I opened my eyes enough to work out that I was lying in a pile of feathers—actual feathers from real birds, not angelic wings or anything—but as Azazel spooned up behind me, his bare skin warm against mine, I decided I was quite happy staying half-asleep. His caresses were unhurried, his breath soft in my ear.

"My Milja, my love," he murmured, kissing my shoulder, and I smiled to myself, letting my eyes drift closed again. Somewhere deep inside me that knot of fear that I'd been carrying since Athens slipped loose. He was safe, and he had come back to me.

And he was eager, of course. I could feel the hot, stiff length of his erection rubbing up against me as he snuggled closer. Hard against my ass cheeks and the softness of my thighs, incorrigible in its probing quest between them, silky where I was wet. Tracing up and down the split of my sex. Eternally curious, never satisfied—a cock for exploring all of Creation, but right now focused on me. I liked that. I liked the way he was pretending that he didn't need to rut *right now*, so that I could pretend he wasn't disturbing my sleep. I liked his restless appetite and his disingenuous gentleness, his simultaneous impatience and patience, his primitive optimism. I liked the way he rubbed against my clit and my labia and the hidden well of my sex, the way it made my body tingle and ache.

Arousal stirred inside me like a serpent uncoiling. My eyes strayed open. The feathers were mostly white like those of gulls, but a brilliant blue one drifted just before my nose like a slice cut from the fabric of Heaven.

Azazel had a hand down there now, guiding his stiff flesh more precisely. He nudged into the tight mouth of my sex and I shifted my hips to engulf him further, inviting him deeper into that wetness as I moved my own fingers down to my clit. My inner flesh had to make room for his bulk. For a moment I held him in my wet and willing embrace, as we rocked gently against each other.

Then he slipped out once more, slicked with my juices. Again the slow luxurious rubbing—down my pussy, up the cleft between my bum-cheeks—as if he needed to feel so much more of my body than just that one wet hole. I didn't mind. I was in no hurry, still woozy with sleep. It felt good, his cock massaging my every intimate inch. Even the muscled iris of my rear declined to clench, enjoying the firm pressure.

I could feel my own wetness gathering, slippery beneath my fingertips.

His movements were more urgent now, though still contained, still subtle. But I could feel the lock of his muscles, the gusts of his breath on my nape and ear growing deep and harsh. The push of his cock was denting my flesh, threatening entry at my virgin whorl, never quite enough to force it but putting on an increasingly relentless pressure, and I could feel that portal softening and dilating in response. There were shivering little pulses of need waking within me, in places I was not used to, and a strange feeling of hunger inside as if an undiscovered emptiness needed to be filled. But all was dreamlike, all slow-motion, all muffled by feathers and sleep and his warm embrace.

And then he came. I felt the shudder run through his frame, heard the groan in his exhalation. A hot wet slickness surged between us, creaming the half-furled rose of my bottom. For a moment I held my breath, savoring the sound he made in his throat and the sigh that followed. My own pulse thumped in my ears. My empty sex ached like a collapsed star.

I had no time to feel disappointment. Azazel took a deep breath and, riding the wet tide of his own making, pushed full on into my rear hole. My guard was entirely down. Before I could remember to be afraid, before I could dread any pain or revulsion, he was already inside me. And the shock was as vast as his girth.

He felt like he was filling me, every part of me from head to toe. He was huge, and he fitted to perfection. This was physical closeness on a scale I had never experienced. Every nerve-ending sang. And when he moved, sliding deeper…I came, in a wave of sensation so shameful, so wonderful, that I couldn't stop myself.

My cry echoed, not deadened even by all those feathers.

"Yes," he whispered. His left hand, no longer needed for guiding his cock, slipped around to stroke the wild sleep-mussed hair from my face for a few tender moments, though whether he was rewarding me or reassuring me I could not tell.

Then, still sheathed in my ass, Azazel shifted his bulk to sit up over me, his knee ploughing through the mound of feathers. I still lay on my side, limbs loose, but he was kneeling astride my lower thigh now, his spread knees bracketing the curve of my rear. I looked up past my left shoulder to see him stooped over me like a mountain eagle, his eyes black with hunger. With his dark hair hanging down in sweaty tails and his skin glossed with perspiration, he looked like the eidolon of some ancient priapic cult, and though I knew he was a false god my heart shook in worship.

Somehow he got his hand down between us, and his thumb into my neglected sex. Then he began to move into me, slow and fierce, his cock slippery from his first ejaculation but no less hard, no less needy for all that.

Like I said, not human.

Every thrust of his cock taught my body new things about pleasure—where it could come from, and how little it had to do with dignity or decency. He was turning me inside out and his movements tore great long inarticulate pleas from my throat. I was soon sobbing under that shuddering assault on my ass—but not with pain, instead delirious with a pagan ecstasy.

When he felt his second climax approach he pitched forward over me. Sweat droplets spun in the air, spattering my skin. My eyes were unfocused, barely open; I saw his locked forearm thrust into the feathers before my face as he braced himself, the muscles beneath his skin standing out like carvings. I heard the grunts of release resounding deep in his chest.

Then slowly he eased down, muscles slackening from their

ferocious rigor. Sliding off and out of me, he stretched out face to face, cradling the curve of my waist in his hand. Already his eyes were back to their depthless quicksilver and I could see my head reflected within them, dark against the feather lining of our nest.

Azazel smiled as I pressed my palm to his panting chest, feeling the thud of blood beneath. My own heart was pounding like it wanted to jump out of my breast and join his. I was still in shock, to be honest, and floating on endorphins. I couldn't quite believe what we'd just done, nor that I'd survived such a hammering unharmed. I pictured his semen drifting like iridescent smoke in the dark caverns of my body, and a small part of my mind wondered what sort of alchemy it was working on my flesh. For a long time we lay there just gazing at each other. A downy feather, barred scarlet and yellow, drifted down to land on his shoulder and cling to his damp skin.

"Good morning," he said, the skin around his eyes crinkling.

"Wow." I had no words for the collision of feelings, both physical and emotional, within me. "Some guys would start with a cup of coffee."

"I can get you coffee, if you like."

"No. Don't." The last thing I wanted was for him to leave. "You're okay?" I whispered at last, lifting my palm to cup his cheek and feeling the rasp of his stubble. "You look tired." He should have been radiantly smug after what he'd just done to me, but he really looked like he could do with a proper night's sleep. Or whatever was the angelic equivalent. And there was gray streaked through the darkness of his unruly hair.

Well, I could fix that. I tilted in to kiss him, letting my concern for him and my desire for his wellbeing flood through me from head to toe. By the time I finished the kiss, his hair was midnight and raven wings once again.

"My little witch," he laughed softly, running his hand over my waist and up the curve of my hip.

"I was scared, Azazel. I thought…"

"Scared?"

"Did you fight with M—" I bit my words off. "With Mr. Row-the-Boat-Ashore?"

He laughed again, but his eyes darkened to a pewter glint. "I ran. This is my life now. I run, he follows. I hide in places he won't think to look. I see you when I can. I keep moving." He cupped my breast, holding it as if it were some fragile treasure. "I wish it were not like this. I wish I could stay with you day and night."

That confession shook me, and I traced my thumb across the rasp of his jaw. With all his power, all his resources…yet he lived the life of a hunted animal? "That's what was going on in Athens?"

"I would fight any of the archangels one-on-one, but they do not fight fair, and they will call in allies if they think they're losing. I'm too outnumbered."

I bit my lip. "But I heard you tell the Lightbringer that he didn't have the Host to back him up."

I meant Uriel, whose name means *God is my Light*. He's often pictured carrying a flame in his open palm. Of course, *Lightbringer* is more often rendered in Latin as *Lucifer*.

"Hnh, yes. *He* doesn't have backup. He doesn't appear to be working together with the Boatman—and I don't know why, to be honest. I'm somewhat out of the loop." He snorted. "You look in your Old Testament; Satan barely appears and when he does he is an obedient member of the Court of Heaven. Yet by the New Testament he is the great enemy, doing ill everywhere. Something has happened since I was around."

"Well duh—he was cast down from Heaven." Except that he'd told us he hadn't been: *"I never fell."* And Uriel still featured in the iconography of the Church as an archangel.

"I think not. He's certainly not on the side of the Watchers. He's no rebel."

I wrinkled my nose, acknowledging the truth. Every word Uriel had spoken to me reeked of unctuous loyalty to God. He was sarcastic, snobbish, a little bitter, yes—but not a rebel.

Azazel shook his head. "I don't know what's going on."

That worried me. If Azazel couldn't work it out, who could? Who exactly were we up against?

"So… How did the Boatman find us? Was it the consecrated ground?"

"Yes. He hounds me. He's made it his special mission not to leave me in peace, and is trying to provoke me into combat. To prove once and for all that he is the greater warrior." He blinked slowly, and touched the huge old scar that angled like a lightning strike across the right hand side of his abdomen. "He was never disposed to like me…not even when we served together. There was always rivalry."

I didn't wholly understand, but I slipped my fingers amongst his, feeling that hard puckered scar tissue, that one wound that had never entirely healed. It was Azazel's only disfigurement.

Michael did this? What sort of a monster is he? But I knew that Michael was the implacable enemy of evil, the great warrior-angel who led the armies of Heaven. He wasn't going to be a model of compassion, not with that resume. An itch of anxiety blossomed between my shoulder blades.

"Will he find us here?"

"Perhaps not. The Host don't have much imagination." He snorted. "It's almost their defining feature."

"But if they know where *I* am, where I live, they can find and trap you, surely?"

He misunderstood my alarm. "You're safe, don't worry. The unfallen Host have to abide by certain rules. They can't do anything to you directly without orders from On High, or else your own permission. Unless it's to save your life, of course. We have always been allowed to *save* people on our own initiative." He grinned. "That's where all the trouble started, to be honest; your kind are so irresistibly vulnerable. But the Host can't take you anywhere, and they can't hold you prisoner. Don't be frightened."

"I'm not worried about *me*."

He pulled my forehead to his lips, breathing the scent of my hair. "Sometimes I worry it is too much to ask of you," he said indistinctly.

No, really? I supposed that was a good sign, if only a tiny one.

Then he went and blew it. "Your little life is so fragile, like a house of sticks."

I let out a sigh and rolled back to put a little gap between us. "I have a new job, thanks for asking. Same employer though. She wants to meet you, in fact."

Azazel cocked an eyebrow. "Why?"

Because you're hot on camera. "She has a thing for angels. She's a bit weird, to be honest. I don't trust her much."

He grinned wickedly. "Is she pretty, by any chance?" The unspoken accusation was loud and clear.

"What?" I was affronted. "She's ten years older than me, at *least*."

He laughed. "But still beautiful…"

Damn, he was too sharp.

"I'm serious. She knows a lot—maybe too much. I told her I'd ask you, but that doesn't mean you should agree to meet up."

"Now you've got me really intrigued." He wasn't hiding how much he was enjoying my discomfort.

I sat up, but rather ruined any show of dignity by having to pull a sharp quill out from beneath my ass. For the first time I looked around the tiny room we found ourselves in. It looked like the interior of a giant concrete egg. The walls arched in overhead, and were braced by concrete struts. "So where on earth are we?"

Azazel propped himself lazily on an elbow. "Brazil."

I rolled my eyes at his obfuscation. "At least we're indoors," I muttered. "You need to be more careful. Less posing about on rooftops. No more shagging in churches. Or cafes."

He grinned. "Come on. I couldn't resist."

"You're a giant show-off, you know," I admonished, but I laughed. And that made Azazel pull me down again and kiss me.

"You have to be joking," I giggled, feeling him hard against my thighs. Good grief, how would I cope if his visits weren't constrained? I'd spend my whole life as a sex zombie.

"Not joking," he murmured, sliding down the length of my body, nuzzling between my breasts, his lips hot and fervent on my nipples and then my belly.

"Wait!" I yelped as he neared the point of no return. "I've something important to tell you."

Azazel looked up from between my open legs, crooking one black brow.

"Penemuel," I blurted. "I think I've found Penemuel.

Your friend, right? The other one of your three? He's in Ethiopia."

Okay, that got his attention. He sat back up on his heels. "How do you know?"

I told him—about Roshana and the exhibition at the Chicago Institute, about the old *Book of Enoch* and the illustration therein. I didn't mention Egan. There were a bunch of things about Egan that I'd never told Azazel, largely because I thought it would be a whole lot safer for the man if the angel never found out.

Maybe because I was ashamed too. A bit.

"The book came from a church in a town called Lalibela. I looked it all up—there are a whole bunch of really old chapels cut out of the living rock there. But the book's even older than the churches—it dates from the previous dynasty."

Azazel listened to every word, his expression as intense as a hawk's, then rose to his feet. "Wait," he ordered, and vanished in a clap of displaced air and a whirl of dislodged feathers.

"Oh right," I mumbled, too late. I was on my own.

The first thing I did was check how much of a mess Azazel had made of my tingling bum—which turned out, to my relief, to be none at all. Then I stood and looked around our little love-nest. I had absolutely no idea where he'd brought me. There was barely any room in here—Azazel had had to stoop a little when he stood upright. Just enough room for a mound of feathers to stretch out on.

I imagined Azazel plucking feathers from wild birds in flight. Not that I'd ever seen him fly, but it wasn't something that would have surprised me. He definitely gave the impression of wings sometimes.

The only light in the cramped chamber came from a barred vent in the dome of the ceiling over my head. I could see blue cloudless sky and hear, beyond the warbling throb of the wind blowing over that vent, birds singing and the faint honk of traffic. The pallor of that sky made me think somehow that it must be early morning, maybe dawn.

Brazil makes sense. Same dateline.

Standing, I tried to peer through the skylight, but it was too far over my head. I paced the very small circumference of my prison, trying to ignore the creeping sense of claustrophobia.

"Come on, Azazel," I muttered, to no avail.

When I leant against one of the concrete rafters I could feel it vibrating faintly. *Machinery...or wind?* I bit my lip, then scrambled up between the two inclined braces to the grill overhead. A bolt held the metal bars in place. Even with my face up against them, I could see nothing but sky.

I worked the bolt back, dropped the grill on its hinge, and pushed my head out into the light.

"Oh *no*."

The breeze tore at my face, making my eyes water. I saw a domed concrete shape, the exterior of our little chamber, falling away around me. I saw a blue bay hugged by green mountains, and a city far below me, clustered in the hills' embrace. I saw a gigantic concrete arm to my right, stretching off for a hundred feet over the gape of the air. And I recognized it all.

The colossal statue of Christ the Redeemer, towering over Rio de Janeiro.

We're camped out inside Jesus' head.

I'd barely pulled back in and dropped to the floor when there came a faint *whumph* of air, a sudden scattering of feathers, and there was Azazel again, hunched beneath the curve of the dome, the open codex in his hands.

Still naked.

"I'm not sure that this is such a great idea!" I tried telling him, but he wasn't listening to me.

"*Qāla barakat za-Hēnōk za-kama bāraka ḥərūyāna wa-ṣādəqāna 'əlla hallawu yəkūnū ba-'əlata məndābē la-'asassəlō kʷəllū 'əkūyān wa-rasī'ān,*" he read out. "Written for those who will be alive in the Days of Tribulation." He flicked through the pages and brandished the familiar double illustration at me. "That's what you saw?"

"Penemuel is the angel who taught mankind to write," I said. "That's him, isn't it?"

"Yes." He stared as if dazed. There was an expression on his face I was unfamiliar with, and it took me a moment to identify.

Hope.

It tore at my heart.

His finger stabbed at the second picture. There was a word inscribed on the hillside. It was very short—only two letters—and written in the clear discrete alphabet of Ge'ez. "This says *Roha*," he told me.

"Okay. That's the old name for Lalibela." I'd been doing my research.

"Lalibela," he muttered, tossing the priceless antique aside into the feathers. "I will go look."

I crossed swiftly to where he stood and wrapped my arms about his neck, pressing my bare body against his. The heat of his skin, the rough caress of his chest hair against my breasts, his hardness against my softness—it was only natural that I mold my flesh against his, and just as inevitable that his hands fall upon the curve of my back and then down to the swell of my bottom. I looked hard into his eyes. "Take me with you?"

His lashes swept down like a fall of soot. "It's too

dangerous, Milja."

"You said the angels couldn't touch me!"

"Dangerous for me, not you. But if I'm taken prisoner, I would not have you abandoned in a strange country."

"If you're taken," I told him fiercely, "I will find you again. Wherever it is. I will find you and free you—I've done it once and I'll do it again."

He smiled, but his silver eyes reflected light like raindrops on a day of wintery mourning. "Don't promise that, Milja—such a hope would keep me alive for years."

"But that's a good thi—"

"No. If I'm taken again, I would rather you forgot me. Find another man. Let me die."

"Don't say that!"

"Love is their weapon, Milja. They created it. They use it against us."

I pressed my face to his throat and he slid his arms around me tight. *I can't face losing you*, I wanted to say. *Don't go. Stay with me.*

But I couldn't say that. I couldn't ask him to live like a rat trapped by a dog. I couldn't chain his immortality to my fear. It would be cruel and stupid to even express such feelings.

"Please be careful," I whispered.

༄

"This looks good," said Roshana, tossing her tablet down on the sunbed next to where I sat. "I'll get John Ellis to start work on it, put a team together."

And just like that I was an architectural engineer. I suppose I should have felt happier. As Roshana wandered over to the little table nearby and poured out two icy mojitos from the pitcher, I looked around us. We were sitting near the pool on the third story roof garden of the Aqua skyscraper, because

Roshana kept an apartment there for when she was in Chicago. A few other people strolled in the distance or sat talking, but not close enough to impinge upon our privacy. In daylight, if I squinted hard, I might be able to see through the forest of high-rises to the marina on Lake Michigan. Right now, over my head, a vast undulating façade of white balconies and black glass soared over eighty floors into the evening sky, reflecting the city lights. It was a stunning building, and the tallest in the whole world designed by a woman. I couldn't shake off the guilty feeling that Jeanne Gang had earned her opportunities and her plaudits the honest way, unlike me.

"Now," said Roshana, coming back with the tall glasses, "let's talk about something more interesting." In deference to the unseasonable warmth of the October night she was wearing a casual sundress with keyhole cleavage that I found quite disconcerting. "Have you spoken to your boyfriend?"

I took a sip of my mojito, appreciating the sourness. "Yes."

"And?"

"He's...not unwilling. I mean, I didn't push him."

"Of course you didn't."

"But yeah, he's sort of interested in seeing you."

Roshana sat down abruptly on the sunbed facing me, and put a hand over her nose. I could see the flash of her wide eyes.

It startled me into asking, "You're scared?"

"Of course I am," she gasped, then recovered herself. "I've never met an actual angel. You're used to him."

"I suppose so." It was a little shocking to think what I took for normal now.

She smiled. "And aren't you nervous when something you've dreamed of all your life is about to come true?"

"I... Uh." *Yes. Of course.* I'd spent so much of these last few months in a state of excitement or terror—and sometimes it had been impossible to tell them apart.

"So where shall we meet? What about my ranch? I have something to show him that I'm sure he'll want to see."

I couldn't help the arch, suspicious look I threw her. "I think something more like neutral territory would be better."

"As you wish. When?"

I made an irritated gesture with my glass, feeling hounded. "I don't make his timetable. Azazel has lots of things to do, you know. He's—" Then I stopped short as her eyes widened and she stood, her gaze fixed over my shoulder.

He heard me. Oh...

I turned. The terrace pool had been empty of swimmers, spot lit from below the waterline to a brilliant azure. Azazel, as ever a master of the inconspicuous, was standing in the pool. On top of the water. The light from beneath his feet had bled up into his silvery eyes, so that they blazed blue.

Oh well, that's that then.

At least he was back in some clothes.

He strolled toward us across the water, tracking bare wet footprints onto the slabs of the surround. I stepped aside with studied politeness.

"Azazel, this is Roshana."

And then something happened. It happened in his eyes first, as the blue turned to crimson. Every one of the bulbs in the pool imploded as the water rose to a hissing boil, and then all the ambient lights on the terrace winked out with a fusillade of shattering glass. I heard little shrieks of surprise from people in the near-distance. The air around us suddenly grew so tight I could hardly draw breath, and a magma glow from the clouds overhead provided illumination to the scene.

IN BONDS OF THE EARTH

Roshana pulled herself upright, head high, chest lifted proudly.

"Az—" I gasped.

He wasn't even looking at me. He had eyes only for her. He stalked right up to her and grabbed her by the throat, forcing her jaw high. I could see the fear in her eyes—fear and a strange lustful defiance. I cringed inside as he stooped over her, thrusting his face to hers, his lips almost brushing her cheek and her shoulder—*sniffing her*, to my absolute horror, in a manner that was more bestial than angelic.

Then he pushed her away hard and she staggered, clutching her bruised throat.

Azazel shoved his hands into his wild hair, staring like he'd been stabbed through the heart. I could see the glint of his bared teeth. "Avansha," he said. "*No.*"

The hairs on my arms and nape crawled at the broken horror in his voice.

Roshana set her feet. She was still unbowed, though her eyes shone wetly. "Hello, Father," she said.

The air around us pulled into tight striations and then, with a thunderclap as of huge wings, Azazel vanished.

Six

PENEMUEL

"Why on earth are you asking me?" I might have sounded like I was wailing, but that was because I was clinging to a railing at the top of an ancient brick tower that leaned at an alarming angle over the city streets a hundred feet and more below. Of course I didn't doubt that Azazel could catch me if I started to slide, but I wasn't one bit comfortable.

"I want a human perspective." Azazel sat right at the edge of the roof, his back to me and his bare feet hanging into thin air. His agitation was visible as a shudder in the air around us. "She wants to see me. She keeps asking. What should I do?"

"A human perspective?" I didn't know where the hell we were, but the terracotta rooftops and pillared colonnades below looked Mediterranean to me. The regular tourists in the taller second tower behind us—the one that still stood vertically—were pointing through their safety wire and shouting at us, but of course my lover was oblivious. "Uh. If she is your daughter, then you should go see her. She deserves that much. You should see her and tell her you love her."

"I don't love her. I loved her mother, Ansha. I loved my two little boys and my little girl. I don't know this woman. I don't know what to think about her."

Okay, full marks for honesty, Azazel. "How old was she, last time you saw her?"

He twisted to glance over his shoulder at me, looking perplexed. "I, uh…small. Maybe six or seven?"

"Then please, you have got to apologize for abandoning her, at the least."

"I didn't *abandon* her—I was imprisoned!"

"You think a six-year-old knows the difference?"

"She's not six now. She knows what happened!"

I shut my eyes so he couldn't see them rolling. I'd had to cope with Roshana's frigid, brittle *sang-froid* since their horrible first meeting, and I could only imagine what emotions she was trying to bottle up.

He's never been a child. Remember that, Milja. He has no idea what it's like. He didn't grow up; he was always like this. He talks about his brother angels, but they're more like fellow soldiers than family.

"You asked for a human perspective," I said, keeping my voice steady. "Well, if she's your daughter then, *humanly* speaking, rejecting her now would just be incredibly cruel. It would break her. You have to take my word for that."

"Why do you keep saying 'If she's my daughter'?"

"Enoch said the Nephilim stood three hundred cubits high. That's like four hundred and fifty feet tall."

He snorted. "Does that seem likely to you? How would such a creature stand upright, Milja? Use your common sense."

I caught my breath, biting back sarcasm. *My common sense gave up a long time ago, Azazel, and is off quietly drinking itself into a stupor in front of reality TV.* I contented myself with, "And he said explicitly that they only had a lifespan of five hundred years. If Roshana's telling the truth, she's more like five thousand."

"Hm." His eyes narrowed.

"You should know, shouldn't you?" I tried to sound casual. "Ansha was just your last human wife, wasn't she? I'm sure you've had a bunch of other children over the years?"

He sighed. "Our children were...difficult. They grew up quarrelsome and very ambitious, and they fought each other. Most died violently, even before the divine purge. I admit, our grandchildren fitted in better with human society."

That made sense. The vision I'd had of his two sons had suggested boys with extraordinary powers. I could imagine that going to a young man's head very badly indeed. No human mother could hope to curb them, and—forgive me for being a little judgmental—I doubted very much that the Watchers had made for good fathers or role models.

And yet here, if she was to be believed, was one of the Nephilim who had somehow escaped the divine genocide and kept a low enough profile to survive down the centuries.

Hell yes, Azazel owed her his attention. But she also represented a terrible danger to him. Roshana's body, if it fell into the wrong hands, was literally a weapon. On a brutally practical level, his best bet would be to kill and cremate her as soon as he could.

I didn't want to ask if that had occurred to him too. I felt dizzy, and it wasn't just vertigo.

"How did it go in Ethiopia?" I asked—anything to change the subject.

"Not well. The old part of the city is almost entirely consecrated ground—even the dry river bed." He shook his head angrily. "I need to take you there to look for his cage. To try to talk to him. But they're waiting. I put one foot in there and they will know I'm coming."

I switched my weight from one cramped hand on the railing to the other. "Can't you use a cat to sneak in?" I hated to use the word *possession*, but I'd seen him use a cat's body before to infiltrate a monastery unnoticed. It hadn't ended well for the animal, mind.

"Someone's worked that one out. There's not a cat left alive in the town."

"Some other animal then?"

"It would have to be an animal allowed free movement. Of those, only cats are both willing and strong enough."

I bit the inside of my lip. "What about…"

"What?"

"When I was at college in Boston, you…stayed in contact. Through my dreams. Could I talk to the Watcher that way?"

"You've no connection with Penemuel."

"But you do. If you came with me… Could you reach out to him?" I wasn't going to mention the torrid occasion on which I'd inadvertently dragged both Azazel and Egan into my dreamspace. The less said about that the better.

Azazel jumped up onto the edge of the roof, balancing thoughtlessly on the crumbling stone in a way that made my stomach lurch despite everything. "Yes," he said. "Maybe. You're smart, Milja." He smiled. "And I will talk to Avansha, if you think I should."

I tried to smile back, though a big part of me wanted Azazel to have nothing to do with Roshana. I distrusted her less now that her interest in him was clearly not sexual. But I didn't feel good about this sudden change.

Then the sunlight turned golden around us—everywhere

but in Azazel's eyes. His upper lip lifted in a snarl.

I glanced around and caught the briefest glimpse of Michael standing at the far end of the roof, his long hair billowing around him like a goddamn shampoo commercial, before Azazel lunged forward and seized me.

"Time we were gone," he growled.

༄

"Is this some place you know?" asked Azazel from behind my shoulder.

I looked around my dreamspace. "Not really," I said, conscious of the light press of his fingers at the small of my back in a way that threatened my concentration and thus possibly our entire endeavor. "It's just a library. I thought that if we were trying to summon Penemuel, it'd help to have books."

"I don't like that word," he said, "but you are right. Summoning is what we're doing. So can you find me a knife?"

I twisted to look up at him, wanting some explanation.

"A knife," he repeated innocently.

"Okay." I glanced around us again. My subconscious had actually outdone itself in creating this cathedral of books which, though reminiscent of the Bapst Library back in Boston with its soaring collegiate-gothic arches and its stained glass windows, was a riot of architectural complication unlikely to be found in any real place. Stairs of polished wood crisscrossed the vertiginous spaces overhead with their many balcony levels, and I could see through the gargoyle-carved arches there into nooks crowded with bookshelves. The long hall in which we stood was flanked with reading desks sporting lamps with green glass shades. Presiding over them was a more magnificent desk like a pulpit—so high that you'd have to stand at it, not sit—built of onyx and green copper.

Concentrating on my intention, I ascended the spiraling marble steps, took a deep breath and slid open the drawer in the lectern. Inside lay a knife with a long two-edged blade.

I picked it up gingerly, between fingertips of both hands. "Will this do?"

Azazel nodded, his eyes lambent. "You realize that if this works, I will be able to use you to find all my brothers? Even Samyaza himself!"

"And I don't like that word. *Use*."

For a moment he lowered his eyelids in acknowledgement. "Now," he said, laying his fingers on his ribs just to the left of his sternum. They looked dark against the bright white of his shirt. "Stab me here. Deep."

"No way," I whispered.

"For a summoning there must be a blood sacrifice," he said. "Blood is life. Blood conducts intent between the spheres. And it is only a dream, remember."

"You think I want to hurt you, even in a dream?" My voice shook a little.

"Trust me, Milja."

Egan had urged me to trust him—and look how that had turned out. I drew my upper lip through my teeth and considered refusing. But I am terrible at defying Azazel.

He took hold of the point of the dagger and drew it to his chest, dimpling the fabric. "Concentrate on his name." Azazel swept his other hand around to grasp my nape. He stared deep into my eyes. "Penemuel."

"Penemuel."

Gripping my hand tight on the hilt, he pushed the blade home.

I felt surprisingly little resistance; the dream-blade must have been sharp. It was no more difficult slicing between his ribs than piercing the skin of an orange. Azazel gasped. I looked down and saw a thick crimson seep around the buried steel.

"Penemuel!" he cried, yanking the knife out of the wound and staggering back from me.

I flung my hands over my face, staring through the bars of my fingers. *Oh god oh god please be okay—*

Blood spurted from the stab-wound, hanging in mid-air. Except that it wasn't blood. The drops looked more like flakes of burning ash. They blew outward on an unfelt breeze, spinning in lazy curlicues as if in the updraft from a bonfire, forming a long tenuous ribbon of scarlet that stretched away down the hall and floated through one of the many gothic archways.

"Follow," Azazel gasped under his breath, one hand pressed beneath the crimson fountain. "Find him."

I dithered helplessly, all my instincts telling me to stay, to hold him, to help him. But he waved me away with frantic motions.

"Hurry! Don't lose him!"

Stifling a dry sob of protest, I set off after the shimmering aerial clue that wound under doorways and about corners, leading me through room after room of bookcases in a labyrinthine dance. The droplets looked less fiery now, more like crimson petals, and they flew more sparsely. By the time I tracked them up a winding spiral staircase and across an arched bridge and under a low lintel into the footings of a great hollow tower, there were only a few velvet flakes left in suspension, and these last few fell softly around the shoulders of a figure in white who crouched in the center of the tiled floor.

I stopped and caught my breath. He knelt with his head

bowed. I could see one bare dark shoulder contrasting with the loose drape of the bleached cotton robe; the familiar garb of an Ethiopian priest. I saw hair close-cropped around a delicate skull and fine-boned cheek. I could make out, as I approached, the open books spread out all around him, their pages flecked with blood-red petals.

Of course it's hard to read in dreams, but I doubt that I could have deciphered these tomes in the waking world. I recognized elegant Arabic calligraphy and thick Germanic black letter and boxy Hebraic; scripts in a dozen unknown languages.

The man's long elegant hand swept out to brush the pages near his knee, sweeping aside a single drop of crimson.

"Hello," I said softly. "Penemuel?"

He glanced up, strain written across his handsome face. But it was not until he rose and I caught sight of one bare breast that my brain shook itself and I realized that the lithe frame in front of me was female.

Penemuel, if this was she, was most definitely a woman.

I tried not to stare.

"What are all these?" she asked, her voice husky. "All these…" She lifted her face and indicated the interior of the tower over our heads—a hundred receding tiers of leather-bound folios and quartos and octavos in balconies threaded together by a web of slender wooden ladders. "Are they *all* books?"

"Uhuh." I remembered Azazel's fascination with my father's small private library when I first freed him. Such a thing was undreamed of all those millennia back when they were thrown into captivity. "All your fault. You taught us."

She spun slowly on her bare heel, neck craned.

"*Of making many books there is no end; and much study is a weariness of the flesh,*" said Azazel from behind me. He was quoting one of the sourer verses from Ecclesiastes. "Hello, Penemuel."

He'd caught up then. I felt a rush of relief to see him on his feet and smiling.

It was as nothing to Penemuel's reaction. She lurched past me to face him, her golden-brown eyes wide with recognition. Thrusting one palm flat toward him, she met his hand as if pressing against a mismatched reflection in a mirror. She was as tall as he was. I'm not used to women taller than me.

"Azazel," she breathed in wonder. "You're alive."

"World without end."

I noticed that the red stain across his shirt was no longer weeping new blood, and that he seemed to have recovered from his ordeal. I found myself hovering awkwardly, an unnecessary adjunct to their conversation.

"We didn't know that you were still with us. We thought you might have been unmade."

"That would have been a kindness, wouldn't it? Never trust a God who keeps telling you how merciful He is."

"Azazel." Her face fell. "Don't."

"It's a bit late in the day to start being nervous, I'd say."

She laughed sadly. "You haven't changed."

"Well, *I* haven't." He looked her pointedly up and down, his silver gaze lingering on her breasts. "This is…new." Judging from his expression he was appreciative if somewhat perplexed.

She stared down at herself as if reading a book of revelations. Where their hands touched, a golden light leaked from between them. "This? It pleases me better."

"You had a mortal wife last time I saw you."

"And a husband. They both stood and tried to defend me

when Gabriel attacked." Her smile looked broken. "Can you imagine?"

His own expression struggled not to shatter as he shook his head sorrowfully.

"You were the first to be taken, Azazel. You missed the slaughter. The years of war and devastation."

"I did not miss it all."

Pain flicked across her face to match his, as if she was reading his memories. Quite possibly she was; they stood pressed palm to palm as if about to hurl themselves into an embrace. "We looked for you, Azazel. We thought if we could find and free you then we stood a chance. But you were nowhere to be found. Zaqel said you'd been taken toward the Black Mountain and we sought there, but we found no way in, and then the Host were upon us."

"I cried out. No one answered." His face hovered over hers, almost touching. "Where was Samyaza taken to?"

"I don't know. We were separated."

"Ah. A pity. We will find him, though."

"How did you find me? This is a dream, isn't it? Hers?" She didn't look at me. "That's cunning."

"For the moment it is a dream. But I am free, Penemuel."

Her eyes widened. "Free? How?"

"My Milja cut me loose." He indicated me with a glance, and for a moment she actually stared at me before her attention swung back to him like their faces were magnets. "I walk the earth just as in the old days. Soon you will too. We will find you and we will free you."

"But the Host?"

"Not what they used to be. They've grown slack, sister."

"That can't be."

"They haven't dared come to battle," he assured her—not

entirely honestly in my opinion, as it certainly looked like Michael was spoiling for a full-on fight.

I think Penemuel had enough sense to doubt him. One eyebrow arched. "What are you planning?"

"We will free you, first of all. Then Samyaza and all of our brothers. Tell me where you are—Are you in Lalibela?"

She looked uncertain at the name. "I am still in the Land of Punt," she hazarded. "Beneath the earth. The rock is red. The sun and moon stand over my head."

"What do you know about your prison?"

She shut her eyes as if listening intently. "I hear singing," she whispered. "And prayer. Prayer day and night. Men with bare feet. I hear the hooves of donkeys, but beyond them a rumble I do not recognize. It is a place of many voices." The golden light between them was growing.

"What do they say when they pray?" I asked, feeling gauche for interrupting. But there were at least eleven rock-cut ancient churches in the Lalibela cluster according to my research, each with its own patron. "I mean, anything specific to the place?"

"They call upon Maryam and Gebriel and Giyorgis to protect them from the evil beneath their feet."

Mary and Gabriel and George. "Well," I said, pulling a that-information-is-a-bit-too-vague-to-help-us face, "the church of Saint George is where the book came from. We could start with him."

"Your wife is clever," she told Azazel. "Her head is full of books." I couldn't tell if that was supposed to be a compliment or a joke, given our surroundings. "I am glad our work was not in vain," she added. Her bare breast was almost brushing his chest.

"You cannot imagine what we have wrought," Azazel said.

"But I promise, you will see it."

"I am glad you are free."

The light was almost too bright to look into, now. It streamed from between them, blurring their bodies, almost as if they were losing physical coherence. I could feel myself trembling in every limb. I knew with a piercing certainty that I should not be watching—that this was not for my eyes.

"Don't lose hope, Penemuel."

"I never held on to hope. I have longed for death. I only wish I had been forgotten millennia ago."

"It will all be worth it. You will walk in the sunlight again." They were both taller now, stretching into shapes less than human. I shaded my eyes with my hand, ashamed as a child is ashamed when he sees his parents embrace. This was a mystery not meant for me.

"How can we fight God, Azazel?"

"I don't know, but I will not stop trying. I will never give in."

I couldn't make out his face anymore. Their forms seemed to be fluid and curved within the nimbus of shuddering golden light. Flickering vanes suggested the vibration of great wings. They were huge—twenty, thirty, fifty feet tall and still growing, etiolated. I couldn't even tell Azazel from Penemuel; they seemed to be coiling around each other in a spiral. It dawned on me that the Bible verse, *in the resurrection they neither marry, nor are given in marriage, but are as the angels of God in Heaven,* did not mean what I'd always been told it meant. Angels were not sexless even in their ethereal state. The library throbbed with the ache of their power and their desire —but it was a passion divorced from flesh, nothing to do with cocks or vulvas, male or female, pleasure or kink. It was the rush of great powers in primal motion, so alike in nature that they couldn't help but pour together and co-mingle; more nuclear force than lust. It was holy as a vast waterfall is holy, and as inexorable.

Stretching up into the great vertical space of the tower, they had become a living helix of light—a caduceus coiled about the pillar of the world. Flinching beneath their effulgence, entirely forgotten, I thought of the legends from all across the world. I thought of the Garden of Eden and the Great Dragon of Saint John's Revelation, stories bookending the whole of human history.

Oh dear God—is this what they looked like before they took human shape? Giant golden serpents? Winged snakes? Is this what angels are?

There are fairy stories in my homeland about the *zmaj*, dragonish creatures of incredible magical powers and ancient wisdom, with a marked yearning for human women. They are said to have fathered many of our mythical heroes. I'd never made the connection. It seemed obvious now.

The bookshelves were catching fire.

Tighter and tighter they twined, writhing. I could not bear it. I could not bear to see him joining with her. It hurt my tiny selfish human heart.

I stretched every muscle in my head and forced myself awake.

I came to on my bed in my apartment. A split second later Azazel blinked into existence and crashed down onto the mattress next to me, nearly wrecking the bed frame. He was stark naked and wide-eyed.

Also he had the most epic erection, even by his generous standards.

"Milja?" he gasped. "What—?"

I reached out and grabbed his length, squeezing brutally

hard. I wanted that hot, engorged cock. I wanted his full, velvet-skinned balls. I wanted his beautiful muscular body.

"Why did you stop the dream?" he groaned.

But most of all I wanted him to be hard and hungry and elementally undeniable for *me*. Not goddamn Penemuel.

I jumped up, straddling his hips. I was still plumped and slippery from what he had done to me before I fell asleep, and I impaled myself upon him with ease, feeling every inch. His girth stretched me deliciously, and he grunted.

"You made me wake up," I lied, running my hands across his chest. There was no sign of any wound between his ribs. "I was so hurt I couldn't help it."

"Hurt?" Spread-eagled beneath me, he looked baffled. "When did I hurt you?"

"Fuckssake, Azazel!" I moved my hips, starting to grind him, and was rewarded by the look of almost panicked need that shot into his eyes. "Do you think I *want* to watch you screwing someone else?"

"You're jealous?" he gasped.

I rose and sank upon his beautiful thick length, ruthless with him but crueler to myself. "Yes I'm jealous!"

"Why?"

"I'm human! That's how we are! That's what we do!" I dug my nails into the skin of his chest, scoring red lines. "I don't want you to be with other people!"

He clenched one hand in the bedding and pushed back up into me, meeting my thrusts with his own. "You're afraid I won't want *you*?" he growled, catching both of my nipples in the splayed fingers of his other hand and pinching possessively. Sparks flared along my spine, cold-hot flashes, but I was too aroused to flinch.

"Your gigantic fucking cock wants me," I answered, my

hips pumping and my teeth bared. "But it's not picky. You're stiff 24/7. You're ready to spurt at the first sniff of pussy."

"Your. Pussy. Sends. Me. Crazy."

"Anybody's does. You're just a dirty horndog, Azazel."

His eyes were rolling backward under his lids. His spine arched, heels digging into the mattress.

"Slutty little angel," I hissed, knowing I was dancing very close to the edge of disaster. But there were fears roiling in my belly that could be expressed no other way. I'd always thought it was possible he was banging his way around the globe when he wasn't with me, but I'd tried not to think about it. I'd pushed the picture into a cupboard in my head and bolted the door, just because there wasn't anything I could do about it. "Wasn't that the whole point of becoming flesh?"

"Yes," he grunted, face slackening as his crisis built.

"All those bouncing tits and those fine round asses and lovely wet little pussies—you just couldn't resist dipping your wick, could you?"

He was past the point of speech.

"Come on—shoot your load, you can't fucking help yourself. Your balls are bursting. You need to fill cunt. You want to drown every woman in the world in your jizz. Come on and fuck me like you mean it—Ah!"

He roared as he came, and I held on for dear life as he bucked and erupted into me. He took me with him. My nipples were on fire in his broad, hard hand. My toes tore at the bedding. I could hardly breathe for the flames in my head.

Then he released me, sinking back into the pillows. As I came back down from the fiery heights I steadied myself, hands braced on his heaving chest.

I love you so much. Do you understand that? How I feel? There had to be some way to make him see it—of making it *real*, something as objective and indisputable as a rock held in the hand. Saying it wasn't enough; words could lie, or could be taken back. I ached to find some way of conveying meaning beyond mere words, some way that was solid and irrevocable. When I was an adolescent I thought that sex would do that—younger still, and I'd imagined that it was a kiss that made all the difference. But it eluded me still, and frustration prickled my fingers. He looked so desirable that, God help me, my base impulse was to slap him over and over. I wanted to shake him and to eat him up whole—and I didn't understand any of these instincts.

Slowly his eyes regained focus. I could feel his cock pulsing inside me.

He reached up one arm, hooked the back of my neck and pulled me down on top of him. For a moment I tried to resist. I felt his free hand snake around and cup the splayed curve of my ass firmly, fingers brushing the sensitive places bared between my cheeks. Then he pulled my lips to his and kissed me. Long and slow, like he was eating my wild words and taking possession of my tongue. And that was when I came again, whimpering like a small animal and crying out and trying to save myself but failing altogether.

Desire did not die with my orgasm; I wanted more. He was still hard inside me and I took advantage of that, pushing down on him. Then I sat up, catching his wrists in my hands as he released me. They felt solid as oak under my narrow fingers.

Azazel's hot-metal eyes widened and he went very still.

I should have seen the signs. I should have heeded the warning, as the room temperature plummeted. But I was too high on being fucked, and on wanting to fuck him more. And he didn't resist. He could have stopped me easily, but he didn't try. Not in time.

"No," he whispered.

I thought he was joking. Pushing his hands open, I bent to kiss his lips, grinding my pussy on him. He was as hard as ever, after all.

He twisted under me, fast as a snake, and slammed me onto the mattress. "No!" he cried, recoiling convulsively. For a second almost all the light fled the room, and in that instant I thought the walls towered in around us, huge slabs of rock. The smell of stone and water and blood hung on the dank air. An eagle screamed overhead.

Then the light came back and there was Azazel hunched on the very edge of the mattress, rubbing at his wrists with knotted hands as if there was something awful on them. The look on his face was a scramble of terror and shame. Then pride slammed down on both, smoothing his features to a bleak insouciance and pushing his shoulders straight.

"Never do that," he said thickly. "Never. It makes me… uncomfortable."

"I'm sorry," I whispered, crimson with guilt. What the hell had I been thinking of? Memories of his tortured incarceration must still be imprinted in his very flesh.

Warmth leached back into the air. He crawled over me across the bed, using his weight to pin me. He gripped my wrists in exactly the way that he'd so objected to me doing to him, and I made my whole body relax, yielding to his far greater strength. If he wanted to break my bones it would take him no effort at all. I looked up into the blackness of his eyes.

"I'm so sorry, Azazel," I told him. "I should have thou—"

"Shush." He smiled, mollified by my submission, but I could feel a tremble vibrate from his bones into mine. His lips stooped to mine, then brushed my cheek. "I love you," he growled in my ear. "Never doubt that, Milja."

"Okay," I whispered, drowning in the scent of his skin, his hair, his heat.

But why? What am I but a lanky monkey who's always scared, always angry, and liable to screw up at any time? At least I used to be sweet and innocent. I'm not even that anymore.

༶

I woke from my doze when I suddenly lost Azazel's spooning warmth at my back. I don't think it'd been more than a few minutes since we last spoke. I looked around, wondering why he'd left without a word or a kiss. Then I saw the golden light coming through from the other room and I knew.

Wrapping the cheap cotton throw from the foot of the bed around my bare body, I padded through to the doorway. The Archangel Michael stood in the middle of my small apartment, looking about him at the book shelves and the pictures. A paperback copy of *The Girl with the Dragon Tattoo* slipped from his hand back onto the low table.

"Hello, Milja. Nice place. Has he moved his toothbrush in yet?"

It was like waking to find a giant bird of prey in my tiny living room; he looked wildly unsuited to a domestic setting and way too big for it, even with wings furled. In fact, with that Roman nose and those unblinking amber eyes, there was something distinctly golden eagle-like about him. If he stretched out he could knock over walls, I thought.

"What do you think you're doing?" I asked. "This is my *home*. You can't just come barging in!"

"You're right," he said, looking startled. "I have to have your permission. No, hold on, wait…that's vampires. Shame."

I pursed my lips. "Well, God certainly did not hold back on the sarcasm when he made you guys."

He smirked. If you're that good-looking, even a less-than-warm smile can be a weapon of devastating charm. Turning to the couch, he sat down with arms draped over the back and knees spread. It was not so much an invitation as a claiming of territory.

"What do you want?" I kept my voice hard, even as I thought of the icon of Saint Michael that had stood guard over the key in my father's church. That holy painting had always made me feel nervous as a child, and he was no less intimidating in the flesh. His piercing gaze rested lightly upon me, with all the gentleness of a sword-point.

"Nothing."

His rigger boots were caked in dried mud, I noticed, and flaking on my rug. I wished he would blink. It still creeped me out, even though Azazel should have inured me to it. "Angels aren't supposed to lie. What are you doing here?"

"Waiting."

"So, what…you're sitting guard over me until Azazel comes back? Is that your plan?"

"He's too much of a coward to face me. Runs every time."

"If that's the way you want to call it."

He looked at the kitchen door. "I see you have a kettle. You got any tea? I like that Earl Grey stuff. Tastes like flowers."

"I know the rules, you know. You can't actually do anything to me."

"True enough. And I'm not stopping you leaving, if that's worrying you."

"I can move out. Get a new place."

"That's fine, I'll find you. This apartment's a bit small for the two of us, to be honest."

I clenched my jaw, weighing my options. "Okay," I said,

and dropped my wrap to reveal my naked body, in all its postcoital salty glow.

That wiped the smile off his lips. "Don't play those games," he growled, sitting up and looking away from me.

Love is Azazel's weak spot. Shame is theirs. They're terrified of their own human flesh.

"What? Does this make you uncomfortable? That's a pity, seeing as how it's my house and I like to walk around it naked."

"You are shameless." His gaze was sliding all over the place, not daring to settle on me.

"I've got nothing to be ashamed of." I hefted my breasts and jiggled them. "They're my tits. In my apartment. If you don't want to see, clear out."

"Put your robe back on," he rasped.

"Oops," I said. "Did I drop it?" Turning my back to him, I spread my feet and, straight-legged, bent over to pick the fabric up again. Nice and slow…

He moved so fast he'd launched me across the room and onto my bed before I even realized he was out of his seat. The abused mattress twanged in alarm. It knocked the wind out of me—and more than that, shocked me half to death. I wasn't in the least bit hurt, not even bruised, but I hadn't expected him to touch me at all, under the rules. Maybe the Boatman sailed closer to the wind than I'd bargained for.

"Don't do that, whore!" he barked, leaning into my face. He looked furious. I knew why. It takes a human decades to learn how to deal with all the things that come with an adult body—all those hormones and instincts—without losing control. Angels never had the advantage of a gradual introduction.

I had two choices: surrender or fight. I bared my teeth and

snarled right back at him, matching his rage and contempt. "Or what? You're going to *rape* me? 'Cause I think that might just count as a fall from Grace, don't you? And then you'd be royally *fucked*, Mister Michael."

He recoiled, drawing himself up in undisguised horror. I took advantage of the gap between us to roll over and pull the drawer of my bedside cabinet open, pulling out the silicon rabbit sex toy I'd been given at my graduation party. I hadn't used it in months, I couldn't even remember if there were any batteries in it, and I certainly wasn't feeling horny, but I wasn't going to let that stop me.

"Wanna watch?" I asked, spreading my legs wide. "Because that's what us girls do when we're home alone these modern days. You can go into the other room if it squicks you out to see. Then you'll only have to listen to the noises I make."

He turned on his heel and stomped away, slamming his hands into the doorframe hard enough to crack the wood. But he didn't leave altogether. He was just that bit too stubborn.

And the buzzer rang. My apartment has a concierge service; his light was flashing.

Sitting there stark naked on my bed with a bright pink sex toy brandished like a weapon against an archangel, I caught my breath and tried to stave off realizing how ridiculous we must look. I couldn't help listening to the buzzer. It was really annoying.

Michael was clumping around the living room again, out of my line of sight. I heaved myself off my mattress and went to the wall unit, thumbing the button.

"What is it?" I snarled.

"Milja Petak?" came the crackly voice. "Parcel delivery for you downstairs. Needs signing for."

Now? Why now!? I rolled my eyes. "Okay."

I was in my T-shirt and panties before I had second thoughts. I padded through to the other room and glared at Michael, who was staring out of the window at the pigeons with an expression of affronted determination. "Hold on," I said, suspiciously. "Would that be you, by any chance? Are you making fake calls?"

He looked at me over his shoulder, one eyebrow raised. His ruffled feathers were almost visible. "You'll have to find out for yourself."

"That's pretty devious," I had to allow. I was, after all, at least partly dressed again, and my bubble of defensive rage had popped. An uncomfortable awareness was growing in me of just how badly Michael could mess with my life if he wanted to play it that way. Just so long as he left all the wrong decisions to me.

Well played, Michael.

I let my pent up breath out in a huff. "Look, let's talk about this. You're staking me out like a goat on a wolf-hunt, aren't you? You can't catch the wolf, so now you're waiting for him to come to you. Well, I've been there; done that."

Michael snorted, but granted me another sidelong glance to show he was listening.

"It's not going to work, you know. You can't hurt me, so you can't force him to show himself."

He swung around, tilting his chin arrogantly. "The Scapegoat will turn up, sooner or later. You are his whore. He will come for you."

"Okay, I'm not loving the Biblical insults." I shrugged off the irritation. "But you've got it wrong. Azazel doesn't have to come back for me."

"He needs you."

"No he doesn't." I took a deep breath. "He might not have worked that one out yet, but he doesn't. He needs love, care…attention…or he starves; yes okay. But he can get that other places. There are other people who can fill in for me just fine." *Roshana now. Penemuel.* "Oh, Michael—you really don't get human nature, do you?"

"What do you mean?"

"We're built to fall in love. We do it at the drop of a hat. D'you know who my first love was—apart from Azazel? Prince Marko. He was a hero in our fairy stories in Montenegro. He would ride around on his piebald horse Sharatz and save princesses and kill bad guys. I never met him, never saw him, but I was hopelessly in love with him as a child. Then when I was fifteen I fell in love with Prince Andrei from *War and Peace*. A novel, you know? I mean, I had my own boyfriend at college too, but that didn't stop me swooning over Andrei. We can't help ourselves—even a couple of lines in a book is enough to set us off, never mind a living breathing handsome hero like the ones we see in the movies. The fact is, Azazel could find another woman anywhere he looked."

Michael looked dismayed. I pressed onward, feeling a bit sick despite my studied disdain.

"He doesn't even need to find himself another girlfriend. All he has to do is put a couple of videos up on the Internet and let it go viral—tying his hair up in a man-bun, or rescuing a bunch of kittens from a fire or something, I dunno—and he'd have hundreds of thousands of fans. Little girls, old ladies, every horny woman in between—oh, and the gay guys… They'd all *love* him. I'd put money that that would keep him going way better than a few priests doling out rations and prayer."

"You are all wrought of lust," he said, appalled.

"Yep. Pretty much."

"But he is obsessed with you, and that is what matters."

"At the moment, yeah," I agreed, biting my lip. "It won't last. It can't. I'm going to get old and fat and menopausal and I'll stop wanting sex and then I'll die. And Azazel will carry on without me."

He frowned. "Doesn't this…hurt you?"

"Hell, yes. Of course it does."

"Then…then *why* do you damn yourself eternally for his sake?"

Oh boy. I spread my hands helplessly. "Because what I have now makes it all worthwhile."

Michael shook his head slowly. He wore the expression of a man who finds dog mess smeared on his shoe and can't understand where he picked it up from.

"So you're wasting your time," I concluded. "If Azazel can't get to me he'll give up eventually, and go off and find someone else. And you'll never get your hands on him. You'll just sit here watching me play with myself for nothing."

"Eventually." He seized on the word, but weakly. "You underestimate his stubbornness. I think he will come for you."

"No, he won't." I walked over to the kitchenette and put the kettle on the hob. "I've made sure Azazel was listening to every word of this conversation. He knows what you're planning and he knows the solution, and right now Azazel knows I think he should stay the hell away. Do you still want that cup of tea?"

Michael didn't answer. I looked over to see him staring at me, his brow knotted with a look of utter dismay.

So handsome, I thought. *But not nearly devious enough.*

With a shake of his head the archangel vanished. Golden dust hung in the sunlight, settling onto my rug.

I sat down at the kitchen table, quite silent, as the kettle fizzed. Then I put my face in my hands and stared out wide-eyed from between my fingers.

It was all true, every word. And I'd used the names often enough to be sure Azazel had heard. So now he knew, if he hadn't worked it out before.

I'd given him step by step instructions, pretty much.

Sooner or later Azazel would have to move on from me. I'd pronounced my own doom.

Seven

THERE WERE GIANTS ON THE EARTH IN THOSE DAYS

We went out to meet Roshana at her ranch, which wasn't in Illinois but in the Minnesota North Woods region. She was sitting on a swing at the front of the sprawling modernist wood-and-glass building when we arrived, so intent on the tablet in her lap that she didn't see us when we first appeared. Not until we crunched across the track did she glance up and stand quickly, laying the computer aside.

Azazel cleared his throat.

Roshana was wearing jeans and cowboy boots and a tight yellow T-shirt, which made her look very different from the businesswoman I was familiar with. She stood with fists curled, and the expression on her face was one of trepidation, like a teenager seeing a father she didn't know for the first time since his release from years in prison. It occurred to me that that was what she still was inside her head—a young girl orphaned by violence, bereft of both mother and father, now making contact again with a family she hadn't dare hope for in years.

Still, I couldn't help feeling that her T-shirt was inappropriately tight for this reunion.

"Father," she said quietly. She hadn't looked at me—possibly she hadn't even noticed I was there.

"Avansha," he answered. He was so tense about this meeting that, for once, he hadn't even screwed me when he picked me up. And I still wasn't sure whether it was guilt or the resurrection of bad memories that troubled him. Maybe he just didn't want to get involved with family.

I bit my lip, feeling like a spare wheel. I'd only tagged along because Azazel looked unhappy enough that he might bail on the encounter. I didn't want to be here. "I'll go for a walk," I suggested into the silence that hung over us. "Find me when you're ready."

For the first time Roshana's gaze flicked briefly to me. "You can sit inside if you like."

"Nah. I'd rather just hang out here." I touched Azazel's arm briefly then set off down the track between the front yard and the paddocks, and only then did I let my breath out in a long sagging sigh of relief.

It was a lovely place Roshana had here—farmland nestled in a river valley between wooded hills. I don't know how much further north we were than Chicago, but it certainly felt cooler, with an autumnal freshness to the air despite the warm sun. The birches that lined the road margins were starting to shed their golden leaves. The unpaved road was tough on my feet in their inadequate indoor shoes, so I dropped to an amble and stuck my hands in my jeans pockets.

I couldn't hear anything from back up at the house, so at least they weren't shouting at each other.

Oh God, what're we going to do about her? She's a

IN BONDS OF THE EARTH

Nephilim, and they are bad news; everyone says that. Even Azazel admits it. And if the Church gets hold of her...

After a few hundred yards I came across some grazing mares with foals in a paddock with a white-painted steel fence. I know nothing about horses, and couldn't tell if the ones visible in every field were racehorses or not, but they looked vast and leggy and magnificent to me, and their noses so velvety that I longed to touch them. I leaned my arms on the top rail, watching as a glossy foal nursed from its dam. It made me feel a little weird, watching their warm and peaceful bond. Roshana's mother had been killed by angels; mine had died from pneumonia one long bleak winter. I'd been nine at the time, nearly ten. I remembered her wistfully, but with no great clarity. After her death Papa and I had been the only family members left in the Old Country. He'd never remarried because he was a priest, and they must remain widowers until death.

It occurred to me for the first time how lonely my father must have been, in that tiny house and that tiny chapel cut into the mountain wall, with only his daughter and our silent, terrible prisoner for company. The responsibility cast upon him, to raise a child and guard a demon, must have been almost unbearable. And then when he'd sent me away to America at eighteen, to keep me away from Azazel, the loneliness must have become so much worse. He'd been without the comfort of family for five years, almost until his death. All because I was too wayward to obey his warnings.

I'd let him down, beyond words, but he'd never stopped loving me.

I wondered if it worked the same way for a daughter let down by a wayward father.

Then I wondered what it was like for Azazel, to love

mortal women and father children that he would inevitably see grow old and die. Could he really love them, as a human man loves his family? Wouldn't there always be that resignation to loss, an emotional distance?

Shivering a little, despite the brightness of the day, I pulled myself away from the fence and turned down another track, toward the river.

There was a figure walking up toward me.

I'd seen ranch hands from afar around the buildings, and out with the horses. This figure, even at a distance, struck me as different. It was very short, and seemed to be wrapped in a drab blanket. I could make out thick dark hair and a dark face, but no other details yet. But it seemed to be making shuffling steps and staggering a little, as if exhausted or dizzy or both.

I slowed in my tracks, unaccountably wary, just as the figure—was it a child?—pitched forward onto its knees and then sank down, too weary to rise again.

"You okay?" I called, not as loudly as perhaps I should. I jogged a few hurried strides forward—and then blanched as a squirrel, startled from the base of a tree by my motion, ran across the track and *right through the figure* as if it weren't there at all.

"What the—" I started to mutter, but I already knew. All around me the autumnal landscape was bursting with color; the green of the grass, the gold of the turning leaves, the shining white of the birch boles, the blazing reds of distant maples. But this figure was gray as dust, just as if I was looking at it—and only it—through the lens of an overcast wintery day. It didn't belong under this bright sunshine, it belonged to a day long buried in the past.

I hadn't seen any ghosts since coming back to the States. And as I watched, this one sank down and became a shadow among the other flickering shadows cast by the birch canopies, and then leached out and became nothing at all.

I walked forward, feeling cold inside. There was no stain on the crushed rock road, no sign of an unmarked grave nearby.

Why did I see that?

"Milja. We're done."

I whipped around and there was Azazel close behind me, his arms folded and his shoulders hunched. "Did you see?" I demanded.

"See what?"

That gave me pause. I'd never discussed my ghosts with Azazel. I'd seen my father the last time we were back in Montenegro, and that seemed altogether too private a moment to share with him. He'd disliked my father a great deal, with justification.

I took a deep breath. "Never mind. Just a squirrel. Were things okay with you and…?"

"We're okay," he said flatly. I could read nothing in his mirror-shade eyes.

"Are you sure?" I asked, laying my hands on his forearms. Inside me, I admit, hope sparked that it was over, that we'd never have to see Roshana again.

"I apologized. She accepted my apology."

That seemed a little weird to me. I blinked, waiting for something more. Shouldn't that conversation have taken a lot longer? Shouldn't there have been shared reminiscences and tears and whatever? "Okay," I said doubtfully. "Are you two going to get on together?"

"I don't know."

"Give it time."

"We have that, at least."

All the time in the world. I squeezed his hard arm-muscles. "Well, congratulations, I guess. You have a daughter! And…I dunno…any grandchildren? Has she got children of her own?"

He looked perplexed. "I did not think to ask."

"Right then…maybe that's a conversation for another day." *He doesn't understand. He doesn't know what it means to have family, to be a link in a chain from forebears years past, and leading on into the future. He can love his children, but they are not his legacy, because he's immortal. He's just himself. So isolated.* I stretched up and kissed his cheek, thinking that with each iota of new understanding I gained, he became that little bit stranger to me. "What now?"

He looked back up the track and jerked his chin. "We're going for a ride." There was a chunky Nissan pickup trundling down the road toward us, all shiny ox-blood paint and glittering chrome. I could see Roshana at the wheel.

"Where?"

"Not far."

I took a deep breath. "You know the Boatman showed up in my apartment last night? We talked for a while."

"I heard." He brushed his fingers across my cheek. "You outwitted him."

"Yeah, I…"

The pickup stopped and Roshana put her head out of the window. "Jump in!"

There was enough room in the big cab with its bench seat for all three of us, but Azazel only glanced in before vaulting lightly onto the flatbed behind and parking his very fine ass against what I took to be a gun-rack.

Roshana's face fell a little.

I was forced to be a bit more practical about transport, so I climbed in with Roshana, trying not to show my own reluctance. "Everything okay?" I asked, wincing at my own words. How could everything be okay?

"We're just fine." She looked away, checking her side mirror.

We set off, taking the track up the valley. Soon the fenced pastures fell behind us and we were driving on unpaved roads among stands of aspen and oak and dense, dark conifers. An uncomfortable silence reigned in the cab. I could only think of two obvious topics of conversation, and one was too intrusive. So I broke with, "Where are we going?"

"There's a Watcher grave on my land."

"That's…lucky."

"Not even slightly. I bought this place because of the local stories." Reaching to the tablet stashed on the dashboard, she flipped the cover and—driving one-handed—went through the password page before brandishing it at me. "Take a look."

I found myself staring at a PDF that seemed to consist of a lot of scanned newspaper columns. Very old newspapers, from the looks of them—most were dated between the 1870s and the First World War.

"Did you know that the States has a tradition of giant legends?"

"Paul Bunyan?" I asked, remembering a cartoon I'd seen whilst a student. The newspaper clippings had titles like *Giant Skeletons Found in Mound* and *A Race of Giant Indians*. They came from places as disparate as Ohio and Utah and Kentucky.

"More archaeological than that. In the nineteenth century antiquarians and treasure hunters started digging into pre-colonial mounds. Mostly they just found pottery and ordinary bones, but all around the country there came reports of skeletons and mummies too big to be human—nine, twelve, fifteen feet tall. Some even had red hair. It was assumed then that they dated from ancient races that existed before the Flood."

"Huh." I was pretty sure Azazel gave no credence to the idea of a worldwide Deluge. *Floods*, yes, in the plural—and earthquakes and volcanic eruptions, when the loyal angels and the Watchers fought. It had been a bad time for everyone. I wrinkled my nose at the dossier. "Really? Where are the bones now then? I've never seen any in a museum."

"The bodies crumbled rapidly when exposed to sunlight. Almost all the physical evidence vanished."

"How inconvenient."

"You're skeptical." She shot me an acerbic sideways look. "And yet here we are driving around with a fallen angel in the back of the pickup."

"Okay... What were they then? Nephilim?"

"Some of them were, I guess."

"No offence, but you're pretty short. For one of the Nephilim." *Zmajeviti*, they'd call her back home. A dragon-child, whose task it was to fight the destructive hailstorms that were so dreaded by farmers.

"I used to be taller." She laughed. "Being tall makes you stand out. It's not always an advantage. Don't think you're the only one with extraordinary abilities, Milja honey—You're just Azazel's main squeeze. I'm his blood. No offence."

I was glad to have to hold on to the seat and catch my breath as we took a sudden turn left up a rutted track that was so badly maintained that birch saplings bent under our bull bars and scraped horribly on the underbody. The SUV bounced around wildly, but I assumed Azazel was just fine out there. "Do you remember him?" I asked, figuring that since we were past the being-polite-to-each-other stage that I might as well ask Roshana the rude questions. "From when you were little?"

"He wasn't around as much as he might have been. But yes. I do remember."

"Was he a good father?"

"He never hit any of us, or even shouted. Is that what you mean?"

"Well, uh..."

"And yeah, he looked after us, I'll say that. Until... Well, I remember the day he went to find my brothers, and the ground began to shake."

"What happened?"

"My mother ran with me to the caravanserai and paid a man to take me to Uruk straight away. 'Her father will come and meet her at the city,' she told him. But he didn't. And I never saw her again."

"That wasn't his fault," I said gently. I could see ghostly gray figures amongst the trees at the side of the path. Just a few, here and there. Most were lying down, and others sat over fallen figures as if tending them, or mourning. I shivered.

"No, of course not."

I wasn't sure I wanted an answer to my next question. "What happened to you after that?"

"I survived." The words were a wall.

"Did you get back home?"

"Twenty years later. Our village had gone. An earth slip had taken out the whole side of the valley and wiped every house from existence. Not one of my relatives remained."

The archangels did that? The thought made me feel even colder. "I'm sorry," I said, because there was nothing else to say.

"It was a long time ago." She jolted the vehicle to a stop

and switched off the engine. "We need to walk from here."

Azazel jumped down lightly behind us.

From here meant down the steep slope of a little wooded valley. A dead stump shelved with hoof-shaped fungi was the only landmark on the trackside to show we'd arrived anywhere at all. I winced inwardly as I climbed from the SUV because my slip-on shoes were hopelessly inappropriate for rough terrain, but I didn't dare say anything because I knew Roshana would just suggest that I wait in the car. So I slithered down the incline in their wake, gritting my teeth as leaf-mold worked its way in around my toes.

Azazel seemed quite content to be led, for once.

The trees here were dense and still quite slender, decked in a fireworks display of fall colors. Once we reached the bottom of the valley we turned what would have been upstream, if there had been running water. Thankfully there wasn't, though it was squishily damp underfoot. Roshana launched into a monologue about how she'd bought the land at auction from a logging company, and about how there were still bears and mountain lions around here. I think she had very little idea about how to chat to her father, now she'd met him.

I interrupted her tales with a shriek. I'd looked up as I ducked under a branch and suddenly, there in front of me, was a figure with a face so distorted by pustules that its eyes were swollen shut and its mouth looked like one giant scab. Shock made me cry out loud, but by the time the other two heard me and reacted, the vision was gone.

"What's wrong?" Azazel demanded, appearing at my side.

"Oh hell!" I cried, passing my hand over my eyes as if I could block out the memory of that face. "D'you not see them?"

"See what?" Roshana asked, hand on hip.

"Ghosts! This place is crawling with them!" I looked around wildly, as if those shabby gray figures were about to lunge out at me in jerky J-Horror ambush.

If he'd been Egan, Azazel would have swept me into his arms and comforted me. But he just frowned and tilted his head, waiting for more explanation.

"What sort of ghosts?" Roshana asked, smiling.

"I don't know! That one had a face like a bowl of Rice Krispies—I mean, oh God." My throat swelled as I tried to recall details I'd only glimpsed. "I—I think they were pretty old. I didn't see any modern tech or clothes. They all look really ill. What happened here? Why've you got ghosts?"

"Smallpox," she said, unfazed. "When the white guys first landed east of here, their diseases blazed a trial for them. Millions died before they even saw a white face."

"So this was Native American land?"

"The whole country was Native land," she said dismissively. "Come on."

Azazel said nothing. But he did wait and walk behind me this time as we pressed on. I wished he'd take my hand or something.

Roshana led the way to where a great cloven boulder stuck out of the valley side. It looked as if the rock face had split away centuries ago from the bulk of the stone, and still stood like a wall. Between the two faces of stone there was just about enough room for someone to walk into the cleft.

"Here we are," she said, looking at her father. "Do you want to go first?"

"Go where?"

"Into the cave there."

Azazel looked at the rock face, then back at her, slowly. "I don't see any cave."

It was Roshana's turn to look confused. She put her hands on her hips and jerked her chin. "That one."

Frowning, he turned to me. "Do you see it?"

I nodded. "That gap just there? Yes." The vegetation had been trodden back to make a muddy little path.

Azazel took another long hard look. "I…can't see…what you mean."

We stood in mutual bafflement.

"Interesting," Azazel said thoughtfully. "*Not heard nor perceived by the ear, neither hath the eye seen*. It has been sealed from my eyes."

"How come?"

"I imagine it's intended to discourage angelic visitation. I suppose to stop attempts at rescue, in the first place. And once we were defeated…well, even the Host are subject to the subtle temptations of pity." He snorted softly. "In theory, at any rate."

"Is it holy ground?" I asked, nervous about who might be watching.

He tilted his head. "No. Not now. Maybe…a long time ago." Holding out his hand to me, he concluded, "Lead me in."

"I'll go first," Roshana said swiftly, and strode away into the gap.

I'll admit I felt slightly relieved. The prospect of leading the way into those shadows had not been appealing. I intertwined my fingers in Azazel's, wishing we were away somewhere all alone, slick with sweat and urging each other to new orgasmic heights. Maybe he sensed my thoughts, because he smiled at me. I realized it was the first time I'd seen him smile that day. "Are you all right?" I whispered.

"I borrow your courage," he said, stooping to brush his

lips across my cheek, and it was a moment before I realized that he wasn't mocking me. Maybe he really was nervous of going underground again.

I lifted my hand to his face, longing arcing through my body like electricity. I wanted to slide my hand to the juncture of his thighs and capture his burgeoning flesh. I wanted him to enfold the hollow of my back in his hands. For a moment our lips met, soft as feathers, and I inhaled the warmth of his breath.

I love you, I whispered into the hollow of my skull. *I want you, right now.* It was too raw a confession to speak aloud in this company. But his eyes narrowed a little as he smiled again, his long lashes almost tangling with my own.

"This way," called Roshana. She sounded dryly impatient, and that lifted my spirits.

Trying to ignore the mud soaking into my ruined shoes, I took the lead and drew us carefully between the rock walls. Azazel's grip tightened fiercely on mine for just a moment, and then we were both inside the cleft. A smell of damp stone surrounded us. Just enough light filtered down through the vegetation growing over the gap above our heads to allow me to now make out a low aperture in the rock to my right, admitting us deeper into the body of the cliff.

I took a deep breath, ducked my head, and plunged in.

The cave was bigger than I expected, and not natural. That much was apparent as soon as my eyes grew used to the dim light that seeped in from the hole at the apex of the conical roof. It was shaped like one of the old straw beehives they used to have in the village meadows back home, smoothly rounded as if hollowed by water, yet in a place no river had ever run. The roof was striated sandstone and painted with faint petroglyphs of animals and humans. Human*oids*, perhaps. The floor was rough rock, more crudely levelled, and in the center was a huge rectangular slab of stone.

"There were a lot of bones everywhere when I first came," Roshana explained, "but I had them all tidied."

I followed the casual wave of her hand toward an undifferentiated heap of detritus on the far side of the chamber, disconcerted. A cluster of ghosts sat over it, their eyes gray and baleful. "Roshana, this is an archaeological site. You shouldn't have disturbed anything."

"It's my land. I do what I like with it."

Oh boy, she's her father's daughter. "But the bones..." I thought of all the ghosts outside too. "Human ones? They belong to a tribe, you can't just..."

"The tribe's long gone; nobody now even remembers its name."

I shook my head. "But there are protocols, there are—"

"Which bit of 'It's *my* land' wasn't I clear about?"

I looked to Azazel in dismay, but he wasn't paying any attention. What the hell did he care about mortal propriety and sentiment? He was looking at the rock slab at his feet. He crouched to place one palm flat on the face of the stone, as if feeling for a heartbeat.

"Nothing," he said softly. "No one there. Can you hear anything, Milja?"

"There are remains," Roshana told him. "I had a hole drilled under that corner and sent a probe-camera in for a look."

If Azazel was listening, he didn't respond to her words. Instead he hooked his hands around the angles of the slab and heaved the huge weight aside as if he were flipping a child's mattress.

I couldn't help myself. In fact we all three pressed forward to look into the space revealed below; a rectangular cist maybe a dozen feet long, hewn into the bedrock.

There was a body. It was somewhat taller than human normal, as Azazel sometimes gets when he's angry. It was dark gray in color, and a little collapsed, like the papery remains of a long-abandoned wasp nest. We could see the empty eye-sockets, and the bared yellow-ivory gape of the open jaws. I shrank back. Roshana folded her arms as if in vindication. I don't know what she'd promised Azazel.

The fallen angel clenched his fists. Dust began to whip across the floor, circling him. He stretched out his hand over the pit and I was startled to see a red worm of glowing light ooze out of the cadaver's crumpled ribcage, like a vine tendril questing upward toward the sun of his open palm.

Then, before it could touch him, the tendril faded and fell apart—and without warning the whole body fell into dust.

We held our breath.

"He let them die." Azazel's voice was very low, very even, at least to start with. "Mi—the Boatman... They got sick, but he could have saved them. He is the Pillar of the West—it is his job to preserve and guard and keep the Word. He could have saved them, but he didn't, and when they died out so did the Egrigoroi in their care. Jomjael died in the dark, slowly, buried alive."

He turned to Roshana. His voice sounded like the grinding of rocks, and there was a red light like burning blood leaking from his eyes and his mouth. "You say there are more of these mounds? Hundreds more? More bodies?"

She nodded, for once too cautious to speak aloud.

"Why?" His face was a black mask over seething hellfire as he turned it up to the roof overhead. "WHY?" he roared, and I clapped my hands over my agonized ears. "*Why did you let them die?"*

I lurched backward and crouched against the curve of the cavern wall, shutting my eyes, but even through my closed lids I saw the column of flame burst up around him, boiling against the ceiling. I felt the heat on my skin. For a moment I thought he'd been struck down by the wrath of Heaven. But even in the midst of the burning I heard his voice.

"You were supposed to keep them prisoner until Judgment! What are you doing, Michael? What are you doing!"

Don't call him!

Then it went dark and quiet—so dark and so quiet that I thought I'd gone blind and deaf, though it was only the contrast with the former effulgence and clamor. I could smell my own crisped hair. The backs of my hands were stinging where I'd flung them up to shield my face.

I blinked, trying to bring moisture to my parched eyes. Slowly the dim leak of daylight swam back into view. I could see Azazel crouched on the edge of the grave, a knot of darkness, his head down, his shoulders shuddering. A figure stood over him, silhouetted against the silvery dribble of light.

Michael? I wondered. *He heard! He found us!*

But it wasn't Michael. It was Roshana. She stooped over Azazel, one arm draped across his shoulders, and kissed the back of his head. Through the ringing in my ears I could make out the faint murmur of her voice.

"It's all right. It's all right. I'm here, Father, and I will help you. I will help you make everything all right."

Oh no. Oh no, no, no. I couldn't have her pushing in like that. *Damn it, Roshana—just stop that.*

I staggered forward from the wall. "Azazel, listen. This is awful, I'm sorry. But I've had an idea. I think I know how to get you in to rescue Penemuel."

Eight
LALIBELA

"Someone," said Azazel grimly, "has put a great deal of effort into fortifying this place against people like me."

Ethiopia was nothing like I'd imagined. I'd pictured—oh, an arid dusty plain dotted with mud huts or something. Instead we had mountains all around us, with the little town of Lalibela clinging to the green flank of one to our left, and the land was gloriously lush and alive with flowering bushes, here at the end of the rainy season. Jacaranda trees made a purple haze in the gardens beneath our feet and bright yellow daisy-heads of tickseed sunflowers gilded the grasses. We were sitting at a table in the Ben Abeba restaurant right at the fringe of the town—a building so eccentrically modernist as to resemble something designed by Dr. Suess—because Azazel didn't dare get any closer to holy ground and because it was exactly the sort of place he couldn't resist; high up, completely open, with sweeping curves and platforms of concrete upheld by great iron pillars.

"King Lalibela," I answered, thumbing through my

Ethiopian guidebook. I had an avocado and papaya smoothie in front of me, while he nursed a glass of *tej*, the local honey liquor, and propped his bare feet up on the railing. "He fell into a coma and had a vision of Heaven, and the angels ordered him to rebuild this city as a mirror-image of the Holy Land. So there's a group of churches that represents Jerusalem and another one that represents Bethlehem, and a Mount of Olives and a River Jordan, which I think was dug out by hand. Oh, and a Tomb of Adam, and the three graves of Abraham, Isaac and Jacob. It's like a medieval theme park for pilgrims. So they didn't have to walk all the way to Palestine."

Azazel *hmph*ed. "And all consecrated. Just to protect her prison. Which is sealed from my eyes and my ears anyway."

"You should read these stories...the whole place was supposedly built by men working the dayshift and angels working at night. Saint George came down from Heaven to complain he didn't have his own church, and then supervised one being built. The church of Bet Abba Libanos was carved out in *one night* by King Lalibela's wife and a gang of angels. And there's a pillar in Bet Maryam that's kept completely covered up because it has a full prophetic description of the beginning and end of the world carved into it miraculously by Jesus, and the details are too scary for humanity to cope with. It all sounds a bit crazy." I sucked in my lips. "Or, you know...not."

"Penemuel clearly warrants heightened security." He was gazing down over the hillside like he thought he'd be able to spot her sepulcher among the tin rooftops. "More than ever I did, it seems."

I felt a little affronted. "Maybe the angels just trusted my family more," I snipped. "Which," I had to admit, "was a mistake. Obviously."

"You sound...wired, Milja."

"I'm a bit nervous, yeah. The Church here have had the *Book of Enoch* since whenever it was written, right? Which means they never forgot about the Watchers like we did in the West. So there are...however many...priests down there in town just waiting for their fallen angel to try and break out. They'll be ready for this. Worst case scenario, one of the Host might even have rocked up and warned them you're out and on the prowl."

"Avansha will be there to watch your back. And if anything happens to me, she will see you home."

"If anything bad happens to you, I'm assuming the kill-zone will take out me along with most of Ethiopia."

"You might be right." The grim twist of his lips made my nape prickle.

"Tell me about Penemuel, will you?"

"What about her?"

"You were close?"

"We were brothers." He paused a moment. "Yes, we were close. It does not mean the things you fear."

I flushed. "What's she like? I mean...is she like you?"

He considered the question. "I can only speak about Penemuel as I knew him, years ago."

"Of course."

"He wasn't like me. He thought too much. Worried too much. Always saw the potential danger in every action. Argued with Samyaza constantly over whether we were doing the right thing. It vexed him that your mortal lives are so short, that there is so much for a Son of Earth to learn that he is barely able to teach his own children before he dies. Penemuel thought that there should be a way for your kind to preserve knowledge, so that it might accumulate. Otherwise, he said, nothing would ever change. So he invented the written word. And thus changed *everything*." He cast me a sideways glance. "You owe Penemuel a great debt, if that is any encouragement."

"Yeah. I guess." It didn't make me feel more courageous about what we were planning to do.

Azazel reached a hand toward me across the table and tangled his loose fingers in mine. I clung to them for a long moment, trying to look brave.

"Will it hurt, to have you…riding me?" I asked in a low voice.

"I don't believe so. I will make myself very small and inconspicuous."

"Will you be able to poke around inside my head?"

He smiled crookedly. "Why—have you something to hide?"

I laughed.

"If you prefer, Avansha could play that part, I'm sure."

No. No. NO. "No way. If one of us has to jump in and save the day, it'd much better be her. She's the one with the Nephilim superpowers or whatever. And the money. I'm just the mule."

As if on cue, I caught movement at the corner of my eye and saw Roshana ascending the long curved ramp toward our table. She was checking something on her phone and wore—along with a smirk of satisfaction—a broad-brimmed sunhat and *the* most beautiful long white blouse that managed to be both flowing and figure-hugging.

This is my step-daughter? I asked myself bleakly.

"All sorted," she announced, sweeping off her sun shades to bat her dark lashes at us, and stooping to kiss Azazel on the cheek. "I've changed some birr, and had Mario book us a hotel safely out of town. There's a car on its way to pick us up, and a local guide waiting for us at the churches."

"What, now?" I said.

Roshana smiled at me a little pityingly. "Reconnaissance. I thought it'd be a good idea for us two to get a thorough look around before trying anything funny with Big Boy here. The site's apparently rather labyrinthine."

I wished she wouldn't talk about him like that. Azazel just looked faintly amused.

"Okay," I admitted. "Good idea, I suppose."

"Of course it is." She looked over at her father, arching a brow. "We'll call you when we're ready, shall we?"

"I'll be waiting."

She dropped a pile of what I assumed to be the local currency on the table, and crooked a finger at me to summon me from my chair. "Let's go."

And I obeyed, of course.

༄

We were met at the entrance to the church complex by our guide, Eskinder. He wore shiny shoes, neat slacks, a jumper and bomber jacket, obviously considering the day a little cool despite what—to us—seemed like the pleasant low-eighties warmth, saved only from tropical swelter by the altitude of the plateau. He greeted us with a dignified little smile. "Selam. Hello and welcome to you, Mrs. Smith and Miss Jones."

Well, Roshana had clearly taken the subterfuge bit between her teeth.

I thought that she looked uncharacteristically pale and uneasy in that moment, but she visibly gathered herself and responded.

Eskinder sorted out tickets for us and indicated another man who waited patiently a few yards away. "We must take off our shoes when we go in to the churches, so he will come with us and look after them."

"Hi," I said awkwardly to the unnamed guy. "Thanks."

So our tour began. Roshana wasn't wrong; we'd have quickly got lost if we'd tried to make our own way around, even though she had some sort of map that she tried to follow on her phone while we walked. I don't think any sketch-map could have done the place justice, not in two dimensions. We needed Eskinder to find the churches, and then to explain just what it was we were seeing.

The whole site was excavated into a slope of soft, volcanic rock. The architects had started by digging trenches ten or more meters deep to expose huge blocks of raw stone, which were then carved and hollowed out into churches without a speck of mortar or a length of supporting timber. So the roofs of the buildings were level with the surrounding ground and their red walls were austere, the keyhole-shaped windows kept small to maintain structural strength. Chambers and tunnels had been cut into the trench sides too—chapels, store-rooms, crypts, and water channels to drain the heavy rains of summer down into the River Jordan. Grave niches of priests and pilgrims pocked the exposed rock faces, mostly empty now except for those that held the bedding of hermits. A network of hidden underground passages connected the churches on many levels according to Eskinder, which made Roshana and I look pointedly at each other over his shoulder.

I'd already reminded her not to talk about our mission while we were on holy ground, nor to use any personal names. There was too much danger of being overheard.

But we asked questions. Oh boy did we ask questions. Eskinder seemed pleased with our evident interest. And I can't speak for Roshana, but I was knocked out by the scale and artistry of the site; at first impressed, then awed and moved, and finally really quite cowed.

I'd expected a tourist honeypot—this was after all billed as the Eighth Wonder of the World. But there were very few international tourists and a great number of Ethiopian people, men and women draped in white shawls, moving quietly and with patience. They raised their open palms when they entered a church, and kissed the stone doorposts. Small crowds of boys sat learning their letters ("Religious school is very good for discipline," Eskinder told us,) and from somewhere unseen a choir of young male voices chanted, the sound making my skin prickle eerily. A group of women sat against a wall, winnowing flour to make communion bread. These churches were not just heritage, and they were certainly not museums. They were living centers of active worship, and it was going on all around us.

There were also a lot of flies. I fanned at them with my guide book.

Our guide tried to put it all in context, telling us about how Menelik, the son of Solomon and the Queen of Sheba, had brought the Ark of the Covenant to Ethiopia; how even before the nation converted to Christianity, Judaism was established and influential here. "This is a very old way of Christianity, like the Apostles would have known. We eat no pork in Ethiopia. During services men and women are separated, and all stand. At the center of every church there is a Holy of Holies, which only the priest may enter, and inside that is a replica of the true Ark of the Covenant."

He showed us the narrow staves with the T-shaped heads that priests used to lean on during services that lasted three or four hours, and to beat time with upon the floor as they chanted the liturgy. He showed us boxes of sistrums, like metal rattles with wired disks.

"Egypt," said Roshana, dryly. "The sistrum came from Egypt."

"Yes, there are many connections here with the Coptic Church."

"Isis," she muttered in my ear as he turned away. "They were used in Isis-worship."

It all made me feel like my own Orthodox religion—which we like to claim is the direct and original version of the Faith—was an upstart innovation along the lines of Protestantism.

That didn't mean the churches here were grand. Far from it. The thickness of the walls meant that most interiors were surprisingly small, and lit by bare bulbs on long trailing wires. The thin rugs on the floor were laid directly onto roughly chiseled rock, so that every bump and notch could be discerned by our stockinged feet. *'Tuck your pants into your socks,'* the guide books had warned, *'as some have complained of flea-bites.'* And the sweeping drapes that curtained off each Holy of Holies ran heavily to red sateen and gold chintz. Every interior was dark, slightly dusty, and slightly damp from the breath and bodies of the faithful. The rock of the interior walls was polished greasily smooth between knee and shoulder height from the passage of so many people over so many centuries. But the painting style I'd found so childish back in the Chicago gallery seemed powerful in its simplicity here, the bright colors glowing from the shadows and the wide sloe eyes staring as if into my guilty heart. It was an *old* faith—old in soul, and far too old and too deep-rooted and too sure of itself to care what the outside world thought of it, or to care much about the outside world at all.

Everything that mattered here took place inside—inside

these walls, underground, in the hidden depths of the human heart.

I couldn't tell if my nervousness was claustrophobia, or a creeping conviction of my own foolishness and sin. The smell of frankincense took me straight back to my childhood, and I felt shrunken, all the individuality I'd accrued in my life an illusion. My defiance of God and my desire—even my love—for Azazel seemed petulant and adolescent in this place.

I did try to stay focused. In every church I stood for a few moments and *listened*, hoping to catch Penemuel's stifled voice. But I heard nothing.

And we did try to gather clues narrowing down the presence of a supernatural prisoner. The trouble was that there was an excess of possibilities. Every church seemed to have some unique feature that roused my suspicions. Bet Medhane Alem, the House of the Savior of the World, was the very first we visited and the single largest rock-hewn church in the world, the only one truly cathedral-like in scale. It was barred all around the outside by thirty-six huge pillars in just the way the Parthenon was, though not the least bit Hellenic in detail. Once more I was reminded of a vast cage. Then we passed through a tunnel into the adjoining pit of Bet Maryam, the House of Mary, which was reputedly the oldest church here and sheltered the prophetic pillar that was too dangerous for mankind to read. It was also the one with the most elaborate interior frescos and carvings, and Eskinder pointed out a wall-painting of two bulls in combat.

"The white bull represents good, the black bull represents evil," he told us.

I recalled my vision of Azazel and Raphael's ferocious battle and I shivered.

There was a carved relief of Saint George slaying a dragon

on the western facade. I wondered whether the legend was based on an angel bringing down one of the Watchers, or some later conflict on a more human scale. Saint George seemed to be everywhere in Ethiopia, even on the beer labels in the restaurant.

Fellow dragon-slayer Saint Michael had his own small church, accessed from a steep trench so riddled with graves it looked like Swiss cheese. Bet Mikael guarded the way to a second interior church, Bet Golgotha, which we were not allowed into. All we could see from the connecting doorway were a couple of larger-than-life-sized bas-reliefs of robed and haloed men carved into arched niches in the walls. The gray faces of these saints and patriarchs—if that's what they were—were forbidding, and the crumbling of the old stone had granted them an unfortunate corpselike cast.

A priest sitting on a bench looked up at us mildly and made a pushing-back gesture with his palm.

"No women are allowed in," Eskinder explained. "That is the most holy church of all. King Lalibela is buried under the Selassie chapel there, that is what they say."

Roshana and I exchanged another significant glance. Eskinder tried to make up for our frustration. "Look at this," he said, pointing at carvings high on the corners of the pillars in Bet Mikael where we stood. "These are only found here and one other place. They are angel eyes."

They didn't look much like eyes to me, unless angels had vertical spindle-shaped pupils, but I wasn't going to argue. I wondered if Michael was watching us through his stone eyes, and I retreated from Bet Mikael with some abruptness, retrieving my carefully lined-up shoes.

I was even more unnerved around the corner, near the great hollowed-out block of Adam's Tomb, to see a blue sign pointing into a cave labelled Bet Uraiel.

"Shall we go in there?" Roshana asked.

"No." I shook my head as the word came out with more vehemence than I'd intended.

"It is only a recent church," said Eskinder with a dismissive gesture. "It opened in 1998. Before that, a store room. Come this way."

Uriel suddenly decided he needed a foothold here, did he? I asked myself, wondering if this was what paranoia felt like.

We left that northwestern cluster of churches, the second Jerusalem, though Adam's Tomb and down the broad trench beyond. Some traditional domestic houses, like two-story turrets, stood watch over our retreat. A clutch of small children intercepted us and followed, shouting, "You! You! You!" until our shoe guy drove them off with the threat of a raised hand. I felt relieved and guilty in equal measure.

Bet Giyorgis, the House of George, stood by itself across the road and down the hillside, like a sentinel guarding royalty. It was the most famous of the Lalibela churches, of course, because it was the easiest to take an impressive photo of. A huge square pit sunk into the bare rock framed a cruciform block of a church four stories high. Bright chartreuse and gray-green lichens splotched the pink stone. We stared down at it from above, letting its monolithic sophistication and the sense of implacable faith sink in. I tried to imagine how long it would have taken, hacking down into the rock with hand-tools, to create such a thing. Any mistake would have been permanent, since no stone could be replaced.

The slope of the surrounding rock and the relatively narrow gap tempted me, much against my common sense, to contemplate the possibility of a leap to the flat cross-carved roof. I wondered if anyone had ever made that insane attempt.

This place, I thought, could send you out of your mind. I blinked my dry eyes.

We descended into the pit via a trench that wound around the outside. "Look at this," said Eskinder. "These are the footprints of Saint George's horse." The imprints ran vertically up the face of the rock.

"Wow," I said dutifully.

"Do you believe stories like that?" Roshana asked, with more courage and less tact than I could muster. "You have a college degree, you said. You're an educated man."

Eskinder looked calmly at her. "Only a very uneducated man would put limits on the power of God."

Then we passed under a thick arch of rock and into the sunken church enclosure. Eskinder took us on a circuit of the exterior first. A pair of leathery mummified feet poked out from one niche.

"Look at this. Many pilgrims came here to die on holy ground in old times, from Egypt, Syria, Jerusalem." he said. "Most of the bodies from here have been moved now, but if you go to Yemrehanna Kristos Monastery just outside the city, there are eleven thousand skeletons in the cave."

I couldn't imagine what eleven thousand bodies looked like stacked up.

We shed our shoes once more on the carved steps of the church, and climbed into the interior. For a moment I held my breath, wondering if this was the place we sought. The gallery book had been borrowed from this church after all. Perhaps Penemuel was below our feet right now.

Are you here? My heart thumped against my breastbone.

But the church kept its secrets. Once more the interior turned out to be smaller than it looked from the outside, the pillarless space carved with precision and restraint. The carpet under our toes was a coarse red industrial weave. The glossy curtains strung from a sagging pole shielded the Holy of Holies from profane eyes, but there were portraits of Saint George propped up against the walls, and two huge wooden treasury coffers that were supposedly eight hundred years old, now spattered with wax drippings. I wondered what other books were kept hidden in there.

The priest, wearing ornate vestments and sun-shades, obliged us for a photo opportunity and brought out a tall cross in brass filigree for us. We took our pictures and looked around, and I was the first to head back to the porch. The shock waiting there nearly floored me.

Directly opposite the door, Egan was walking out of the gap in the cliff. I leapt back into the shadows, my heart suddenly hammering.

I'd recognized him instantly. He wore a collarless Nehru-style shirt over canvas pants, and sunglasses pushed onto the top of his head. Unlike every other tourist that walked into the pit, he did not stare up in awe at the church; he instead glanced left and right, searching the crowds. It was the only thing that'd stopped him spotting me straight away.

"We can't go out!" I hissed to Roshana, grabbing her arm.

"Why?"

"Egan's outside!" I tried to keep my voice down, but I could feel my blood racing. "He can't see us! We're finished if he does!"

"Egan?" She frowned. "Oh—your friend from the gallery?"

"He's not my friend." I met her arch, expectant glare and dropped my voice to an even lower mutter. "I can't explain here! But he can't see us. Can you do *anything*?"

She turned to Eskinder, plucked a rolled note out of the

tiny handbag slung across her torso, and pointed it at him. "There's a man outside who was very creepy to my friend in the bar last night. We don't want him to see us. American, yellow hair...what's he wearing, Milja?"

"Blue Indian shirt. Sunglasses on the top of his head."

"Can you go out first and distract him? Take him to see the mummy or something, so we can get past without him seeing."

Eskinder looked pained. "Tip the man who looks after your shoes," he said, waving the money away. But he went out.

Roshana went a minute later, peeking cautiously around the door frame. "Okay, we're good."

I pulled my floppy sunhat down over my head, trotted down the steps, scooped up my shoes from the ranks and scurried in my stockinged feet for the safety of the tunnel mouth, dodging the knots of visitors. Roshana sashayed after me with rather more dignity. We waited in the trench for Eskinder and our shoe guy to catch us up. I was feeling dizzy with anxiety.

Had I imagined Egan's presence, imprinting his face onto some innocent stranger? It had only been a glimpse, after all. But no—I felt sure.

"Are you all right, honey?"

I shook my head. "I can't take this all in. I need a rest. And something to eat."

She pulled out her phone. "I'll call our car." And when Eskinder did reappear, she smiled at him with patrician confidence. "We will tour the rest of the churches tomorrow, I think. We are too tired now, and Miss Jones is very jetlagged. We need to go back to our hotel now."

He nodded, thoughtfully. "You should not hurry. Lalibela

is best taken slowly, slowly."

"Can you meet us tomorrow afternoon?"

"Of course. Will hour eight be suitable?" He smiled at my look of confusion, enjoying his gentle tease. "That is two o'clock p.m. We count time from dawn."

It would be six in the morning according to my Chicago body-clock, but I nodded. "Thank you."

Paying everyone off, we retreated back to our hotel out of town. Roshana and I did not speak in the car. We weren't sure we could trust even our driver. But as soon as we were standing on the hotel forecourt, with metallic blue starlings flitting about the modern glass architecture around us, she said, "I think you need to tell me about the lovely Egan."

I swallowed hard. "He works for the Vatican."

"Seriously?"

"He keeps a watch on me...but I've no idea how he knew we'd be here. He couldn't have checked the flights this time." I twisted my guidebook in my hands. "If he sees us, he'll tell the priests here. No question. He'll try to stop us."

Roshana looked surprised. "So he knows about you and Daddy?"

"Uhuh."

"And does Azazel know about him?"

"Yes." *Sort of. Yes, after the last time they met, in the monastery. Egan made it pretty clear then that they were on opposing teams.* "Yeah. He does."

"Then why doesn't he take the cute Catholic out permanently?"

I was shocked. "Well, he's... Egan's not a threat! He saved my life back in Montenegro, several times." I pulled a face. "I owe him, big time. He's just...not on our side."

"He's a threat now, clearly."

IN BONDS OF THE EARTH

"He wouldn't do anything to hurt us." *Not me, anyway. Just Azazel. He'll do everything he can to stop Azazel.*

"You hope. And he might have a soft spot for you, but there are a hundred priests down there who don't give a stuff about some slutty American witch. Don't forget that."

I could feel the blood rushing to my cheeks. "We just have to stay out of his sight."

"Fine." She shrugged, turning to the hotel doors. "But it's a complication we don't need."

༄

We ate dinner on the hotel patio, watching vervet monkeys play on the rocks nearby while thunder rumbled across the hilltops. Thankfully we were clear of the flies up here. Afterwards I went for a lie-down. My head was spinning, not from the change of dateline but from anxiety. I didn't want to let Azazel down. I didn't want to precipitate a fight with Egan. Or with a hundred priests. Or even one archangel.

I dozed off and dreamed. It was a weird, shallow dream, in which I was still aware of my body lying on the hotel coverlet but I felt like I was somewhere else, somewhere dark and subterranean. Voices muttered in the shadows around me: *Salutations to thee, Raphael, gracious and good, rejoicer of hearts. Salutations to thee, Gabriel, messenger of the King of Heaven. Stand before us against the powers of evil. Save us from the darkness.*

Milja? A woman's voice whispered through the hubbub.
Penemuel? Is that you?
Daughter of Earth... How long? How long before you come?
Soon, I promised.
I suffer.
We have seen. Another voice; a familiar and horribly ominous phrase. Egan?

I forced myself awake, into a more mundane darkness, and found that according to my phone it was past midnight. My mouth was sticky and dry, but the complimentary Abyssinia bottle by my bedside was empty. Not trusting the tap water in my sink, my head still wadded with tatters of sleep, I let myself out into the corridor and padded along to the lobby to seek out another bottle. Rain hissed on the leaves in the hotel grounds.

The corridor opened out into an interior balcony over the bar. I looked down to see that Roshana was down there, holding court. A dozen tourists, mostly men, lounged around in easy chairs. Staff leaned against pillars, watching. She sat on a high stool, her legs crossed under what I'd call an *insensitively* short skirt, and was recounting a story about someone she'd met at a winter party, a Hollywood star, who'd taken her out for a après-ski spin on his snowmobile and then got stuck in a drift and they'd had to beg shelter in a redneck mining settlement. It was a funny story, and they all seemed to hang on her words.

She didn't look tired in the least.

I'd met people like her ever since coming to America. Clever, charming people who fed on adulation and attention. People who thought the world revolved around them—and whose opinion the world seemed quite happy to go along with. I'd had a roomie at college like that. She'd had half the male students in the year queuing up outside her door for the smallest crumbs of indulgence.

Is this what angelic bloodlines look like? Is this what the Watchers gave us?

I snagged a bottle from a cooler unit in the corner of the deserted lobby and skulked back to my room.

Roshana took me into her room the next morning and gave me a rather lovely peach silk dress to wear over my own capri pants. It made an acceptably demure top over my longer torso, though it hung more loosely than on her lush curves.

"We don't want anyone recognizing you by your clothes," she said. Then she sat me down in front of a mirror, unbound my long hair and, with an expression of dire concentration, ran her fingers through it. Her touch wilted my locks from brunette to blonde.

I gasped.

"Stop wriggling," she admonished, pulling her fingers through each tress until they faded, sere as autumn birch leaves. I fixed on my reflection, fascinated and appalled. My brows are black and my eyes dark; they stared out at me now from a frame of wavy gold. There was just too much contrast, like sin revealed in the midst of innocence.

Hair grows out, I told myself. *It's no big thing.*

But when she laid her cool fingers across my cheeks I knocked her hands away and jumped up with a cry. "Don't you dare!"

"Stop being childish," she laughed. "You want Egan to spot you? What if he's been handing your picture around to the priests?"

"I don't care," I snarled. "You're not messing with my face."

"Tchah." She wiped her hands dismissively on the air.

"For God's sake," I said, retreating across the hand-woven rug to what felt like a slightly safer distance. "If you've got these...*powers*..." I ran out of words momentarily, then started again. "You've got goddamn magic. What can you do to get Pen out?"

"Nothing." She sat down on the edge of her bed, folding

her miraculous hands demurely in her lap. "I can't do a thing on church ground. Not without letting everyone know where I am and what. Which will really kick over the wasps' nest, won't it?" She glanced down at her hands. "I can feel it the second I walk on consecrated ground, you know. I can feel it prickling all over my skin. It feels like eyes watching me. Ugh."

I sniffed, trying to regain my composure.

"You have no idea what I'm risking, helping you here," she said in a low voice.

"Yeah. I do."

"I have made an art form of not being noticed, all my life. Yesterday was the first time in five thousand years I've dared set foot on holy ground. I've steered clear since the day I was born."

"Don't exaggerate. Even Judaism isn't that old."

She smiled, eyes narrowed and her crimson lips taut. "Angels are older than Abraham."

"I know that!"

"D'you think monotheism has the monopoly on truth? That this is all about Yahweh?" She shook her head. "Don't tell me, after all this, that you still *believe*?"

I was confused. "Isn't this all proof? How much more do you want?"

"What's it proof of? An all-loving, all-knowing, infinitely wise Father who watches everything you do? Or maybe something a bit more impersonal?"

I bit my lip. "I don't know. God is a Mystery, ultimately unknowable." That was my Orthodoxy coming out.

"But you still believe in Someone, don't you?" She laughed.

"Azazel believes in Someone."

"You think so? You really need to learn the difference between 'I want it to be true', and 'It is true'. One does not follow from the other. Of course you want a universe that knows you and cares for you. Of course you want to be of infinite importance in the scheme of things. Of course you want to be loved without reservation, and to live for all eternity. And that's because you haven't grown up yet, honey. But the truth is that there is no Sky Daddy coming to save you, or to punish him. There is just a bunch of bastards with rules and big ideas—and some of those bastards have wings, and some just have sticks 'n' guns."

"Then tell me—Who is Azazel rebelling against?"

"Let me spell it out for you, honey. There are only two games in town. There's Divine Order, which by its nature creates, and Chaos, which must tear apart. It doesn't matter if you call that Order Jehovah or Ahura Mazda or Zeus or Marduk. All the stories and the dogma, the morality and Commandments, the God-so-loved-the-world shit...that's just fancy paintwork. You obey or you rebel."

I was sure as I could be that that wasn't how Azazel saw things, so I didn't intend to argue further. "Which side are you on, in the end?"

"Me? Screw the game, I'm on *my* side. I was spawned by chaos—and I've had to spend my life working on the side of order so that none of the bastards notice. I've stood in the shadows pulling strings for kings and empires and artisans. I've built up nations and sucked the cocks of tyrants. I have done everything I can to hide my heritage."

"Until now."

"Yes."

"Then why are you helping him now if it's such a big risk?" I snapped, unable to hold down my irritation.

Her eyes widened. "What's your problem, Milja?"

"I don't have a problem!"

"Then why are you shouting?"

I clamped my mouth shut.

She moistened her lips. "He's my father. He's part of me. Not some fancy idealist Heavenly Father, but down here in my blood and my bones. Shouldn't a daughter naturally long to be with her father and to do as he wishes? I mean, I know you didn't, obviously…"

I felt the color drain from my cheeks. "Shut the hell up. You've no right to judge me."

"Sorry, did I strike a nerve?" Her eyes were narrowed. "At least you *had* a father as a child. And your mother and brothers weren't butchered. Do you know what happened to me when I arrived in Uruk and there was no one there to take care of me? Do you want to guess what happens to little girls with no family?"

Shut up, I wanted to tell her again. But I knew she was right. She'd suffered through things I couldn't bear to imagine. I shook my head, helpless and angry. "Let me know when you're ready to head out," I told her, making for the door.

"He loves you," she said, pausing me in my tracks.

Yeah.

"But he's loved so many women. It's not a blood-tie, Milja. Love cannot last. Only blood is forever."

Nine
EMPTY, SWEPT AND GARNISHED

We began our tour of the southeastern cluster of churches with Bet Abba Libanos, the church that had been built overnight by angels. Father Libanos was one of the Syrian saints who had brought Christianity to Ethiopia, and a picture inside showed him striking water from the ground with the tip of his spear. His church was a huge block situated inside a carpeted cave, still attached to the overhang above and the bedrock below. There were more of those purported 'angel eyes' carved inside, and I wondered why here and not in all the churches.

I was so annoyed with Roshana, and so wound up by the fear of seeing Egan, that I could hardly think straight.

The terrain on this side of the Jordan was even more labyrinthine, with many spiraling semi-natural passages and tunnels, some blocked by rough, antique doors. A tall slit-like tunnel led us to a ravine and through that to Bet Amanuel, supposedly the chapel of the royal family itself. Certainly it was the best-carved of all the churches inside and out, with a gallery floor over our heads that we couldn't access, though Eskinder sounded dismissive when he told us that the occupying Italians had restored it in the 1930s.

I found myself looking carefully over all the interior paintings for some clue.

"This is the story of Saint Mary and the Water of Correction," said Eskinder as I frowned at a panel, his expression expectant as he waited for understanding to dawn on me. Unfortunately, I was ignorant.

"What's that?"

He pointed at the picture of the girl taking a pot from some bearded priests. "Mary is twelve, and she is taken to the Temple when they find her to be carrying the baby, the Christ Jesus, but with no husband. They give her the Water of Correction to test her." He blinked at me, waiting for me say *Of course*.

I however was trying not to pull a face at the off-handed assumption that the Virgin Theotokos was only a child. Though that made a horrible sort of sense, of course, given the times.

"If she does not lose the child and die, it is seen that God blesses the baby and wishes it to be born," he explained.

"Wow." My stomach roiled. It was coming home to me how much the Christianity I thought I knew was, in foreign lands, a strange and unfamiliar religion.

We passed from Bet Amanuel to Bet Merkorios, which had lost its front half to collapse and whose remaining rooms smelled of damp. Apparently iron fetters had been discovered here, suggesting it had once been an ancient prison before conversion to a church—a revelation that made my skin crawl. Its patron was also depicted with a spear, but he was using it from horseback to gorily disembowel the evil Emperor

Oleonus. I'd never heard of either. In the forecourt of that building was a trapdoor in the floor.

"Look at this. It is the Valley of Death," Eskinder told us. "We go in."

Roshana fanned herself with a postcard, looking skeptical. "Really?"

"The tunnel runs right through from church to church, one hundred fifty feet. You can use a torch if you like, but to walk through in darkness is to feel the grave. That is what pilgrims think about."

"I see." She winked at me. "We're up for it, aren't we?"

We scrambled down rock-cut steps into the darkness. There seemed to be a choice of ways, but Eskinder led us off to our left, and we lost the light almost immediately as the tunnel curved. The slot was narrow—I found I could easily touch either wall by stretching out my arms—and the blackness absolute.

"Be careful," came Eskinder's voice from ahead. "The roof is low in places. Put your hand above your head."

"I hope there are no bats," Roshana grumbled.

"Yes, bats. But not here."

Bats didn't bother me, but the darkness did a little. It felt too much like the tunnel under Papa's chapel. I was at the back of our little line and it felt like the other two had consumed all the oxygen. I wondered how many of these tunnels there were under the church complex. I wondered how far they stretched, winding above and below each other, and whether anyone ever snuck in and got lost. I wondered if Penemuel was within shouting distance.

Then we heard voices ahead. Clearly another party was coming down the tunnel in the opposite direction. The afterlife was a crowded place, it seemed.

"…passage runs right the way through to a trapdoor inside the House of Immanuel, but that's blocked off and we'll come up earlier, in the House of Mercurios." The indistinct words came in a tone that first sounded weirdly familiar, and then made my heart clench.

It was Egan's voice.

Dear God. He's heading right toward us.

"Hello?" Eskinder called.

"Hello there."

"Hello!" A woman's voice.

"We should pass to the right," said Eskinder.

"Sure, no problem."

What if someone puts a torch on? I shrank against the right hand wall of the passage, putting my hand up to shield my face and hoping that my hat and fake yellow tresses were enough to fool him. The sound of scuffing feet and muttering grew closer. He was with an Englishwoman—no, two of them, who were giggling and panting a little, enjoying their subterranean adventure.

The lights stayed off.

Why's he showing women around? I wondered with a pang, but I knew the answer. Egan's protective instinct was in my opinion close to masochistic. All it would take was for the women to wander past him in a ravine, looking lost or pestered by touts or both, for him to offer his every assistance —and not in any hope of gain, but simply because he was one of nature's white knights.

Then they squeezed past, one at a time. I felt Egan brush my shoulder, an electric jolt through my straining nerves, and he apologized. I caught the scent of his skin, shockingly familiar in this dank underground hole, and it made my insides ache. I held my breath and tried to stop my heart from hammering. *He won't notice me. He won't notice me.*

Then he was gone.

"Thank you." The women smelled of soap and lily-of-the-valley, and their voices as they squeezed past each of us betrayed their advanced years. The wave of relief as their voices faded away made my skin clammy.

I didn't even notice the rest of our subterranean journey, or the scramble through the defiles and staircases beyond. I wasn't paying any attention to our route. It wasn't until we came out under a railed overhang, and looked across a small bridge over a moat fifty feet deep to the slab-like face of the building beyond, that my brain clicked back into focus.

"That's...stunning," I said weakly.

"This is Bet Gebriel-Rufael," Eskinder announced. "It is the oldest building on the site, older than all the churches. It was here before King Lalibela. We think it was a fortress. But now it is two churches, Saint Gebriel and Saint Rufael. Look at this, to the right." He pointed at a huge ramp of rock, a towering narrow knife-edge like a wall blocking off the end of the moat. "That rock is called the Way to Heaven, because it is so steep, so narrow."

"It'd certainly be a shortcut," Roshana muttered. "Look at the drop."

"Look down here. Those two stone hatches in the floor? They are the covers to a cistern underneath the rock, where the rainwater is collected."

I gripped the modern railing and stared down, feeling a little dizzy. There was an inch of water across the bottom of the trench, bright green with algae. Maybe it was the contrast with the claustrophobic darkness of the Valley of Death, but the moat seemed shockingly vast, and the ex-fortress beyond it looming and majestic with its tall arched niches. It certainly looked like a structure built for defense and intimidation.

"This is the bridge over troubled water then, I guess," suggested Roshana. The snark went over Eskinder's head.

"The bridge is new. The old entrance to the church is around the back, down at the bottom. But it is closed now. We go in this way."

We trooped across the wooden planks, and—after shedding our shoes—into the church beyond. The twin rooms inside were irregularly shaped, sparsely decorated and bigger than most of the other churches. It felt to me more like a theatrical stage with most of the sets removed than an ecclesiastical interior. The priest here was neither waiting by the ubiquitous red donation box with a cross for pilgrims to kiss, nor dozing in a corner; he was crouched before the curtain of the Holy of Holies, reading aloud from a hand-lettered book. He ignored us completely.

The drone of his words made my skin prickle, and the longer I paid attention the more uncomfortable I felt. "What's he saying?" I whispered to Eskinder.

"He is praying. The words are in Ge'ez not Amharic, so it is hard for me to hear..." He frowned and after a moment's hesitation had a stab at translation anyway. "Selam to you, Rufael, gracious and good, rejoicer of hearts. Selam to you, Gebriel, messenger of the King of Heaven. Stand before us against the powers of evil. Save us from the darkness."

My stomach lurched. I recognized the words from my dream at once, and I knew better now than to ignore my dreams.

Oh oh oh.

"Are you unwell?" Eskinder asked. My sudden alarm must have shown on my face.

"I want some fresh air."

I lurched through the second chapel and out onto a stone platform overlooking the moat. There was as much fresh air out here as anyone could ask for—and no safety railings this side, I noted, inching toward the edge to squint down. I could see carved steps descending into the hatch of the flooded cistern.

Okay, she's here. Somewhere. God, what if she's underwater there? No...more likely in the bottom floor of the church. The old entrance at the rear.

"Well?" said Roshana, strolling out to join me and popping her sunshades back on the moment the sun struck her face.

I nodded, swallowing my anxiety. "Here."

Her lips formed a tight pout. "Really?"

"Yes."

Eskinder appeared in the doorway, just making sure we didn't topple into the pit or something.

"Eskinder, why was the old entrance to this church shut up?"

"I don't know. I think the way in was very difficult—up a ladder to this floor. The bridge is easier for tourists."

"Can we see it?"

"It is shut," he repeated patiently.

"I know. I just would like to see it from the outside."

He shrugged. "This way then."

We retraced our steps through the twin chapels. I could hardly look at the priest with his white turban and his white beard.

All these centuries you've been waiting for a jailbreak. Girding yourselves against the powers of evil. Now we're here. Two sort-of-American broads in sunhats and sandals. And it's going to be tonight.

Coming, ready or not.

☙

"Are you sure?" Roshana asked, as we sat with our drinks at the hotel. She'd bought me a blue cocktail that tasted of coconut, and I had no idea what it was called.

"Yes." I was sure, and now all my nervousness had disappeared. This was *my thing*—something I could do that Roshana couldn't, it seemed. I liked that.

"Okay." She leaned forward in her chair and took a sip of her own cocktail, which was clear and, I suspected, a lot less sweet than mine. "I'll take your word for it." She poked her tablet awake and indicated the plan of the Lalibela churches that she'd found online. The doorway we were interested in was situated down a black trench cul-de-sac and wasn't labelled, but the steps were obvious in the diagram. "Well, the route from the road looks easy enough, so long as we stick to the bottom of this ravine. What if the door's bolted from the inside?"

"It won't be." I took a deep breath. "Someone forgot to lock it last time."

She opened her mouth to protest skeptically and then saw the look on my face. "Ah. Well, if you can pull that one off…"

"If I can't, we can always get Azazel to break in."

"I'd rather avoid that. Letting Big Boy out will set off all the alarms." She picked up the bar receipt and began to idly fold and rip it. "Save him for emergencies, like getting the hell out of there."

I fingered my plastic loop necklace, the one with the wire-saw core, and nodded. Maybe Penemuel was just tied down and we'd be able to cut her free. Maybe she was buried under a slab too, like poor dead Jomjael. I bit my lip. It was bugging me that Azazel could not hear Penemuel when she called out to him. And that Michael had not responded when challenged by name in the burial mound. If the prison cells were sealed, as we suspected, to angelic eyes and ears and voices, then it would take human guile to cross the minefield of consecrated ground and get us inside. "We can't talk much once we're on site, remember," I said. "It's all audible."

"Yeah, yeah. I remember." She was crafting a crude paper butterfly, it turned out.

"Bring your phone so we can write messages to each other."

"Honey, I'm carrying *everything* of value. D'you think we're coming back here for drinkies when it's done?"

"Fair enough. Okay."

"I'll book a table tonight at the Seven Olives, and we'll get a taxi into town. We can walk from there when it's good and dark." She flicked the paper butterfly off the end of her fingers and it took flight, beating its white wings frantically. We both watched as it bumbled to a nearby shrub, some sort of red-hot-poker, and investigated the fiery orange flower spike—before suddenly falling to the ground, nothing but a lifeless paper scrap once more.

I cleared my throat. "I guess I should go…get ready then."

She smirked. "Give him all my best."

༄

I called Azazel to my hotel bedroom, and he came down over me like the blackest oil, silky and opaque, covering me with a sweet darkness in which all the words of my anxiety and my doubt and my insecurity, written and rehearsed and repeated so often, were blotted out. His embrace was an escape from self. He moved upon me softly, like a shadow made flesh; skin upon skin, breath to breath, his hair a dark veil circumscribing my field of vision, his limbs the pillars of a prison I had no desire to escape.

He didn't even mention my change of hair color.

"Milja," he whispered, all lips and hot breath and barely curbed appetite. Sometimes he is almost too urgent, too impatient—but not that afternoon. This time he held his own desire in check, to indulge it the deeper and more keenly. The voltage of his suppressed power crackled across my skin. He savored my passion and my body alike, making me cry out for him, making me sob with need and release, one and then the other, over and over. I felt like a shimmering jag of lightning wrapped in a thundercloud. He brought me to a place beyond words and thought, a place where I was only ache and flare and shining tumble into more ache.

If he had carried on I would have died and dissolved into him, and the storm would have lasted forever.

But he lifted me off the soaked bed sheets and carried me into the wet room and set my burning slippery body against the tiled walls, my breasts and face and forearms pressed to their coolness as his hands poured over me, as he hefted my weight without effort, as he cupped me in the hot hard nest of thighs and crotch. My toes left the floor and I arched my spine and made room for him, taking him deep. My fingers scrabbled across the tiles, seeking purchase. My breath gusted mist on the glaze.

"Yes," he growled in my ear. He wasn't thrusting, was hardly moving. "Let me in, Milja. Let me in." He kissed my shoulder and my neck, his lips so slow that it felt like delicious torture, and his voice was a thick soft needful murmur that made me run wet. "I'm inside you. You like that, don't you. I am closer to you than the veins in your throat. Closer than your heartbeat. I am part of you, your flesh. I am the fire in your blood. I am the seed in your belly. I am the star-stuff in your bones."

His finger, curled around me, found the point of ignition.

"Yes," I whispered to the tiles as the light caught, flickering through my nerves. I wanted him inside me. I wanted to draw him in and swallow him whole. "Yes!" I moaned, as I felt him swell, rising on my tide.

I opened, willingly, as I came.

I felt him move into me, sighing.

No matter how much I crave his lovely hard cock it's always a moment of doubt, that point when he enters me. There's always a little fear. *Is it too much? Will he hurt me?* And the only solution is to welcome it.

This was like that—but not just my sex or my ass, but in every cell of my skin, in every bone of my spine. I felt something—I don't know what—the slide of huge muscle, the push of inexorable mass. And no, it didn't hurt, but only because I surrendered, only because I was still tumbling through my orgasm. I felt Azazel pour himself into my body, suffusing the cytoplasm, invading the nuclei, twining up the DNA spirals. It was terrifying and joyous in equal measure—and when it was over I stood alone, barely holding myself upright against the bathroom wall.

His spill ran down the insides of my trembling legs. I felt feverish.

Groggily, I reached for the shower handle and let the water gush out over my burning skin. It took a long time for me to cool down to a comfortable temperature, minutes in which I seemed unable to collect any thoughts at all. I watched my hand on the wall and the splash of the water drops, the way they ran down and ran together. It was the only thing I could focus on.

Behind my eyes, somewhere at the back of my skull,

something lurked, vast and watchful; something barely contained.

If he stretches, he will shred me. It was my first coherent thought. I imagined an explosion of bone fragments and blood splattering the shower room, like some horror movie. *Keep still, Azazel*, I told him.

He didn't answer, not in any way I was aware of. But I didn't die—and when I looked down at myself, rinsing off our mingled sweat, I didn't look bloated as I'd feared. Swift worms of water trickled their way over my breasts, fountaining from my hard nipples. I played with the rivulets, letting them spurt over my fingers, dinting the soft pale flesh experimentally, fascinated. Every drop. Every dimple on my areolae. I could see them all. I hefted my breasts in my hands, squeezing them together, delighted at the way that changed the flow of the water over their luscious swells.

I was getting gooseflesh now. That was fascinating too. The way the stippled texture of my skin interacted with the water...

Okay. Okay. What am I doing here? It dawned on me that I'd been standing under the cold flow, mindlessly distracted, for at least fifteen minutes. I flipped the shower handle, stepped out into the bedroom and grabbed a towel. The soft fibers felt glorious on my skin, and it was only a glimpse of my reflection in the full-length mirror that distracted me from patting myself dry with sensual extravagance.

My eyes flashed silver.

Oh, what?

I stumbled to the mirror. For a moment it was Azazel's inhuman eyes locked on me, before they darkened to their usual brown. I shivered. For some reason, that glimpse of my demon lover looking out from my face was more disturbing to me than the whole notion of being possessed by him. I glared at my reflection, half-panicked, daring it to change.

God, I was beautiful. The realization dawned on me slowly, as my focus slipped from my eyes to my face, and then further down. My cold goose-pimpled skin was beautiful, inviting the brush of fingertips, promising so much sensitivity. Those bumpy red insect bites on my shins made a delicious constellation almost the exact copy of Pegasus. My small-breasted body with that embarrassing mole right between my breasts was *perfect*. All that soft kissable skin—the pliant curve of my waist and back—the jut of my hip that cried out to be grabbed. My lips, full and pink and vulnerably soft. *Perfect. Perfect.*

I ran my hands over my stomach and felt a clench of post-orgasmic aftershock deep inside. The sight of my hands on my own breasts, hefting them, pinching those dusky pink nipples, the droplets of water hanging from the curls of my dark pubic hair…It was all unbearably provocative. I thrust my fingertips into my crotch, cupping the flame there, searching for soft, wet, lickable pussy.

Oh that looks so fucking hot. I want that.

My eyes flared like silver searchlights.

"Azazel!" I yelped. "Dial it down a notch, will you?" Forcing myself to turn away from the mirror, I grabbed at the clothes he'd pulled off me earlier. I could feel the burning of blood in my cheeks.

Was that how he saw me? I was genuinely shocked, and not until I had my clothes all back on did I dare look into the mirror again.

Hair and eyes mismatched. Beautiful. Perfect.

I couldn't help smiling.

As I set off down the corridor, my good mood grew. I felt

taller and stronger somehow, my spine longer, my feet more sure. I could imagine a heavy dong swinging at my crotch as I strode along, and the thought made me laugh. A big vervet monkey sat on the open balcony window, staring at me; I walked toward it without feeling a flicker of my usual wariness —just fascinated by the consciousness in its dark eyes—and it turned to jump away into the frangipani tree outside. I paused to watch, at first following its movements among the branches, then distracted by the flowers, each whorl five-petaled and yolk-yellow in its heart. Tiny spiders scuttled over the velvet cushions of the petals and I caught one up on my fingertip, almost cross-eyed as I focused on the workings of its legs and the angle of its gemlike abdomen. How wonderful it was in its miniature perfection, I realized. And so many spiders on so many flowers on so many trees…

The sound of feet snapped me out of my fractal reverie. A woman was coming down the passage toward me, carrying a mop and bucket. She was small and stoop-backed and elderly, slack-bodied and wrinkled and just incredibly lovely. Every wrinkle was a work of art. Each limping step took my breath away. She was a miracle of creation, it struck me, making my heart leap; a living sentient art-form wrought with utmost cunning out of raw atoms which ought really to be nothing more than swirling gases. Every stray hair, every cracked nail, and every lash on her drooping eyelid was fashioned with painstaking artifice.

"What are you staring at, lady?" she muttered as she passed me.

"You are… I'm sorry." I caught myself before I blurted out how beautiful she was, and grinned. "I thought I knew you."

She shook her head and stamped onward. Only then did I

realize that she'd spoken in Amharic—and that I'd replied in the same language.

Holy crap, Azazel, I gasped under my breath. *Is this what it's like for you?*

I hurried into the bar, and found Roshana leaning against the counter chatting to a young man in hotel uniform who was hanging on her every word. She dismissed him with a flick of her wrist the moment she saw me, though, and came across to lead me to a nest of armchairs. Her mouth was pursed tight and her gaze intense.

"You've got him, haven't you?" she said in a low voice, staring at me across the glass coffee table. "He's in there!"

"How can you tell?"

"You've suddenly started to walk like a man, honey. And you're sitting like one too."

Panicked, I clapped my spread knees together and sat up fast from my slouch. "Shit!" I hissed, and Roshana laughed.

"What's it like?"

"Like being a bit drunk," I admitted. "Full of confidence. I feel like punching a lion. And he's got...this amazing ability to focus. Not eyesight—I mean, to notice stuff. There are eighteen pillars in this room, each made of four sections, each with the hotel logo repeated three times. There are fourteen different kinds of whisky behind the bar. There are three hundred and sixty-three sequins on that blouse you're wearing, two hundred links in your necklace, the stone is a fire-opal."

"And there I thought you were just staring at my rack," she said, amused. "I'm up here, by the way."

"No!" Far too late, I wrenched my gaze up to her eyes.

"Well you checked out every woman in the room when you entered."

"I did not!"

"Oh, you did." She flourished a grin. "I think he's *particularly* good at focusing on titties, don't you?"

I didn't answer, just dove into my jacket pocket and jammed on my gloriously dark sunglasses as fast as I could. It might look odd wearing them indoors, but that was the least of my worries. "How the hell am I supposed to manage outside of here?" I moaned.

"Well." Roshana stood and offered me her arm. "Keep your shades on, don't talk if you can help it, and stay close to me." She winked as she drew me to her side. "And honey, do try not to get a hard-on."

☙

I did not enjoy the meal out. To be honest, I don't recall it that well. I do remember that Roshana had to stop me ordering seven different courses because I wanted to try every possible flavor; sweet, savory, spicy, fruity, meaty—I just couldn't make myself chose only one. Azazel's immanence made me dizzy, and I could feel his restlessness. I think he was exploring the other potentials offered by my body too, because I found myself inconveniently—and very uncomfortably—horny, and I had to grit my teeth and cut myself off mentally from my inflamed sex.

But we took our time over dinner. We lingered until all the other tourists had finished and gone back to their rooms and hotels. Then we walked out through town. There was no street-lighting in Lalibela, only that which spilled out accidentally from bars and shops. We kept to the shadows purposefully, hoping not to draw attention. Roshana was carrying a chic little rucksack with, I assumed, all her expensive essentials in. I simply wore the jacket I'd arrived in, its pockets loaded, most of my clothes and toiletries abandoned back in my room.

I'd expected the site of the churches to be quiet at this time of night, long after tourist hours, but we could hear singing as we approached.

"Do they never stop?" Roshana muttered, aggrieved. "There was some sort of service going on at three this morning. I heard it from my room. They had a *loudspeaker*."

Thanks to our reconnaissance and the Internet, it was easy enough to find the approach trench to Bet Gebriel-Rufael, though not so easy to pick our way along it. Our boots sounded horribly loud as we scuffed our way there through the deep shadows. Above our heads a strip of starlit night showed where the rock faces ended, but did little to light our way, and though I'd brought a small flashlight I didn't turn it on in case we were noticed. Just because there were no visible barriers, it didn't mean we weren't trespassing.

If it hadn't been for Azazel flaming inside me I think I would have been terrified, but what I felt in actuality was a wolfish eagerness. The darkness felt like my ally.

We climbed through the arch cut from one section of trench into another. The singing was more muffled back here, and I hoped the service was keeping all the priests occupied.

The bottom-level door to the church was, as we'd previously discovered, a small portal deeply recessed into the rock at the head of seven worn steps. The wood of the door was ancient, cracked and reinforced with big iron studs. I took the lead, reaching up and pressing upon the boards.

It didn't yield. It didn't even shift.

For a moment I was genuinely nonplussed. Hadn't I leaned on Chance to leave it unlocked? My unnatural luck had been good enough to stop a gun going off before now—how was the door defying me?

Roshana stood on the step below, close enough to waft me

with her perfume. "What's up?" she breathed.

I shoved my shoulder against the door. It didn't rattle on its hinges. "I don't know."

She groped around behind me. "Wood's swollen. Let me."

So I retreated a few paces, staring around us twitchily. There was just enough light for me to see her lift her hands and shove the door hard. *Really* hard. The wood let out a loud crack and fell back from the frame, revealing a slot of pitch darkness as it swiveled on a single intact hinge and sagged into the room.

Okay…just how strong is she? She might look ordinary, but that push had been anything but.

"Oops." Roshana stepped through into the dark and I followed a moment later. We were both conscious of the noise we'd made breaking in, and the first thing we did was grope about until we had the door between us, lift it back into place, and wedge it against the door jamb. I'm sure Roshana could have managed that on her own, to be honest, but I was trying to gloss over the fact that I'd noticed. And that I was slightly annoyed that she was stronger than me.

"Okay?"

"Uhuh."

Then she took out her phone. The pale glow of the screen seemed incredibly bright as she played it around the chamber.

"Holy…" I blurted. She lifted an admonishing finger to her lips, then pulled out the phone stylus and wrote on the screen. I read the lines of handwriting she brandished.

'*We found where they stash the bodies then.*'

Ten

BLESSED ARE THOSE WHO DIE IN THE LORD

I could only agree with her verdict. We were surrounded by corpses, dried-out and fragile-looking, stacked so high that the ones at the bottom must have been flattened by their brethren. The easiest features to make out were feet and skulls; everything else was a leathery dusty mess of disintegration, draped ineffectually in chintz curtains.

I pulled an *Ewwww* face, baring my teeth. Hundreds of empty eye sockets looked at us, the shadows shifting within them. It took an effort of will not to work out exactly how many.

Roshana seemed a lot less perturbed. She glanced over the piles curiously, shining her light into dark corners. There was no particular smell in here, thank goodness—just a dusty church aroma—so the bodies must have all been really old. Nevertheless, I found myself trying not to breathe too deeply.

With the tip of her finger Roshana indicated a long ladder of warped poles that led up to a square aperture in the ceiling.

'*Church up there,*' she wrote on her screen, and I nodded. '*Where's the lady?*'

For a horrible moment I wondered if Penemuel had just been stashed under all the bodies, a needle in a macabre haystack. But she hadn't mentioned cadavers when we'd talked in my dream, only red rock.

'*Not under this lot,*' I wrote. Gingerly, trying not to step on anything that would give me nightmares forever, I plucked the little flashlight from my pocket and picked my way across the rocky floor between two piles of ex-pilgrims.

I found an interior door easily enough. I judged that it faced back toward the so-called River Jordan. A device was carved into the rough rock of a lintel that threatened to smack the forehead of anyone entering: a deep U-shape cupping a ball. I stared at it, wondering what it could mean. It didn't look Christian. It looked a lot older, somehow.

Roshana nudged me. '*Sun and moon*' said her phone screen. Her lips quirked smugly.

Oh. Penemuel had said "The sun and moon stand over my head"—and I'd assumed she meant she was near the equator. I touched the carvings gingerly, noting every tiny pit in the stone.

There was a padlock on the door, but it looked rusted. I glanced back at Roshana and she didn't need telling; she snapped it off the hasp with one pull and dropped the broken pieces. Beyond the door was the narrowest of stairways which descended steeply into the dark.

Azazel's impatience shriveled a little.

Down we go then, I told myself, and instinctively took the lead. Not my own instincts, of course—Azazel's. Personally I'd have been happy to be in the rear when it came to meeting danger, but he felt strongly he should go first. Roshana pulled the door shut behind us. The stairs were not constructed for someone as tall as me; I had to arch my spine and crane my head back from the overhang of the roof. That angle and the worn stairs, scalloped by the passage of feet, made the descent precarious, and I considered sitting on my ass and sliding down.

That plan was discarded when my feet hit water. I squeaked in shock and recoiled. Roshana hissed as I fell back against her shins and she poked me in the shoulder in an interrogative manner.

I shone my torch down and oily-looking blackness gleamed up at me. I reached over my shoulder for the phone and—clenching the flashlight in my teeth—wrote, '*Flooded. Looks like the passage levels out tho.*'

'*Is there room?*'

'*Think so.*'

'*Go on then!*'

I hated her right then more than anyone else in the universe. The dank, stale air of the passage felt claustrophobic, and I was sweating despite the cool stone against my palms. Azazel, I'm sure, would have much rather faced a thousand armed enemies than this rock squeeze. My inner heat in no way encouraged me to touch that lightless sump water. I wondered how long it had been standing in the tunnel, growing stagnant. Gritting my teeth, I eased down, step by step, into the tepid seep.

At least I don't have to worry about waterborne tropical diseases, I told myself. *Leeches, maybe. Do you get leeches in caves?*

Ankles. Shins. Knees. *Ugh!* Thighs. And *ah*—now it levelled out. Luckily the roof was high enough here to allow me to stand upright, with caution. I played the torchlight from side to side as I waded slowly forward, testing my footing each time. The tunnel was wide enough for only one person to pass comfortably and there was a line of grave-niches on either side, all of them occupied. Those were above the tide mark, thank goodness. Or at least I *hoped* there were no open graves under the water, because that was a mental picture I really wanted to keep out of my head as I sloshed through the turbid fluid. It smelled like old dishwater, but I tried to be glad it wasn't worse.

Skeletal remains gaped at me like confused drunks, half-woken by the flash of my torch. *Sorry*, I told them.

The tunnel was long, and nearly dead straight. It was going under the trench of the Jordan, I surmised, with more confidence than I'd ever naturally feel. We were heading back toward the northwestern group of churches.

And there ahead of me, thank goodness, was a short flight of steps leading up through a rock arch. I gave Roshana a thumbs-up sign over my shoulder and felt hope as well as water surging around my strides. There was a chamber beyond the arch. It couldn't be far now...

But the chamber was not a prison cell, or even a single room. It was a labyrinth. For a moment we stood, pressed into the doorway, confused by what it was we were seeing—many corridors, or one complex hall? Great rough pillars had been hewn out of the living rock, with graves chiseled into every face and bones stacked high in every slot. Between the pillars narrow little passages wound about to create a catacomb that reminded me, more than anything, of the shelved area in my old college library basement. The walls were painted all over with pictures of patriarchs and saints in a style now familiar, though down here the bright colors had all degraded to shades of brown.

'*FFS*,' Roshana wrote succinctly on her phone screen.

I could only nod.

'*Where?*'

I shrugged, and set off hoping she'd stick close. It would be all too easy to lose each other in here, though I tried to keep a straight line heading forward. Like some monstrous snail, we left a wet trail behind us, but the drips from our sodden clothes died off as the distance wore on. This catacomb was vast, though there was no grandeur to its rabbit-warren structure. There must be tens of thousands interred down here; articulated mummies no more, just anonymous piles of skulls and femurs and less identifiable bones.

Azazel hated this—the low roof in particular. I could feel his rebellion throbbing inside me.

Every so often we'd hit a pinch-point, where the tunnels would end in a blank wall that had only a single entrance to the next, near-identical-looking chamber. This feature was the only thing that kept me pressing on with any hope that there was some sort of linear structure to the maze.

Then we came at last to a dead end, with no egress before us. Just a plastered wall with a huge fresco of Saint George slaying the dragon, surrounded by scenes of his three hundred martyrdoms. The princess in the main story, I noted, had very wisely hidden up a tree.

Roshana surveyed the dead end with an expression of extreme annoyance that needed no words. She looked like she had been personally affronted by the architects. Then she shot me a look that said, *Well?*

Trying to gather my wits, I let my gaze flit over the wall-painting as I leaned back against a knurl of rock. I was busy thinking about how many doorways we might have passed to either side without realizing. The visual part of my mind was meanwhile parsing pictorial torture after torture, noting how the pagans were always depicted in profile while the good guys were full-face, counting the speckled scales on the dragon, seeing the faint horizontal striations under the surface of the plaster...

I caught my breath.

Stepping forward, I laid my hand on the flank of the stallion that George rode. The broad wash of white paint did not hide what lay underneath so effectively as the darker, more complex parts of the fresco. My fingertips could not discern the pattern, but there was the faintest visible discoloration.

Frantically, I signaled for the phone.

'*Blocks,*' I wrote. '*Not rock.*' An opening here had been walled up and then plastered over to hide the aperture. I started to scratch at the paintwork.

Roshana understood my message at once. She made a fist and punched the horse right below the strappy harness on its rump. A big piece of damp plaster cracked away, and when she pulled it out we could see a line of mortar between squared stones.

I nodded wildly, and helped her pull the decaying plaster away in plates. Detritus covered our shoes. Together we revealed most of a blocked-up archway, by which point I was panting in the stale and humid air.

Stand right back, her hands signaled me. And when I obeyed—reluctantly—she started to attack the wall. Her fine little hands should never have been able to take that sort of abuse. Every bone in her wrist should have been broken at the first blow. Her shoulders should have been dislocated. But what actually happened, in front of my wide eyes, was that the rotten mortar gave way and the hewn stone shifted and the weakest block crashed back into the space revealed beyond.

IN BONDS OF THE EARTH

After that she got her hands in and pulled the stones out one at a time into the room with us, tossing them aside.

It all made more noise than I'd have liked.

At last the hole was big enough to climb through and even Roshana paused for breath. I stepped up to shine my torch into the void.

There was a big empty chamber behind the wall. There was something else too; I saw it in that fleeting moment that my flashlight wasn't pointed directly within. A faint reddish glow, instead of utter darkness. The shine of a candle, or a lamp turned right down low, hidden out of my direct eyeline. I backed away.

Roshana saw the look on my face.

This was no time to beg for the phone and write anything. '*Light!*' I mouthed, pointing.

She leaped through that hole like a jungle cat. Shocked, I scrabbled to follow her form with my flashlight, though God knows whether or not she needed it; she might have been able to see in the dark for all I knew. I think she hit the ground with her outstretched arms and flipped into a crouch, but maybe I was conflating my hopeless glimpses with memories of movie stunts. I certainly saw her stand and start to turn back to face me—just as the priest hidden to the side of the portal stepped out and swung his staff at her head.

Roshana slammed her arm up and caught the pole, twisting beneath the swing and wrenching it from the priest's hands. Effortlessly she extended her pivot until she was face-to-face, then punched him in the diaphragm. No... *Through* the diaphragm. She thrust her hand right up under his ribs, buried almost to her elbow in his soft insides. He didn't scream. Maybe she'd collapsed his lungs or something.

I dropped the goddamn flashlight in my shock.

By the time I retrieved it, the fight was over. I scrambled in an ungainly fashion over jagged and tumbled stonework. The beam of my light cruelly spot-lit Roshana as she stood up from the still spasming wreckage of the priest's body, spattered in gore, and lifted her bloody hand to her face. She licked her fingers, then wrinkled her nose in disappointment.

I didn't see that. I couldn't have seen that.

I could feel the clamminess of my clenched fists.

"What?" she asked harshly. Her eyes gleamed like polished jet. "If he'd hit *you*, Daddy would have come out and killed him. If he'd escaped, he'd have just gone and got his friends. How many do you want us to have to kill?"

I couldn't answer. I should have felt terrified and nauseated by her brutality, but mostly I was just full of rage. He'd been an old man, with a white beard. She could have put him down without killing him, surely? My desire to slap her was so strong, and my hands so twitchy, that I could only fix on the smallest criticism.

I put my finger to my lips to reprimand her for speaking out loud.

Roshana shrugged dismissively. "This room isn't consecrated. That feeling of being watched? It stopped as soon as I came in."

The room sure as hell *was* consecrated, though it was unlike anything we'd come through yet. It was round, for a start; drum-shaped and plastered and painted a deep bloody red. There were no central pillars, though there was a broad wooden staircase leading up to a trapdoor in the roof at the opposite point to that we'd entered. Around the walls were painted four angels, their huge extended wings touching at the tips, left hands held up in warning, right hands wielding swords. Their black almond-shaped eyes seemed to exude a tragic foreboding.

But I believed Roshana when she said she didn't feel under surveillance anymore. *Dead air*, I thought. *Heaven's Faraday cage.*

There was nothing else in the cave—nothing except the lit stub of a candle near the wall, the corpse of a priest that I could not bring myself to even look at, and a round disc of stone in the center of the floor, like the dais of a fountain that wasn't there. "I'm going to be sick," I muttered. I wanted to make her feel bad for what she'd done.

"No you're not. You're going to find the Bookworm. I'm just here to do the heavy lifting, remember. Come on, honey, what now?"

I stalked over to the dais. It was a single piece of stone exactly three cubits in diameter, my angel-tripped brain told me—which I interpreted as less than five feet—and about ankle-high. Incised deeply into the center was another cup-and-circle symbol. Ancient symbols of heavenly order standing watch for untold centuries, long before Christianity or even Judaism came to this land. *The sun and the moon stand over my head.*

"She's right here." I pointed at the flagstone. "Under that. Can you shift it?"

"Hmph." Roshana dropped to a squat, gripped the edge of the disc with her hands and gave it an experimental shove. The stone didn't shift.

Oh Jesus Christ forgive me, she is covered in blood. I can smell it, like copper pennies.

"It's a plug," she mused. "I have to lift it."

"There's a chip in the stone this side," I said, not looking, trusting to luck that I'd be right. "You can get your fingers under." Because if she couldn't lift it I'd have to call Azazel out, and then there was no saying how far things would escalate. Backing out of the way as she came around, I watched as she felt for purchase, clenched her jaw and, with a grunt, heaved the stone up. A gush of fetid air issued from the gap beneath.

"Careful," I warned, as she flipped the stone disc right up on its edge. "We're right under—"

Too late. The flipped lid fell backward with a crash of stone that echoed around the cave.

"—the churches," I finished, wincing. The uncannily attentive part of my mind had correlated the distance and direction we'd walked, compared it to all the maps and diagrams we'd seen, and reckoned we were close to Bet Maryam and Bet Mikael.

Roshana examined a split nail, frowning, and didn't seem to hear my words. Then she looked into the pit revealed at her feet. "That her?"

I bent forward to see, and my throat closed up until I couldn't catch a breath.

Oh God—Azazel got off lightly, didn't he?

At least during his incarceration he'd been able to see the distant sky. At least he'd been able to breathe, and speak to his captors. Here before us a shaft barely wide enough to accommodate a human body had been plunged vertically into the earth. Its occupant had been dropped in feet-first, and sealed—airless, lightless, alone—in a living tomb. For five thousand years, with only the muttered prayers of guardian priests, working shifts, to mark the torturous passage of days.

I could see a pair of dark, bare shoulders and the back of a slumped, close-cropped head.

That's unbearable...

"Penemuel," I said softly, reaching down to touch her

scalp. "It's me."

She heard. Tilting her head back, she looked up into my face, her teeth bared in a rictus around a thick leathery gag, her eyes as black as the darkness she'd stared into for millennia. Her dried lips were cracked and bleeding, but I knew the angel-woman from my dream. A wordless hiss issued from her throat, and then turned into a moan.

This was beyond cruelty.

"Get her out of there," I gasped.

"Coming up," Roshana said, and reached in to grab her by the shoulders. I heard Penemuel whimper and I wanted to stop my ears and gouge out my eyes.

Penemuel's long naked body slithered out of the hole as if some bizarre birth were being enacted, with Roshana as the bloodstained midwife. Not actually tall enough to lift the Watcher all the way, Roshana got her rear up onto the lip of the shaft and then dragged her horizontally across the floor. The fallen angel wasn't in any shape to assist in her own rescue; it was immediately obvious that her arms were bound against her torso with a long crisscrossed rope of dried rawhide which was wrapped tight round her body from shoulder to ankle, and which strapped her legs together. The gag was knotted cruelly underneath her ear.

"Snap these," I demanded.

"No." Roshana, weirdly, didn't seem to be upset by any of this. Her expression was as disdainful as if she'd just pulled a handbag out of a sales pile and then decided she didn't like the look of it anyway. But she deigned to explain, for my benefit. "If she can't then neither can I. It's not a question of strength, it's about blood. This is a job for"—and goddamn if she didn't smirk—"pure-bred monkeys."

"You think this is funny?" I gasped, whipping off my

plastic necklace.

"More...ironic."

I decided to stop talking. Peeling away the sheath to reveal the wire core of the necklace, I slid the flexible saw behind the bonds at Penemuel's ankles. There was most space between rope and flesh there. And yes, it saved me bending over more disconcerting parts of the bound and naked and twitching body of a still-beautiful woman who was making bits of my brain do backflips. I swore under my breath, knowing just how much hard work this was going to be.

But I'd done it before, in releasing Azazel. The vile bonds were tough, but I could feel the tiny titanium saw teeth bite as I went to work. I could do this.

Roshana stood with her less-bloody hand on her hip, tapping her toe as she watched. Overhead, a muffled chanting had begun, and an unidentifiable shuffling. Neither of us remarked on the new noises.

"There!" With sweat beading on my temples and my fingers sore from pulling the tiny handles, I finally snapped through the hardened flesh rope that bound the angel. That left me the job of trying to unwrap her, tugging the stiff cordage from her skin. It had been bound on so tightly that it was stuck to her flesh, tearing away to reveal raw pink patches that made my stomach lurch.

Penemuel moaned from behind her gag, and twisted her legs apart. I tried not to look.

Roshana, with a glare at the trapdoor, strolled over to where the priest lay dead and picked up his staff. She snapped it across her knee effortlessly, and the broken ends looked wickedly sharp. "Hurry up," she muttered, twirling the improvised weapons in a casual *kata*. In the half dark, barely illumined at the margins of the flashlight, she looked like a

IN BONDS OF THE EARTH

vampire-slayer preparing for the next wave of incoming monsters.

Except of course, I realized, *we* were the vampires in this story. The good guys were the ones in the church overhead.

That was the moment the trapdoor was flung open from above. Light—electric light, from many bulbs—flooded in, making me blink. I stared up at a ring of priests clustered around the doorway at the top of the stairs. Voices poured down on us too, from that group and from others unseen in the church nave, and I could hear every one of them and understand every word. Most were praying, calling on Saint George to defend them, but others were less pious.

"What is happening?"

"Has he escaped?"

"Women! Why are there women there?"

"Where is Brother Yohannes?"

"Blood! Can you see the blood?"

I glimpsed the gray wall behind the trapdoor, carved with the crude haloed figure of a saint, and in recognizing it I knew exactly where we were; underneath Bet Golgotha, the holiest church on the site. Its embargo on women made more sense now, given my own history.

The first priest started down the stairs, and as Roshana closed to meet him others looked ready to follow suit.

"I don't think we're getting out of here without help," she said. "Time to call Big Boy out."

Instead I hauled Penemuel into a sitting position. I was still trying to free her of her bonds, my hands tugging ruthlessly, my head whirling with hot thoughts like flames. She writhed and I knew I was hurting her, but now I couldn't take time to care. I was thinking that if I could release Penemuel then she could take us far away without involving

Azazel. *He* was churning inside me, longing to rise, blotting out my caution. I wasn't afraid of the priests—they were only men. I'd seen how Roshana dealt with them, and they died easily. Yes—there went that next one, and it wasn't even shocking anymore. I was sure she could hold them off until I joined her—and then I'd show her what I could do. I was convinced that I could handle a few old men easily. I wanted to fight. I wanted to smack down those interfering priests and rescue Penemuel so that she would adore me, and stride out of there the victor leaving Roshana gaping in awe and then—

And then I won't have to let Azazel go.

The realization hit me. The hot parade of my reckless thoughts, that clotted intermingling of his instincts and mine, suddenly struck me as near-insane. I'd been inflated like a balloon by the demon inside me, his confidence and his pride and his eager lust, until I was terrified of shrinking back to human proportions.

I was tripping on Azazel and I didn't want to come down.

"Milja!" roared Roshana, thrusting the slumping body of the priest aside. "Call him!"

But it wasn't her command that forced me into action. It wasn't the sight of another of our victims bleeding all over the floor, or the horror in the faces of the priests hesitating at the foot of the stairs, staves raised, shouting at us to surrender the demon. It was a glimpse I caught of the stone relief in the room above and beyond those stairs. It was cracking like a pie-crust, as if under sudden terrible pressure *from behind*—and a twisted black limb was thrusting its way out through the crumbling rock.

The priests still in the church scattered the hell out of sight of the trapdoor, yelping.

"Azazel," I whispered. "Please, quickly!"

He came out fast, much faster than he'd entered me—and it hurt beyond anything I could have imagined; it hurt like all the fires of Hell tearing through my flesh. I let go of Penemuel and slammed to hands and knees, screaming as I felt him erupt from the whole length of my spine. I was convinced he'd physically split me open. I think I blacked out for a few seconds, because I opened my eyes to find myself curled in a fetal position on the rock floor, wet with sweat.

Everyone in the chamber had gone deathly quiet all of a sudden.

Azazel, stark naked, was crouching over me. He cupped my face, his eyes concerned. "You're not hurt, Milja," he said gently.

If I'd had a voice I might have begged to differ, because every cell of my body still felt that fading agony. But I couldn't speak, and could barely draw breath. It was like he'd sucked all the strength out of me with the force of his departure. I was a pair of wide eyes in a body paralyzed by the physical shock; not just a mere human again, but the weakest and most helpless of specimens. "Unh," I said, drool pooling under my cheek.

"Mmh!" chorused Penemuel, still gagged but doing better than me, in that she was at least sitting up, mostly.

At that cry he swung from me to her, and knelt to lift her face in his hands. I might have felt hurt if I'd had time to think about it. But his turning away allowed me to see the staircase, and see what was descending it toward us.

The saint had answered their prayers.

Three hundred martyrdoms had left very little of Saint George that could be considered human. No eyes, for a start; just empty pits. He was mostly bone and charcoal now, crusted and black, though still draped in the corroded remnants of the scale armor he'd been buried in. God alone knows how he was still capable of animation, but I guess that goes without saying. Miracles are not always pretty.

The priests, who'd been trying to retreat back up the stairs away from the fallen angel suddenly arrived amongst them, took one look at their divine ally on way down and just fell sideways off the steps, scrambling for the wall.

"Oh for fuck's sake," came Roshana's disbelieving voice from somewhere beyond my field of vision.

Penemuel struggled weakly in Azazel's embrace, her eyes wide with fear. She had seen what he had not. I would have screamed a warning, but I had no strength. There was barely any air in my lungs, so I just gasped like a dying fish.

The holy revenant carried a spear with a wicked iron head in his right hand. And as I watched he hefted it, aiming straight at Azazel's back.

Azazel turned. Maybe he did note our collective panic, or maybe his warrior instincts were just that finely tuned. He turned with inhuman speed and grace, reaching his hand out to whatever weapon was aimed at him. He had no reason to fear—he knew after all that nothing metallic could harm the father of weapon-smithing. I'd seen him catch bullets before now, and he was almost casual despite his speed. He backhanded the spearpoint as it descended, swatting it away.

Well, he would have, if that narrow iron head had been capable of being blocked. Instead, angled downward in flight, it punched straight through his hand, through his stomach, clear out of his back somewhere in the kidney region—and pinned Penemuel through the chest. For a moment the two of them were skewered together, and everybody in the room froze in shock.

Everyone except the saint, who drew his rusting short-sword. He had no face, so it was impossible to discern his expression.

Azazel, hunched like a crow over the shaft impaling him, uttered a surprised groan. Then that became a roar of pure rage as he unsheathed his own flaming blade out of the air. Blood and hellfire steamed crimson in an atmosphere suddenly too thick to breathe.

We're going to die now, I thought.

Step by step, writhing in pain, the fallen angel walked himself up the length of the spear-shaft, leaving a slick of blood up the ancient wood. He walked himself right off the end, and then he lifted his sword and launched himself at the stairs.

I shut my eyes. I knew what was coming; I had seen this before. A wave of heat blasted across my skin and I tried to curl into a ball, while the screaming rose around me. It wasn't a huge chamber, so there was nowhere to go to escape the flaming sword, or the two inhuman antagonists whirling around it. And they didn't give a damn about collateral damage. The only reason I survived, I'm sure, was that I was flat on the floor and most of the fire went over me. I knew from the noises that people were running and struggling with each other, but that didn't last long. Even the cries of pain didn't last long.

There was a terrible smell of burning hair and charred meat.

I opened my eyes to a room full of stinging smoke, and started coughing weakly. Through the filthy haze limped Azazel, a great shadowy titan, with his mutilated hand crushed to his bleeding torso wound and his face gray with pain. He looked around him, and his gaze swept over me, but I can't say for sure he even saw me. Instead he staggered over to

Penemuel, who still knelt with knees spread and the spear angled through her chest. Her head was slumped, but her hands were free of her old bonds, and I saw the weak stir of her fingers that showed she was still alive.

Azazel slid to his knees at her side and wrapped his arms around her. The smoke billowed as they vanished from this world.

I could feel myself swimming in and out of consciousness. I tried to raise myself up, but my arms would not obey me. "Azazel," I whispered, but heard no answer. "Roshana," I tried, in vain.

I lay there waiting for him to come back and save me, while the smoke oozed out into the church overhead and the sound of distant singing rose and then faded. Strange lights bloomed on my retinas. Sleep seemed by far the easiest option. Azazel would come back for me, I told myself, as soon as he had healed; any moment now.

He didn't.

I shut my eyes, because there wasn't anything to see. The world faded.

Briefly I re-opened them once, when the sound of footfalls paused in front of my nose. I was looking neither at bare, sculpted feet nor dusty Ethiopian sandals, but at a pair of very shiny, very expensive-looking lace-ups. This surprised me, faintly.

One of the toes lifted, hooked under my shoulder and rolled me over onto my back.

"Milja. Oh dear." Uriel shook his head at me and tutted. The handsome silver fox of an archangel hadn't changed a bit since I last saw him, and the lingering smoke even gave him an ethereal halo, as if he'd just descended from the clouds of Paradise. "What did I warn you?"

I realized that he'd used his feet because his arms were full. He was carrying Roshana, though I only recognized her because I was familiar with her little chartreuse designer rucksack. All her lovely thick hair was gone and her face was a raw red-and-black mass of burns. I could see most of her teeth.

Uriel looked annoyed, I thought. Not furious, not defeated. Perturbed.

"I'll tell them to go easy on you," he said, and as I finally blacked out, my last vision was of him, an Armani-clad Richard Geresque psychopomp with Roshana's body draped over his arms, climbing the stairs through the haze toward the light.

JANINE ASHBLESS

Eleven
DELIVERED THEM INTO CHAINS

I woke up in Hell, and it was full of women.

I lifted my head, because the blanket under my nose stank of sweat and feet. That movement taught me that my body was working again, even if my head thumped and my throat was parched. I was lying on a rock-hard bed. The room was full of beds—I mean *full*, no gaps at all between the frames, like a great bed platform—and they filled it almost to the door, which was metal and stood wide open to admit brilliant sunshine.

The place was hot and sticky and crowded and full of voices. I looked around, blinking the grit out of my eyes. As the smell of sweat receded I caught a whiff of open toilet. The room was crowded with Ethiopian-looking women wearing long skirts and headscarves, who sat on the beds and stood in clusters on the scant floor space. There were children here too, mostly really young ones. Babies shrieked. Toddlers tumbled around.

What is this? A hospital? A really awful hospital?

If the priests had dumped me at a hospital, I supposed I had cause to be grateful.

Some of the women were watching me, now that I'd started moving. Their faces displayed a strange immiscible expression of both curiosity and exhausted disinterest, as if nothing I did could have any meaning.

Slowly I rolled to the nearest edge of the bed and tested my wobbly legs on the floor. Quite a few children stopped what they were doing and stared at me, but I ignored them. My eyes were on the outside door.

Where am I?

I staggered out into the sunshine, trying to draw moisture to my dry mouth. I was standing in a rough courtyard, hemmed in on three sides by buildings which also stood open to show roomfuls of women. There was a standpipe with a concrete curb, and for a moment I was tempted to run for that, but I forced my attention to the fourth wall which framed a steel gate, which was closed. There were a few people in faded uniforms, hanging around watching the civilian women as they sat in the sunshine talking and working at small domestic tasks. There were men among the uniformed ones, the only men in sight.

Guards. They've got guns. Oh no.

"Azazel?" I croaked.

Nothing happened.

I moved toward the big gate, my legs sagging beneath me, and a guard detached himself from the flirtatious conversation he seemed to be having with a young woman in a bright headscarf. He intercepted my path and waved the muzzle of his shoulder-slung rifle lazily.

I couldn't understand a word he said anymore. My

linguistic intuition had deserted me along with the angelic possession, but I did grasp the general gist, which was *Not this way; fuck off.*

My brain caught up at last. This wasn't a hospital. It was a prison.

"Do you speak English?" I tried.

He rattled off more Amharic and repeated the gesture with the gun, which made me back off, hands raised in placation.

"Does anyone speak English?" I asked, raising my voice and casting around. The hubbub of voices faded a little as people paused to stare at me. "I need to speak to your captain," I tried, turning to the guard, and backed that up with a lie: "I'm American. You can't hold me here. I need to talk to the American consulate."

Not even the lie worked. The gesture with his fingers was utterly dismissive.

"For God's sake—" My voice rose with my frustration and fear. But the result was exactly counter-productive, as for the first time he frowned and this time he really barked.

"*Hiğği!*"

I flinched, then obeyed best as I could. "Azazel," I said to the empty air as I retreated across the courtyard, arms clenched around my torso for comfort. "Azazel, please come and get me!"

He wasn't listening, it seemed, and my mouth felt full of glue. I was desperate for a drink, so I lurched toward the standpipe. A short length of hose hung from the faucet, dripping into the concrete basin, and I fixed my eyes on that luscious promise. It didn't matter if the water wasn't clean; I was betting that my witchy body wouldn't succumb to any germs.

I almost had my hand on the tap when I registered the shouting behind me and turned. It wasn't the guard, but it was one of his uniformed female colleagues, waving her arms and gesturing angrily at me.

"I don't speak goddamn Amharic," I said through gritted teeth.

She tapped her wrist and made a fierce shooing gesture in my face, still shouting.

Really? What the hell kind of place doesn't let people drink in this heat? "This is insane," I said. She didn't appear to be waving a gun, so I grabbed at the tap, and that was when she slapped me hard across the face, hard enough to rock my balance.

"*Iyyy!*"

Well, I'd picked that up in the last few days—it just meant '*No.*' Stunned, I clutched at my ear, which was ringing, and tried to blink away the red stars flashing in my vision. I didn't resist as she grabbed my blouse and manhandled me away from the standpipe, shoving me back toward the center of the courtyard, and then gave me another couple of slaps for good measure until I cringed away and kept retreating.

I couldn't stand up to them. These people were armed, and I've never fought, not even as a child. I couldn't fight, and I couldn't argue, and I couldn't even burst into tears. I didn't understand what was happening and it scared the hell out of me.

Azazel!

She stopped hitting me when I ducked and held my hands up and made it clear I wasn't going anywhere near the tap again. She stood and watched me as I shuffled back toward the room I'd come from, blindly seeking shade. She didn't smirk sadistically or anything. She just looked self-righteous and a bit irritated at having had to put some effort into putting me in my place.

Every tissue in my body howled for water.

Where the hell was Azazel? Was he okay? And if he was, why hadn't he come for me? From the position of the sun beating down into the courtyard it was near noon, which meant…oh, at least twelve hours since the fight under Bet Golgotha. That was easily long enough for him to heal up and come back. And this place wasn't like the monastery in Montenegro; it wasn't consecrated ground, surely? So he ought to know exactly where I was. He ought to be able to hear me when I called his name.

Thoughts churned through my dehydrated brain. My fallback champion in a crisis was supposed to be Roshana—but she was dead. Maybe. My brief glimpse of her burnt body hadn't been enough to confirm that. But if she wasn't actually dead then she had fallen into Uriel's clutches which meant *he knew what she was* and she'd be dead really, really soon. Uriel would stop at nothing to recapture Azazel. I didn't want to imagine what was happening to her now.

There was no third backup plan.

Shit, this situation was disastrous. What the hell was I supposed to do? *Where was Azazel?*

I returned into the crowded, stinking barracks and the bed I'd woken up on. Another woman was sitting on it now, dandling her baby, so I perched on the very edge. At the other end of the room a squabble had broken out and several women were screaming at each other. I bowed my head, not wanting to look, not wanting to be a part of this. I was trying not to panic.

I touched the side of my face, feeling the puffy swelling around the orbit of my eye. A lock of scorched and stinking hair crumbled when I ran my fingers through it.

The kick caught me in my back right over my kidney, and knocked me off the bed onto the dirt floor. For a moment I had no idea what had happened, and then I managed to look up and see the mother's barefoot sole pointed at me—before the agony surged so fiercely that I couldn't focus on anything else at all. I half collapsed, keening with pain. I could hear myself swearing in both English and Montenegrin. Lights flashed behind my eyes.

And when the tide of pain receded at last, it revealed a long red shore of rage. What the hell were they doing treating me like this when I'd never done a thing to any of them?

When Azazel comes for me I'll...

And I pictured with avidity the whole prison levelled to smoking ruins and burnt corpses. The guards and the prisoners alike, the mothers and their skinny little babies, the deranged old crone sitting over there talking to herself, the lumpen teenager banging her forehead repeatedly against the concrete wall—all of them, without exception. *I wanted to teach them a lesson.* In that moment I wanted to kill them all.

I'll show you bitches.

Then I caught myself. A vertiginous shame at my fantasies oozed up from the depths, though I resented it because it felt so much less comforting than the rage. I had no idea what these people had been through. I had no idea what transgressions or misfortunes or injustices had confined them here. The red judgmental rage—what right did I have to that?

Is this what having Azazel inside me does?
Is this what the righteous wrath of angels is like?

I couldn't cry, so I dry-heaved.

When I looked up, there was a cluster of women standing in front of me. They looked like any of the other inmates, thin and shabbily clad, but it was obvious that one of them was the boss and that she was giving another—a young woman in a red headscarf—instructions. I stared blearily.

Were they going to attack me? Was it safer to defend myself or just take it?

Oh crap…

I wondered if I was in any state to get to my feet and fight back. My body was on fire with pain already. I grabbed the edge of the bed and tried to pull myself upright.

The girl with the red head scarf took a half-step toward me. "What is your name?" she demanded.

For a moment relief was enough to overwhelm my pain. "Milja Petak," I groaned.

"You are American?"

"Yes." Again with the lie, but I had vague thoughts that the USA might have enough international clout to tip the balance in my favor. More than a small country in Balkan Europe, anyway. "Thank God you speak English. I thought… What is this place? Where are we?"

Her lip curled. "This is Sekota Prison. Why are you here, *feranji*? Why did they put you in here?"

That wasn't the easiest of questions to answer. "I behaved badly in a church," I admitted, hoping that wouldn't sound too reprehensible.

"In a church?" Her eyes narrowed. What did you do?"

"Nothing much…" *Lies lies lies. If they knew they'd kill me.*

"Where?"

"Lalibela. Are we far?"

She relayed this in Amharic to the other women. Then she laughed in my face. "Stupid tourist! You come here and think you can do anything you like? And now you will get away with it because of your white skin and your passport? Hah! This is our country, not yours."

I didn't answer that one, couldn't even meet her eye. What could I say to defend myself? I'd murdered people, hadn't I?—or brought in the agent of their death—and I *had* expected to get away with it, because I had an angel on my side and because might makes right.

She held out her hand. "You have a passport?"

I shook my head. The last time I'd seen my passport it had been going into a hotel safe in my cousin's room in Montenegro. Since making it back to the States I hadn't bothered to get a replacement. Azazel doesn't have to pass through border control, after all. "It's gone. I need to speak to the prison governor. I need to get out of here."

She just sneered at that. "Of course!"

"I need a lawyer!"

"Maybe I can speak to someone. Have you got money for me?"

I patted my pockets, knowing it was in vain. "Money—no, not on me." Someone had removed my jacket while I was unconscious; that jacket with all the useful pockets that held my money and my camera and everything I needed, down to my goddamn emergency toothbrush. It felt so unfair. "If I can get out of here I can get you money," I promised desperately, though even that probably wasn't true. Where the hell I'd find an ATM around here I had no idea. It was dawning on me just how alone I was, and how vulnerable.

"Yes, I am sure," she said, and mocked me over her shoulder at her friends as she passed on my pathetic plea.

"Please, has anyone here got a phone?" Though who the hell I'd ring...

"What can you give me?"

"I…I don't have anything."

She shook her head. "When you think of something, we speak." They started to walk away.

"Please!" I didn't care how coldhearted she was, at least I could talk to her. Just to be able to communicate felt like divine grace right now. "What's your name?"

"Fuck you, American bitch," she said cheerily, not looking back.

☙

I moved back out into the courtyard, and sat in the tiny strip of shade against a wall, my arms around my knees and my head sunk on my breast. There was nothing I could do except keep out of everyone's way.

I'm not an extrovert. When I panic I don't run around shrieking; I lock down instead. And I was panicking now. I'd survived incarceration at Father Velimir's hands, but he had at least locked me in a private cell and kept me fed. He'd wanted to keep me alive. Here I couldn't even get something to drink. There was every chance that I could die of dehydration here, I thought sickly, and no one would care. I'd been forgotten by the world.

Had Azazel forgotten me too?

He'd need me eventually, whatever he was up to, I told myself. He'd never stayed away for more than a week or so, and I could survive a week here, surely? *Perhaps.* Sooner or later he'd come for me. If he was okay.

Maybe he's more than okay, said the treacherous voice in the back of my mind. *Maybe he's happy with his soul-mate Penemuel and he doesn't need you anymore. They're out there chasing comets and having massive jiggy angel-sex and he's never coming back.*

My mind's eye kept spooling the scenes from the crypt.

Saint George, dead yet walking. The blood. The flames, and the savagery. Azazel had gone crazy when Saint George ran Penemuel though with his spear. He hadn't worried about collateral damage, not to me and not to his own daughter.

What sort of a man acted like that?

Friendly fire, I thought bitterly.

Christ, Roshana had looked really badly burnt. Was she alive? Conscious? However much I searched my memories, I couldn't be sure one way or the other. And yes, my feelings about Roshana were not exactly uncomplicated; it wasn't as if I really liked her or anything. But I didn't want her maimed and suffering like that.

I certainly didn't want her in Uriel's elegant hands.

I have to warn Azazel.

I rolled my head. I felt like I was going mad. How could it have all gone so badly wrong? How could I be so helpless, so useless? If roles had been reversed, I berated myself, if I'd been the one killed and Roshana the one dumped here to rot, then she would have worked this. She'd have talked her way into an alliance with Red Scarf and her clique already. She'd be up there now flirting with the guards, miming her way to a mutually beneficial relationship. She'd be organizing a prison breakout. Whilst I was just sitting here, wobbly with thirst; inexperienced and terrified and clueless.

I only had one good card left to play.

They'd taken away my jacket, and reduced me to pants and blouse. But they'd also left my hidden security wallet on. I could feel the nasty nylon strap that ran under my bra. If I knuckled myself under my breasts, I could feel the bulge of the pouch there. It wasn't very big, but it was supposed to be emergency backup if we ever got mugged and needed a taxi back to the hotel.

So, in theory, inside that pouch was our hotel card, four hundred and forty birr in bills—twenty dollars more or less, maybe enough to bribe Red Scarf, assuming she didn't just rob me, but not enough to buy the prison warden or a lawyer—and most important of all, my rubbishy old phone, the one that I barely used because I didn't have anyone to call. I'd brought it along in case I needed to text Roshana from my bedroom. I couldn't remember charging it since we got to Ethiopia, and I was already cursing myself for my negligence.

There was no point in calling Roshana; that ship had sailed. But I had Egan's number on my SIM.

I didn't dare look though. Not with everyone watching.

So I sat and I concentrated, squeezing every mental muscle. *I have connectivity. I have connectivity. I have bars, and battery, and the phone is still working. And Egan's still here.*

Yes, I knew it would be a desperate move, to throw myself on the Church. But I *was* desperate.

☙

As the sun started to dip over the compound wall, people began to file into the yard and queue up in front of the standpipe carrying plastic washbasins and old Abyssinia and SPA mineral water bottles; maybe a couple of hundred women along with their children. I watched Red Scarf and her gang strut their way to the front of the line, along with those young women who seemed to be in with the guards. But most waited their turn patiently, and when the guards came around and turned the tap on, I joined the queue near the back.

Just standing up made me feel faint.

Slowly we wended our way toward the front. As women turned away with full bottles and basins, they headed across to a second line on the far side, where some sort of food was being doled out of big aluminum pots. I couldn't even think about food right then—all my focus was on the tap and its glorious gush of life-giving water, growing closer moment by dragging moment.

Then I spotted the female guard watching me. I couldn't read her expression, but she said something in an aside to her colleague. And I saw one of them glance at his plastic wristwatch, and look up at the setting sun.

What if they shut it off just as I get there? I thought. Then: *they're going to throw me out of the queue, aren't they? Just to put me in my place.* The headache contracted around my skull like a twist of string.

I glanced behind me at a young woman in a teal flower-print skirt. She was holding a baby in one arm while a little boy, barely walking age, clutched at that pretty skirt. Her face was masklike, but I could see the anxious flick of her eyes, measuring the distance before us.

I couldn't bring myself to speak through my sticky mouth, but I stepped silently to the side and gestured her in front of me.

There was a stir amongst those few behind her, and the next person, an old woman, pressed forward. I didn't stop her, or the ones who followed. I didn't object. I just dragged my feet across the packed earth and broken concrete to the back of the line.

And I waited.

Maybe my siren body doesn't need water. Maybe it's that good. Maybe drinking is just a habit.

When I got to the standpipe, the last of all, the woman guard stared me in the face. I met her eyes only for a second, before ducking to plunge my hands under the flow.

She didn't stop me.

Perhaps I'd just been paranoid. Perhaps...no, I don't

know.

The ungumming of my throat was almost painful, as if I was tearing something. I had no bottle and no bowl to fill. I just knelt and sucked water from the faucet until my stomach ached, and it was a pleasure I'd rank right up there above all others—above sex with Azazel, even.

When I'd drunk all I could I went and sat down a little way away, picturing the fluid soaking through my insides and rehydrating my aching muscles. I was only surprised from my stupor when someone moved in front of me, blocking the light.

It was the mother in the teal skirt. She sat down before me and handed over a large, grayish pancake pocked with holes. She handed one to her son, and kept a third for herself.

For a moment I didn't know what to do, and then I remembered to smile. "Thank you," I husked. I pointed at my breastbone and ventured, "Milja."

She smiled tentatively. Her hair was bound up in complicated knots and her cheekbones were sharp, but that smile lit her eyes. "Deborha," she said.

"Milja. Deborha." I gestured questioningly at her toddler.

"Emanuel. Menas." That was the baby.

I nodded, smiling, as we tore pieces off our pancakes and started to eat.

I'd tried this food before, when I first arrived in Ethiopia. It was *injera*, the staple carbohydrate of the country and reputedly packed with nutrition. I'd found it truly disgusting, like a piece of cold carpet underlay soaked in vinegar, but here in the prison it seemed to taste a whole lot better. But now my stomach was full of water, and after eating two thirds I handed the rest of my *injera* over to Emanuel.

"I can afford to lose some cocktail calories," I said.

IN BONDS OF THE EARTH

He didn't understand a word, of course.

☙

After our meagre dinner the guards locked us back in our barrack. Deborha made room for me on her bed, which was beyond kindness as far as I was concerned.

As soon as I'm back with Azazel the first thing I'll do is get him to come here and free her. No—I'll get him to bust the whole place wide open. He'll enjoy that. He hates cages.

I spent the evening in that stifling room curled up with her children. I had to get up once to use the toilet, which was a stinking squat-style hole in the ground, in a cubicle off the main room. There was no door, not even a curtain, and a whole semi-circle of children formed to stare at my weird white body, but I didn't care by this point. I'd shut down every emotion except a focus on my plan for tonight. That was the only thing that mattered. My dignity could go take a flying leap.

I will have bars. I will have battery.

It was easy not to sleep. The room was so humid with body heat, and so airless and crowded, that my great worry was that no one else would be sleeping either. Children cried and adults bickered. Insects—whether fleas or mosquitoes or something else, I had no idea—were having a go at any patch of exposed skin.

It doesn't matter. I will keep going.
I have bars. I have battery.

When it all went quiet at last, and the moonlight had disappeared from the slit of a window, I reached furtively beneath my clothes and—so slowly, so cautiously—slipped my phone out of the hidden security pouch. When I woke it from sleep the eerie blue light of the screen lit my face, making me blink, almost blinded, and I rolled over to huddle above it, trying to hide that giveaway illumination.

I had only a few moments, I knew.

And I did have a bar of connectivity—but only the very last sliver of battery life.

Not enough to call. Shit.

I fumbled desperately down the menus to Egan's phone number, my thumbs tripping over themselves as I texted:

SOS SOKOTA PRISON HLPM E PLS

A hand shot over my shoulder and grabbed the phone. I rose with a shriek and threw myself on the thief—it might have been Red Scarf, but to be honest I didn't see and didn't care. I punched and ripped and kicked at her until she dropped the phone and then I grabbed it back.

They descended on me after that, taking a collective revenge with fists and feet, and they took my phone away for good, but I didn't care by then. I'd hit the right button and got *Message Sent*.

Twelve
A COMPLICATION WE DON'T NEED

They came for me two days later. I heard the word *feranji* being shouted around the yard and then they came in, two guards with guns slung, and ordered me to go with them. They flanked me while we passed out of the main gate and into another building and down a concrete corridor. I didn't resist or show any emotion, not even fear. To be honest I didn't dare let myself *feel* any fear, or any hope, or anything at all. I just walked and watched and listened, waiting for the next jolt on the track of my fate.

Until I walked into that room and saw Egan standing by the desk, that is. There was a man sitting behind the desk too, wearing some sort of uniform, watching me with studied disdain, but all I could see was Egan—and *that* was when the fear hit me, the terrible fear that hope would be snatched away once more and this time forever. He was my last and only chance of freedom. My knees nearly buckled beneath me.

I think he was the most beautiful thing I had ever seen, and at the same time looked absolutely terrible—his face swollen and bruised up one side, his left eye half-closed and flooded pink with blood. There was a dark split in his lower lip. He still managed to frown when he saw me, just for a moment.

Oh, it's my goddamn bleached hair, I thought, a sudden irrational terror sweeping through my veins that he wouldn't recognize me at all.

"This is your sister?" the man behind the desk asked.

"Yes. He held out his arm to me—just one arm, because the other one was in a cast and sling. "Oh yes—Milja."

I lurched into his lopsided embrace and the guards didn't try to stop me. I pressed my face to his shirt, feeling the hard chest beneath. He smelled amazing—a scent of clean skin and laundry soap that I could hardly remember. I wanted to burrow into his chest. I wrapped my arms around his waist, clinging to his shirt.

"Are you okay?" he said, low and urgent into my hair.

I couldn't speak, but I nodded. My heart was banging so hard it hurt.

"Well," said the man in charge. There was a shuffling of papers and feet. "All is well, then. Take her away. *Ciao*, Mr. Kansky."

That was it—incredibly brief. One moment I was the prisoner, the next I was under Egan's wing being steered out through a door into the light and across a street toward a dusty 4WD whose driver was standing watching us with arms folded across his chest.

"Are you okay, Milja?" Egan repeated. "Did they hurt you?"

He meant *rape*, I strongly suspected. "No…no, I'm okay."

One foot in front of the next across the road. Pause to let a donkey clatter past. I didn't dare look up, or meet the donkey-owner's gaze. Was it all a cruel joke? Would they rush out behind me and haul me back into prison?

"I came as quick as I could. Your man back there said he didn't have your passport. Is that true?"

"I haven't had a passport since Podgorica." And Egan had been there for that disaster.

"Just like old times, heh? You don't make it easy for me." He snorted. "Still, he pretty much cleaned me out there already. I probably couldn't afford your passport too."

I leaned against the car as we reached it, twisting to look up into his face.

"You bribed him?"

The skin creased around his one good eye. "Sure, the accountants are going to kill me when I get back."

I reached up and touched his injured face gently. "Thank you. Thank you for coming for me. I mean it."

He grimaced, his gaze holding my own. "One question: where's the Fallen?"

"I don't know." I took a deep breath. "I genuinely don't know. Something's gone wrong, some—"

"Okay, not here." He ran his hand over my faded locks, cupping the back of my head. "Get in the car. We'll talk later."

I obeyed, grateful to slide onto the old rug spread over the back seat. Egan climbed in beside me, moving his injured arm and shoulder gingerly, then passed me a bottle of water from under the seat.

"What happened to you?" I asked. "Are *you* okay?"

"Alright so," he told the driver. "The airport now."

That gentleman rather pointedly started to wind the windows down.

"No, keep them up," Egan snapped.

"I'm sorry," I mumbled, between glugs of water. "I must stink."

"That you do," said Egan, without the slightest interest. As we bumped down the unpaved street, away from the unassuming facade of the prison, he checked through all the vehicle windows, as if worried someone might come running after the car. Only when he was satisfied did he lean back in the seat and return to my question. "And this? I got mugged a couple days back. Greenstick fracture, nothing to worry about."

I felt sorry for anyone who'd tried to get the better of Egan. He might look mild and easy-going, but I'd seen how he fought. If they'd damaged him this badly they'd been putting real effort into it. I put my hand on his in concern. "You sure?"

"Yeah."

"Where are—"

"Talk later." The merest flick of his eyes suggested that the driver might be better not overhearing anything. He knotted his fingers in mine and squeezed my hand. "Get some rest, Milja."

I did more than that. I hadn't slept properly in days, and my head was swimming. I passed out before we even left the town boundaries and slept, slumped against him, until we reached our plane.

⁂

Calling it an airport was flattering it, to be honest. In the pre-dawn murk it looked like a strip of flat dust scraped into the surrounding weeds. A single plane sat there facing away from a concrete hut, its twin propellers pointing at the hilly horizon, and it wasn't a big plane either, by any description. I stood around yawning and shivering and watching the red streaks of sunrise as Egan paid off our driver and talked to the man who seemed to be in charge of the aircraft. He didn't look Ethiopian, I thought; too heavyset. And from the way he and Egan greeted each other with backslaps, they were old friends.

Then Egan hustled me up through the plane's rear door. There were only seven seats in the tiny passenger cabin, and he gestured us into two that faced each other. He slung his rucksack into the seat beside him; that was all the luggage we had between us, it seemed.

There were no other passengers.

I had to help Egan buckle in, because he was down to one arm and even attempting that for himself made him wince. In fact, studying his pallid face and the prickle of sweat on his upper lip, I thought he was in a lot more pain than he'd let on.

"Are you okay?" I demanded. "You look awful."

He pulled a grin, lopsided so as not to split his lip again. "I had to discharge myself to come find you. Probably need some more meds. One of the guys who came at me had a machete...and I don't think it was very clean." He gestured at his bandaged side.

"*What?*"

"It's not as bad as it sounds—I mostly managed to keep out of the way. Just some nicks, really. The other guys looked a lot worse by the time we were done."

"I bet." I tried to swallow.

"Yeah, a bit strange, that." He rested his head back as the props kicked into life. "I've been here weeks walking around, and not a hint of threat. Not unless you count my shoes being shined to within an inch of their lives. Then...bam. They weren't trying to grab my wallet; they were trying to take me down."

We lurched into motion, and I was glad of the excuse to

look nervous about takeoff and not to answer, because a horrible conviction had seized my guts and I felt quite nauseous. *Roshana. Oh my God, Roshana. I told her you knew and were trying to stop us, and then... It must have been the day after, tops. She hired those guys.*

'*A complication we don't need*'—that's what she called you.

Would she really do that, knowing that I owed him my life? I had made that clear, hadn't I? I'd told her I didn't want Azazel to harm him. Oh Christ—would she really do that? Pay to have someone taken out? Pay to *kill* someone she knew I cared for?

The fact was that I knew very little about what Roshana's conscience was capable of. Self-defense was one thing; this was something else again. But she'd survived five thousand years on her own in the face of implacable enmity; and thrived even. And that did not suggest any lack of ruthlessness. I just hoped Egan couldn't recognize the guilt in my wide, averted eyes and my compressed lips.

I didn't try to talk as we gained height. To be honest I'd never travelled in a plane this small and it really was hard to think about anything but how insecure it felt. Only when we'd levelled off and settled on a course did I raise my voice above the engine. "Where are we going then? Rome?"

I think there was a part of me that would have welcomed that. A part of me that felt I needed to pay for all the horror I'd wrought. I'd surrendered myself into the hands of the Catholic Church in order to escape incarceration, and now they could do what they liked with me.

I probably deserved it.

But Egan smiled and shook his head. "In this? No, we're heading for Djibouti."

I'd seen Djibouti on the map—a tiny country on the

coast, east of Ethiopia. That was literally all I knew about it. "Why?"

"Because there's a big-ass American military presence there, which means I can call in some favors and get the nice gentlemen to ship you home without passing Border Control."

"Home?"

"Chicago. That's what you want isn't it? Safe and sound and free again?"

I swallowed, not daring to trust him. "Is this some sort of creepy Catholic lie-by-omission thing? D'you mean 'safe and sound after my people torture you for everything you know and cut off your legs,' or something?"

He actually winced. "No. I told you, I recused myself from any use of you against your will. It's unconscionable to torture you to save others. 'The greatest happiness of the greatest number' is a humanist ethic, Milja—God isn't counting."

"Really? That's what the Church thinks?"

He leaned on his good elbow. "Ah, you want to know the truth? The truth is that I'm acting well outside orders right now, and I'm going to be up to my neck in shite when they find out I'm doing this for you."

That startled me, but I did my best not to show it. "Well I'm sure you can confess it all away with a few Hail Marys."

He gnawed his lip. "Being with Azazel has made you a bit cruel, Milja."

Oh, that stung. "No, it's made me less tolerant of bullshit," I said, but I knew the steel had gone out of my eyes. I didn't want us to fight. "Your people don't know where we're heading?" I asked after a moment.

"They don't know you're here. They don't actually know I'm here." He fixed me with a droll squint. "Kill me right now and you've got away with full deniability."

I couldn't help snorting, following it up with a helpless set of giggles. Egan's lips crooked in a smile that warmed his battered face and turned my defenses to matchsticks.

Oh God, how I'd missed that smile. It seemed to light up the air around us.

"You're an idiot," I told him, my grin shyer than his.

"Okay, we're being honest, I get it."

"I'm glad though. I'm glad you were there."

He nodded, letting out a long sigh. "I have my uses. There's some bottled water under your seat by the way—would you open one for me, please?"

I obliged, and we both drank. Egan wiped his damp brow with his sleeve and pressed the bottle to his forehead.

"Is it too hot in here?" he asked.

"No." It was actually pretty cold in the cabin. I had gooseflesh creeping over my arms, which I showed Egan.

"Ah grand, I'm running a temperature," he muttered. "Okay, no bullshit, no jokes now. I'm taking you home, Milja, and I wish to God you'd stay out of this mess because, win or lose, it is not safe for you, and my resources are going to dry up the moment someone spots how far I've gone off piste."

"I see."

"And I'm not forcing you to say anything, but I would sincerely appreciate it if you could tell me what actually happened in Lalibela, so that I know what on earth it is I'm going to be dealing with from here on."

"Haven't the priests told you?"

He snorted. "The Ethiopian Orthodox Tewahedo Church tells the one true Church of Rome sweet feck-all, believe me. What I know is that the place is locked down and crawling with police and that His Holiness the Patriarch flew in to

Lalibela yesterday. Whatever you did, it was *really* bad, I'm guessing."

I pursed my lips. "Yeah."

"Will you tell me?"

"So you've got a better idea how to capture the one I love?" My voice cracked on the last word, and I saw the hurt in his eyes.

But he kept his cool. "So I can try to save lives, Milja. Yours and others. You think a war of the heavenly powers is a good thing for any of us? Is the end of the world what you're after? No? *Maybe* there's a way out of it. Maybe there can be a negotiated solution—has your man there thought of that?"

Okay, that one sideswiped me. I stared at him, but all I could see was the blood that had been spilt. Blood on Roshana's hands, and on her raw scalp. Those old priests, slaughtered. Father Velimir, burnt to ashes by Azazel's blackest wrath. Blood around my cousin's mouth where she'd cut off her own tongue. My father, collapsed on a hospital gurney.

I thought of little Emanuel and Menas. I wished I'd managed to get money to their mother before I left, and the fact that I'd walked out with my emergency cash still hidden in my belt made me feel sick with guilt. I didn't want them to live in a prison. Nor did I want them to be butchered in some final Apocalypse as the Great Beast arose from the sea and the moon turned to blood and angel fought angel. Maybe that was part of the Divine Plan as promised, but I'd long since stopped subscribing to any plan like that, I realized now.

The blood on my hands and in my eyes seeped down to my throat and made my voice rusty. "If you know nothing, then how come you were even there? Why were you waiting for us?"

"Ah come on." For a moment he looked pained. "A big

naked guy appears from mid-air and steals the Lalibela *Book of Enoch* from a public art gallery in front of staff *and* CCTV? It was obvious you were gunning for the Watcher hidden under the churches. I was on a transatlantic flight by lunchtime. I've been here weeks—and I am so fed up of spiced food I cannot tell you."

"You've been waiting for us?"

"I've been waiting for *you*, Milja. Your boyfriend's bulletproof. Literally. You... I thought that maybe I could persuade you to keep out of danger. But I guess I was too late. What happened?"

I didn't know whether to answer him or not. I felt like I was crumpling from within, just at the taste of those memories.

"Sure, shall I help a bit? We know it's the Watcher Penemuel, the angel of the written word, down there. Did you manage to release him?"

"I don't know. Penemuel was really badly wounded in the fight." I could picture the spear thrust through her like a skewer and the thought made me sick. "Maybe dead, I don't know. Can they die?"

"Fight?" he said, countering my question with his own.

"There are holy relics, aren't there? You know that—like the Nails of the True Cross that you used on Azazel. They can hurt angels. Can they kill them?"

"Uh... I honestly don't know the answer to that." His voice was gentle. "Tell me what happened."

I met his eyes, blue and bloody. "You want us to cut the BS? You want me to be honest and open with you? Well I know nothing about you. *Nothing*. If we're going to talk, you have to start the ball rolling. Who are you? Who do you work for, really? What—" I lost all words, my hand flapping back forth to point at his chest and then my own.

What do you think is going on between us?

For a long time, he just looked at me. "Well, you know about my family," he said softly. "My sisters, Siobhan and Brigit—I told you about them."

"That's not enough, Egan."

He looked down at his free hand, into the crease of his open palm. "I had another sister, Mary. She's dead now."

"I'm sorry." I meant it. "What happened?"

"Suicide."

"Oh."

"The others still live in Ireland. My father's American, but he didn't stay long with us; he went back home to New Mexico when I was six. We lived in Monaghan, up near the border with Northern Ireland—that's the British bit. You don't know much about Irish politics, I'm assuming?"

"No."

"Doesn't matter, really. My distant family had had some involvement in things back during the bad days, but the Good Friday peace agreement was signed in 1998 so the Troubles were over by the time I was a teenager. More or less, anyway. But the paramilitaries didn't all just put down their guns and go back to watching the footie. Right so, when my sister got pregnant by this boy she'd met... You have to understand, where I come from you do *not* have a child out of wedlock. They were getting married before the birth, come hell or high water."

"How old were you?" I asked when he lapsed into silence.

"I was sixteen. Mary was two years older than me."

I grasped at the only thing I knew concerning Ireland. "Was the boy a Protestant?"

"No, but he was a bowsie bastard, ten years older than

her, and he dealt heroin. There were plenty of people did not like that. The paramilitaries on both sides made a big show of being down on pushers, keeping the streets clean, you know. Anyway, my Ma was heartbroken but the wedding was organized. Mary was really happy, and no one cared whether that arsewipe of a boyfriend was happy or not, because he was going to do right by her whatever he wanted.

"So, we come to the wedding day and they're walking out of the church after Mass, and this guy walks up and kneecaps him."

"What does that mean?"

"Puts a shotgun round in both his legs. He'll never walk properly again. Seems the local Direct Action Against Drugs organization wants to send a strong *Just Say No* message."

"That's…extreme."

"They were a front for the Provos, everyone knew that—so business as usual, actually. I wouldn't give a shite, except Mary is knocked over in the panic and falls on the steps, and she's twenty weeks pregnant when she miscarries." He sighed.

"I am sorry," I whispered. He wasn't looking at me.

"Fecks up her whole life. She's got no baby but she's married to this useless cripple bastard. She stuck it out a few years, but…" He drummed his fingers on the arm rest and swallowed hard. "Anyway, two months after the wedding, I get approached by this guy I've never met, and he introduces me to someone with an American accent, and they have a proposition for me. This guy represents an international Catholic educational charity, he says. They offer me a chance to go out to the States and finish my schooling there. Stay with my dad. Learn a trade before I come back home. They'll pay a nice stipend to my family, as well as all my fees."

"I don't understand."

"Charity my arse—he's intelligence, FRU working with the Americans I suppose. They want a Catholic insider they can use when things get hot again in Ireland, and they want someone pissed off enough with the Provos to do it. Which I am."

"These people recruit children?"

"Depends who your dad is, maybe." His mouth twisted. "So I go to the US, which I've always dreamed of, and they put me through military school and some fairly specialist training, and when it turns out nothing much is actually kicking off back home—much to everyone's amazement—they're not going to waste their investment so they shift me into a unit that does odd jobs, all around the world. Sometimes under the NATO umbrella, sometimes UN, sometimes...not."

That was very much the truncated version, I realized: no names or numbers. But given the bits of paper they'd have made him sign it was the most I was going to get.

I wasn't quite right.

"So I end up in Central America, in territory belonging to one of our shittier allies. You realize this story goes nowhere else, don't you, Milja?" For the first time since he'd started his story he looked into my face. His good eye looked weirdly dilated.

"Of course."

"We're detailed to look for an American Catholic Bishop, and his local counterpart that he'd been paying a nice cross-cultural visit to. Specifically, we're looking for the insurgent cell who've abducted them. Leftover communists maybe... I don't even know what the local political angle was. The news has not yet leaked to the press and we're there to get it sorted before the American ends up on the front pages with his head hacked off. This is, thank God, in the days before people started doing it on YouTube."

Again, his fingertips drum.

"It goes more-or-less to plan, to start with. We've got intel that the clergy are being held in this village in deep country, so we insert and we locate the target and we start picking off the insurgents on guard quietly because we don't want the hostages killed or moved out. They're amateurs; they've not even wired the perimeter. But they've been killing villagers, because we find a few bodies strung from the trees, heels up and heads down, their throats cut. Freaky. And I head on in the back with two other guys and we actually get into the house where they're being held because someone's in there already shouting at them, and nobody hears us.

"He's this big guy, it turns out. I mean I get eyes-on and he's *huge*, over seven foot and built, way taller than any of his men. He's shouting at the hostages in English, really old-fashioned English like he learned it from some… God knows where he learned it, it's all, 'Wouldst thou defy me?' and stuff. And then he suddenly *knows I'm there*, because he turns round and shouts 'Mine foes art upon me!' or somesuch shite.

"So we drop him." Egan shook his head. "He dies just like anyone else would with several rounds in him, lies there flopping about on the floor—which is fine, autonomic nervous system and all that. I go over to see that the hostages are okay and not grenade-trapped or anything, and I don't see there's anything weird at first. Until one of my buddies calls a warning and I turn and I swear this cunt is *trying to get up*, like some fecking zombie, even though you could stick your fist into the hole in his chest. And I think that's funny, but my buddy steps in to do the *coup de grace* with a headshot. Which works. All this is real noisy mind, so seven shades of shite are kicking off outside and now we have to get *out* before we're looking at a full-on bloodbath."

I sat there, pinned to my comfortable leather seat by his horrible story. The Egan I knew didn't normally use obscenities. He didn't clench his fist and boast about killing people. He didn't talk about himself much at all, let's face it.

"We drag the two bishops out of the hut and we're laying down fire to clear a route to the tree-line. Then my buddy staggers back, looks around him all wild for a second, yells, 'In the midst of my enemies I stand triumphant, for none is like unto me!'—and he opens fire with his M4 on everyone in sight. Including me. I go down with a hole through my pelvis here." He pointed at his crotch and I recalled the scar there I'd seen in my dream, a long time back.

"I don't understand," I said very quietly.

"Do you know where possessing demons come from, Milja?"

Hell, I'd assumed. I shook my head.

"They're not nearly as common as fuckwit evangelicals fear they are, but they do exist. If you kill one of the Nephilim their spirits are strong enough to take other bodies nearby."

I didn't say anything to that. A great cold hand seemed to clutch my insides.

"I'm still carrying my 9 mil, so I ice my buddy. I have to. Then that *thing* jumps into an insurgent soldier. And it keeps going. The whole situation's a nightmare. Every time its body gets shredded it just moves on, and everyone is turning on everyone else, and I know it's only a matter of time before it gets me.

"You understand, Milja—I'm a real angry young man back then. I've not been in a church since Mary killed herself and the bastards froze my whole family out. I've given up believing, so I thought. But right then I crack and I call on the Holy Virgin and Saint Michael to save me from the Devil, and it *works*. He comes to help."

A year ago I might have been skeptical. Now I only nodded.

Egan laughed, wretchedly. "He looks like Lou Diamond Philips. *Young Guns*, you know… I'd seen that when I was a little kid. He wears this shiny armor like in the stained-glass windows, and carries a shining sword, just like I wanted him to. And when he kills the guy carrying the demon at that moment, Lieutenant Gill burns up like…like a match-head. It works. What can I say?"

I leaned forward in my seat and clasped his hand, unable to bear the darkness I saw in his staring eyes.

He blinked. "We get both bishops out. I get a medical discharge, and then a total mental breakdown to back it up. I spend a while in a psychiatric unit. And then…this man comes to see me. He's flown in from Rome. He says he represents an institute within the Catholic Church, and that they might have a role for me if I want a job. So. There you are."

"Vidimus?"

"Yes."

"What is it that they do?"

"Mostly we keep an eye on the imprisoned Watchers, the ones we know about. We try to track down the ones we don't know. And we hunt Nephilim. Human nature being what it is, there have been a few conceived from the prisoners over the years. *Quis custodiet ipsos custodies…*"

Uriel had quoted exactly that at me the first time we met, and hearing it from Egan made my hair bristle.

"*Vidimus* means '*We Have Seen*'. What have they seen, Egan?"

"Shite you wouldn't believe." For a moment looking into his face was like looking into unending night—and then he smiled, sadly, and he was my old Egan again. "There you go. Do you know me a bit better now, Milja? Is that what you wanted to hear?"

Thirteen
FEVER

What I knew was that I wanted to grasp his face and kiss all that pain away. But I couldn't do that. Instead I flipped my seat buckle and scooted right to the edge, reaching across the gap between us to touch his uninjured cheek. His skin burned beneath the blond stubble. There were no words with which to answer him.

Oh God, Egan, you are a mess.

He'd offered me a glimpse into the monsters his life held, both mythic and personal. He'd shown me that he'd been broken, and how he'd been put back together again—and from here on there could be no hiding the cracks. For all he'd tried to care for me, his soul was as crazed and fragmented as my own.

"Egan," I whispered, inaudible above the drone of the engines and only my lips shaping the words. "Oh, Egan, we are so screwed."

He turned his face and pressed his lips to my palm. His eyes fluttered shut, lashes pale, like he wanted to nest there.

"Oh no," I said, snatching my hand away, earning a startled flash of his eyes. "Don't do that—I'm probably carrying dysentery and everything!"

He exhaled, looking relieved not repulsed. I think he'd suspected a much more personal rejection. Then he reached across and rooted in the side pocket of his rucksack.

"I'm sorry," I stammered, hating myself so much that I physically wrung my hands, as if I could rub away the prison germs.

"No, I should have thought of this earlier." He held out a packet of antibiotic wipes, and I snatched them from his grasp.

"I'm so filthy... Oh God this is horrible. I need a shower. I need to wash my hair."

"Don't worry." Egan unbuckled and stood. "We'll be in a hotel soon. I'll go have a chat with John up front. Knock on the cabin door when you've finished."

I tried to smile at him, grateful for his understanding. When I was alone in the passenger cabin I scrubbed and scrubbed at my face and hands with those little moist towelettes, peeling away my foul garments one at a time to access armpits and underboobs, crotch and feet, desperate to feel clean again. I used up every one of those wipes. If I could have cried I would probably have broken down, but the lack of release kept me focused.

It also gave me time to think. To replay everything Egan had confessed. So much violence in his life. Did I still feel safe with him now that I knew?

His sisters. Oh, that was awful. No wonder he was such a white knight—he must still be haunted by his helplessness.

His mission. Vidimus. This wasn't a matter of faith, was it? His enmity toward Azazel wasn't based on blind obedience to Church dogma. He knew that angels existed, he'd seen one for himself; Michael in all his terrible ruthless glory. He knew exactly what the Fallen had wrought through their intrusion into humanity. He'd seen what their children were like. He'd had to kill his brothers-in-arms to put a stop to one.

Did he mean what he said about a peaceful solution? A Good Friday agreement between Heaven and Hell?

Nice idea. What if it falls through? Which way will he jump?

I couldn't bear to put my stinking boots back on so I stowed them at the back of the cabin and padded barefoot up the aisle to knock on the door. By the time Egan came out I was sitting back in my seat, my bare feet tucked under me.

"How are you feeling?" I asked, alarmed by the sweat beads on his brow and the uncomfortable way he slid into his seat.

"I need to scare up some antibiotics when we land. This arm is sort of hot and tight."

"Oh no."

"Sure, not to worry." He grimaced. "Look what I found for breakfast." He pulled two chocolate bars out of his sling and tossed one across to me. A little crease appeared between his brow as he watched me tear the wrapper open and cram it into my mouth. "Here," he said mildly, handing me the second.

"Y'shoor?" I mumbled through the mouthful I was still chewing.

"Go on. I should have stopped the car to pick up some proper food." He shook his head. "Sorry, I didn't think."

I didn't have the strength of will to refuse his gallantry, but I tried to slow down for the second candy bar. I was halfway through when he spoke again.

"So, are you ready to tell me what happened in Lalibela?"

I froze, my head bowed.

"Since we're being honest with each other?"

I had to force myself to meet his gaze. I swallowed carefully. "Egan, I don't think I can. Really. I'm sorry. I know it must have been so hard for you to tell me all that. I feel awful. But I just can't."

He didn't get angry. He didn't even look surprised. He just nodded, sagging a little. "You still can't trust me."

No I couldn't, but that was only the half of it. "If I told you," I choked, "you would hate me."

"I find that hard to imagine." His voice was soft. "Try me."

I didn't want to talk. Anything I said might, I knew, be used against Azazel. That I could talk to imprisoned Watchers in my dreams? That I'd smuggled him onto holy ground by allowing him to possess me?—those tricks were ones we might need in future. That Roshana was there—then why? That she was one of the Nephilim?—then she was his enemy too, assuming she was alive. That Uriel had taken her?—then her body could be bargained for.

But I couldn't shut Egan out. He'd bared a part of his soul to me. We had so much guilt in common. "People died," I admitted.

"Okay." His tone didn't change. "Did you kill them deliberately, by your own hand, with no thought for self-defense or loyalty or love?"

I shook my head, once.

"Then I can't even start to hate you. You know some of what I've done in my time, now."

I wrinkled my nose. "Well yeah, it wasn't that much of a surprise. I remember Ratko."

"Ratko?"

"That guard in the monastery."

"Ah, yes. Well, I do try to feel bad about that one, for theological reasons you understand." His eyes were full of dark memories. He'd killed Ratko for hurting me and threatening my life. "I haven't succeeded so far."

I bit my lip, voiceless.

"Okay so, I'm going to assume the murdery stuff was done by the Fallen. Priests or pilgrims?"

"Priests, and it wasn't like that. It was a proper fight. He didn't just murder them."

"How does anyone *fight* your man there?"

"They summoned Saint George." Even as the words came out of my mouth I felt it was a mistake—and not because Egan didn't believe me. He looked startled, certainly, but interested. Way too interested.

"Really?"

"I think it was George," I mumbled, feeling my stomach turn over. My body was better at spotting when I was making a mistake than my messed-up brain was. "He had a spear." *I've already told him about the spear, haven't I?* "It was vile, this whole *Night of the Living Dead* sort of thing."

"Okay…that's a new one."

I bit my lip hard. *I shouldn't have told him that was possible.*

"So the priests were just collateral damage?"

I nodded, reluctantly.

"You said Penemuel was injured. But could still be alive. Taken away, I assume then."

I had said that, hadn't I? "Uhuh."

"But your man hasn't come back for you since."

I shook my head.

Egan let out a long breath. "Well I'll tell you one thing, Milja, it sounds like you're lucky you were just dumped off in prison without a covering note. Someone was being very restrained."

I've got Uriel to thank for that, I think. Oh hell. What advantage does Uriel gain keeping me safe and alive? "You told the warden I was your sister?" I croaked.

"You're my sister in Christ." He tried to shrug, and winced. "From a broad ecumenical perspective."

"And you wonder why I can't trust you." I smiled sadly.

"Milja, I would give the last breath in my body to save you. You know that." He wasn't forceful, but he was dead serious.

My heart clenched. Yes, I did know that. "Why is that, Egan?" I whispered.

Maybe he didn't hear me over the engine noise. Maybe he couldn't read my lips, or the ache in my eyes. But whatever, he didn't answer.

The plane started to angle downward.

"Are we landing?" I asked, letting him off the hook.

"No, we're just dropping off the Ethiopian plateau. We've got a few hours to go yet. And I think I need some sleep now."

☙

By the time we booked into the hotel in Djibouti City, Egan was feeling so unwell that I insisted on carrying the full rucksack. He asked at reception for the hotel doctor, pointing at his sling, and then we walked through the dark corridors to our ground-floor room.

"You want to keep an eye on me?" I asked, surprised he'd checked us into the one room together. Not displeased, I admit; just surprised.

"You got a passport to show them?" he answered wearily. He hadn't claimed I was his sister, or his wife; he'd just said nothing, and the hotel had let it slide. The place was large but run-down and everything was brown, like some 1970s film set.

Our room was beige too, and rather dingy, but it had generously sized twin beds and an en-suite, and there were dusty palm trees outside the window. It felt stuffy and humid in here so as soon as I'd dumped the baggage on a chair I turned to the air-con control box.

"Please don't," said Egan, sitting on the end of the bed. "I'm feeling really cold."

He wasn't kidding. "You're shaking," I said, going over to put my hand on his forehead. He'd stopped sweating, but he was still raging hot to my touch. "You should get under the covers."

"I'll sit up and wait for the medic." He wrapped his good arm around his chest.

I pulled the top end of the coverlet up from his bed and draped it over his shoulders, tucking it around him. For a moment he leaned into me, seeking warmth, and I slipped my arms about him.

"Milja. I'm sorry. I'll make some calls once I get some drugs in me."

"That's no problem." I stroked his hair. "There's no hurry. Is it okay if I use the shower?"

"Feel free."

"Will you be all right?"

"I'm fine." That was obviously not true. His teeth were actually juddering together.

"Ah—I haven't got a change of clothes." I was musing aloud more than complaining.

"There's a clean shirt in the bag there if you want to borrow that. We'll go shopping later... I'm sorry."

"Stop saying that. I'd be rotting in an Ethiopian prison if it weren't for you."

"Your man is a piece of shite, leaving you there. I hope you know that."

I laughed, unhappily. *I'm sure there's a reason*, I thought, but I didn't say it out loud. And I couldn't guess what that reason might be. Now that my immediate fear for my own life had ebbed away, I could feel the great dark dread lurking beneath. What had happened to Azazel? What was he doing?

"Okay, I'm going to go get clean," was all I dared say.

I dug a folded shirt out of the rucksack and retreated into the bathroom. As soon as I could I tore off my own clothes and threw them into a corner.

Oh God, oh God, oh God.

It felt so good to be naked. I stared at myself in the mirror, bracing myself for the worst—and I got a shock; I didn't look anything like as terrible as I ought to. Filthy, yes. There was a gray tidemark of grime around my throat, and my unnaturally pale hair was rough and staring. But my face, my skin...

Oh God.

There wasn't a single bruise. I'd been punched and slapped and scratched, and my face should have looked just as bad as Egan's. But underneath all the dirt, I wasn't even puffy-eyed. I twisted in front of the mirror, checking my back and shoulders. Not a mark. And my blonde was growing out—the roots already dark.

Witch.

I supposed I should be grateful to my Dorian Gray body, and to Azazel.

It wasn't something I could afford to worry about now anyway. I went and flipped the shower tap instead. My patience was eventually rewarded with warm water, and I took my time to scrub myself thoroughly clean. I shampooed twice.

The sensation of cleanliness was utterly blissful, like some sort of heavenly redemption. While I was toweling off I heard a muffled knock at our bedroom door, and a low, sporadic conversation between Egan and some other man that ended in a "Thank you," the door closing and silence.

Good, I thought.

I pulled the shirt on over my head. It was the collarless one I'd seen Egan wear in Lalibela, and I guess I'd made the wrong choice because it hadn't been laundered since; the scent of his skin was all around me like incense as the garment settled on my shoulders. Something inside me clenched with a sharp, sweet pain, and suddenly my legs were so weak that I had to sit on the toilet lid. The hand I raised to push back my wet hair was shaking.

Goddamn. While I was in prison, the very fear for my life had held me together, but now I felt like I was flying apart in pieces. The fracture lines in my heart threatened to splinter me into a thousand shards. I felt so alone that I ached, physically. More than anything else, I needed to be held. I needed to feel skin against my skin in primal animal comfort. I wanted to be home, safe, secure in my lover's arms—all the things I could not have.

Could never have, perhaps.

Sitting on a toilet in a dingy African hotel bathroom, I felt Azazel's abandonment like a wound under my ribcage.

Slowly, feeling like it was the heaviest of labors, I rolled the shirt sleeves up to fit my arms. The cotton was soft, and brushed loosely on the tops of my legs when I stood. Just about decent.

I couldn't bear to put any of my befouled old clothes on —not even my panties—so I bundled them into the sink, squirted on shampoo and left them to soak in water. My hair still dripping, I walked out into the bedroom.

Egan had got himself, fully clothed, into bed and under the covers. He lay on his right side with his broken arm propped on his ribs and was already asleep, judging by his heavy breathing. I spotted a small plastic pot and a strip of pills on the night stand; I couldn't identify the capsules in the pot from their label, but the strip was codeine and two had been popped out.

I looked down at Egan, biting the inside of my lip even as I smiled, relieved he was getting some rest. The blankets were tugged right up to his neck, and as I watched he shivered visibly and hunched them higher.

Quietly, I climbed onto the bed behind him and spooned up. I was too hot to get under the covers even had I thought that a good idea, so I just snuggled in around him hoping to lend some body-warmth. Egan made a little mumbling noise as I slid my hand around his waist, careful not to nudge his injured arm.

"Freezing," he groaned.

"Shush, go to sleep," I murmured. I liked the smell of his hair. I liked his solidity, something to hold on to. If he could not comfort me, I could comfort him. "Everything's okay." So I lay there, embracing him, until we both dozed off.

I didn't dream. I hadn't dreamt at all since Azazel left me.

※

I woke when Egan floundered out from under the covers at his side of the bed, gasping, and slid onto the floor.

"What's wrong? Are you okay?"

"Hnh. So hot!" The sweating part of his fever cycle had come back with a vengeance; his shirt was soaked. "Help me," he begged, plucking at his sling. "Gotta get this off."

I wriggled over on the bed and dealt with the safety pin.

The arm revealed wore a cast below the elbow and was wrapped in bandages above.

"Shirt. Cold shower."

I helped him wriggle out of his button-down shirt and then steadied him as he climbed to his feet. Given that I wasn't wearing anything underneath my own borrowed garment I was worried about flashing him, but Egan wasn't looking, and to be honest I'm not sure he would have seen anyway. His eyes were unfocused like he was still struggling out of sleep. "Are you going to be able to manage?" I asked as I chaperoned him to the bathroom door.

He nodded, his movements exaggerated as if his muscle control was shot to hell. As soon as he'd shut himself inside I went and turned the air-conditioning on. The old mechanism clunked and hummed, but seemed to be firing up.

Damnit, what can I do? I wiped the sleep out of my eyes and glanced out of the window anxiously. It looked like the sun was easing down toward evening, and I wondered if enough time had elapsed to dose him with more pills. I really had no idea. I sat on the edge of the bed, my lips pursed, feeling helpless.

There came a slithering thump from the bathroom, louder even than the hiss of running water, that made my blood run cold. I dived for the door.

"Egan! Egan, are you all right?"

He didn't answer.

Thank God he hadn't locked himself in. I thrust the door open to find him half-collapsed on the floor, soaking wet and butt-naked, his injured arm raised. The shower was still running.

"Didn't bang my arm," he said weakly.

"Oh, Egan!" I checked his head for bumps and, finding

none, took a moment to turn off the water so I could think more clearly. "Can you get up if I help you?"

"I'm grand," he said, which was blatantly untrue. I discovered when I wrestled him to his feet just how incredibly bloody heavy a man is; his legs didn't seem to be capable of taking his weight and he leaned so hard on me as we staggered to the bed that I was afraid he was going to go down on top of me.

I let him drop on my own untouched bed, and then pulled the sheet from his to cover him to the waist, just to afford him some dignity. He was still running hot under the slick of shower-water, and wouldn't let me cover him any further, thrusting the sheet down with a groan of protest. His pupils were alarmingly dilated.

"I'm going to get you some ice," I told him, once I'd held a bottle of water to his lips and made him drink.

"Ice nice," he said, and snickered at his own rhyme.

"Don't go anywhere," I warned him. "You have to be a good boy."

"Very good," he sighed, his eyes drifting shut. "Do I get a kiss?"

"Ice will do you more good."

I pulled on his way-too-big-for-me cargo pants and cinched them as tight as I could about my hips before running out barefoot to the hotel bar to demand an ice-bucket. By the time I got back, our room felt pleasantly chilled by the air-con. Egan hadn't moved. I wrapped ice in a hand towel, soaked the corner of a second in the cold melt-water, and went to tend him. He started a little when I blotted the cool cloth over his forehead, and tried to focus on my face. "Milja. Can you open the window? It's a bit warm in here."

"Just relax," I said, sitting beside him on the bed and

using the icepack on his chest. He was badly bruised over his ribs and I was as gentle as I could be, wiping a swathe through the slick of sweat and shower water. There was a gash on his right bicep that had been closed with butterfly stitches. *Jeez, you're a mess*, I added—but not out loud—appalled and moved and secretly impressed by the damaged he'd soaked up.

It was strange, touching him like that with such intimate care. His body wasn't darkly bronze all over like Azazel's; it was pale gold where it had seen the sun and just pale elsewhere. His torso and legs seemed almost hairless in contrast to what I was used to, and he didn't have Azazel's lean muscularity or exaggerated definition. Egan was more squarely built, his muscles hard but not showy. Solid and human and touchingly vulnerable. I could feel a pulse at his diaphragm when my fingertips lingered there.

I could feel the heat in my cheeks, too. Egan was massively guarded and private in his self. It was hard to imagine him strutting about naked in public; he had no fierce angelic pride in his own beauty. Touching him felt like being admitted to a mystery, and treading on holy ground. I owed him respect and humility in my care for him. Gentle, unhurried strokes, tender over the blue-black blooms of his bruises. Concentration, seeking out the feverish heat in order to sooth it. Patience, taking my time, returning again and again in my attempts to comfort him and sooth the fire in his flesh.

While a slow burn kindled in mine.

He's lovely. He smells good too, sort of like toast. Azazel is all pepper and smoke. God, my mouth's watering... I wonder what he tastes like. Not that I would, of course. Ever. He'd freak out. Like on the Grlica. I touched him then, but it was a dream. I sucked his... I shouldn't be thinking this. I shouldn't even be looking at him this way. He's ill. He'd hate it.

"I love you, Milja," he said, shocking me out of my reverie.

"That's the fever talking," I said with a hoarse little laugh. "Shush."

"No." He stretched his throat, perspiration shimmering in the golden hollow beneath his Adam's apple. "I see you being put through ten types of shite, pushed places no one should have to go, and in the middle of it all you shine. A rose in a storm. That's what I thought when I met you…a rose in a storm, whipped around by wind and rain. Strong and beautiful, and loyal. Too loyal. Does he even know how hard this is, what he's asking of you? Does he care?"

"Don't." My cheeks were burning now. "Don't talk about him, please."

"Okay. I don't want to talk about him." He shifted his spine on the mattress, and I could feel the strong, beautiful machinery of his body moving beneath my hand. "Let me talk about you. You don't have to do this, Milja. You don't have to carry this burden. The end of the world is not your responsibility, one way or the other. Walk away. Be happy."

Oh, he would break my heart.

"Egan…please…"

"I want you to be happy. Ah, I want things I've no right to want. When I hold you, oh Christ. The temptation. I can't… It's so hard not to want those things."

He lifted his good hand and grabbed mine, his grip shockingly strong. I'd imagined him weak. Startled, I met his gaze. It was wider than natural, almost glassy. My heart was banging against my breastbone. I tried to form words but couldn't bring them to mind.

"Your lips now. I think of your lips under mine. I think of

your body under my lips. I want to fuck you, Milja, that's the truth, because I'm a piece-of-shite sinner and that's how my love feels, all wrapped up in my lust and what I need—and I'm sorry, I can't stop thinking about you. About how much I want you."

"Oh God." My pulse thudded all the way to my sex.

"Do you think about me?"

I'd never realized before that blue is the color of pain. I thought I might be trapped by those terrible blue eyes forever, drowning in his anguish—and mine. "Yes," I breathed, the admission nearly breaking me.

"This?" He pulled my hand down lower, over the sheet, pressed it down firmly against the cotton. Every muscle in my arm contracted in shock—but he did not let me pull away. He held me there, and so I looked. The thin sheet was soaked and plastered against his body, hiding nothing. Not the thick ridge of his erection trapped between my hand and his hard stomach, not even the subtle twin plum-shaped swells of his balls.

Oh. Oh oh oh. My nipples were so hard that the drag of the soft cotton shirt was almost painful. He burned against my palm, a feverish wedge of need trying to push open the doors of possibility.

"Please," he groaned, tightening his fingers around mine to squeeze his shaft and rub up and down.

"Egan…"

"Please, Milja." His hips twisted. "Oh God, please." Sweat speckled his upper lip anew. The ache in my core rose like a heat plume to meet the ache in my heart.

He's gorgeous, I thought, and simultaneously; *This is so wrong*. I reached in with my left hand, grabbing his little finger and pushing it back to break his grip and peel it away from me. I pushed his good hand back up onto the pillow, leaning on his palm to pin it with my weight. He didn't have any leverage to resist me.

My breath caught in my throat.

Poor poor Egan. Aching and desperate and helpless. Pinned on his back while his swollen cock raged and wept for release. Just like Azazel had been before I freed him.

After all these years, the darkness beneath the mountain was still there inside me. I had him at my mercy, and that mercy ran slick and hot through me until it escaped down the inside of my thighs.

My right hand hadn't moved from his cock. I squeezed him again.

"Ah Jesus, yes," he cried. Egan never blasphemed.

You need this? You need this? I wanted to bite his parted lips until they broke again and bled, and if I'd had the reach I might have. I can make no excuses for what I felt, or what I did. There was a dark tide of lust rising in me—and even though yes, I could try to explain, it makes no difference to my guilt. I felt bad for him, yes. He was handsome and sweet and he loved me, yes. No difference.

I loved him, in a way I couldn't even bring myself to think about.

No difference.

The fact is, he was hurt and he was helpless and *that made me want to fuck him right now*.

And that's why I didn't let go of his thick cock. I kept hold of it through the cotton sheet.

"Oh. Yes—Milja!"

I kept hold of it and I rubbed it even harder and thicker, until his heels dug into the mattress and his hips danced. I worked him slow and hard and pitilessly, until his head was thrown back and his throat distended with strain and the blood ran down his chin from his split lip, until he was gasping and rigid and begging incoherently.

Until he came in a long drawn out series of bucks, under the sheet, calling on his saints and his God.

I drank in every cry, every detail. I kissed his bloody lips and lay beside him, cradling his head to my pounding heart. He burrowed his face in the V of my shirt and kissed my breasts.

And only then did I come out of my trance.

I think Egan fell asleep almost immediately. I slipped out from the bed and sat on the edge of the other one, my knuckles pressed to my mouth, watching his chest rise and fall as his bruises faded slowly away like invisible ink.

Fourteen
FROM OUT OF THE STRONG CAME FORTH SWEETNESS

"Milja, wake up."

I wasn't asleep. I hadn't been asleep since I heard Egan rise from his bed and go into the bathroom. I'd lain there as still as a stone, listening to the tap running, watching the dawn light creep across the brown wallpaper. *He's scrubbing himself off*, I'd told myself—and that bit of my mind that never listened to my conscience had wished that I'd seen it last night, that I'd pulled the sheet down and witnessed the gush of his exaltation. That I'd touched him, skin on skin.

It wished that I'd tasted him. It wanted to know.

Now I sat up, pulling the covers around me because I'd dumped his trousers and was half-naked again, and I rumpled my hand through my wild hair.

"Look at me, Milja. What do you see?"

I lifted my gaze slowly. Egan stood there with a hotel towel knotted about his waist. The bandages that had swathed his upper arm were gone and the skin revealed was crosshatched with scars, but they looked pale and shiny, weeks or months old. He bunched both hands into fists, then spread them wide, his fingers moving freely.

He looked well, and better than well. I liked every inch of what I could see, and the precarious towel only served to direct my attention to what lurked beneath. I bit the inside of my lip, unable to bring myself to appear surprised. "You're feeling better?" I asked huskily.

In answer he tore open the Velcro strips of his cast and threw the whole thing across the room to smack against the wall, making me flinch. His face, unblemished now, perfectly healed, was marred only by the blaze of his eyes.

"What happened last night, Milja?" He was whole again. No trace of fever, or infection, and barely a trace of any injury. And he was rigid with alarm.

"I healed you," I whispered.

"How?"

"It's a bit like a miracle." *You're down with miracles, aren't you?*

"Oh I really doubt that. Milja, what the hell did you do?" His rage held something close to panic, I realized. "I can't remember anything."

Horror made my limbs quiver. "Nothing?"

"Only…" He batted at his forehead with one palm, his voice strained. "Flashes. I thought it was a dream. Was it one of your dreams again?"

I couldn't lie to him. "No."

"*Tell me what happened.*"

"We had sex." When he just stared at me, I added nervously, "It turns out I can heal with sex. I thought it was just Azazel, but…apparently not."

Witch.

The blood had drained out of his face. "Why? Why would we do that? I was ill. I was hurt."

His visceral, instantaneous rejection felt like a punch in the guts.

"You wanted it." *You said you loved me*, I thought, but I couldn't throw that at him. Not if he didn't remember.

"Milja, for feck's sake, I was out of my head. You know what they call that, don't you?"

Guilt made me snarl, "You were perfectly lucid! *Insistent*, in fact." Because what else was I supposed to say—other than admit straight up, *Yes, I'm some sort of sadist and I raped you?*

Egan sat down suddenly on the bed facing me. I think he'd forgotten how to blink. "Ah God, no." His voice was clotted with horror. "Tell me I didn't…"

"No!" I shook my head vehemently, the pendulum of my fear swinging wildly back from self-preservation to guilt. Dear God, there was no way on earth or in hell I was going to inflict that sort of recrimination on him. I'd rather take it all on myself. "No, it wasn't like that! You weren't even…It was up to me too. I wanted it. It was…lovely." The lie of that last word sat like ash on my tongue.

"I…I thought you said you loved him."

My heart was thumping so loudly I was sure he could hear it, forcing the blood up my arteries and into my blazing cheeks. "I do love him."

"Then why?"

My mouth twisted. "Turns out I am the Whore of Babylon after all, I guess."

He just didn't understand, that was clear from his expression. How could he, when I didn't understand myself? I'd acted purely on instinct. Some toxic combination of pity and lust and loneliness, I suppose. A perfect storm of weakness. But I had mastered myself again now.

"Pretend it didn't happen, if that's what you want," I told him. *If that's how you feel about me.* "It was just sex. No big deal, hey." But my voice shook, betraying me.

Egan put his head in his hands. "It's not your fault," he said in a low mutter. "You weren't to know."

Well, I might have been able to master myself if he hadn't been sitting with his knees open so that the V of the towel showed a pale teasing slash of skin right up the inside of his thigh. I caught myself staring and wanted to poke my eyes out for shame. *What is wrong with you, girl?*

My brain caught up slowly. "What do you mean? What didn't I know?"

Egan's face, as he lifted it, was gray. He looked like he wanted the earth to swallow him up. "I didn't tell you."

"Tell me what?"

"Milja... When I joined Vidimus, one of the things I had to do was take holy orders."

For a moment it was my turn to look uncomprehending. "You mean...like a priest?"

He nodded.

I seemed to be having terrible difficulty dredging up what I knew about Catholics. "You're a *priest*?"

"Yes. You understand? I've taken a vow of celibacy."

I sat back in my nest of blankets. If I could have got up and left the room with any decency I would have walked out. "Shit, Egan," was all I could say.

"I'm sorry, Milja. I'm really sorry."

☙

We barely spoke over the next couple of days, or on the flight out of Djibouti. Egan had withdrawn deep into his shell, no doubt preoccupied with his need for repentance. When we did have to interact he spoke softly and didn't meet my eyes, his sideways glances radiating muted despair. I didn't know enough about Catholic practices to guess whether he needed to do penance of some sort or just get it all off his chest in a confessional, but he needed *something*. And it wasn't to talk to me, it seemed.

I'd fouled him with my nasty dirty sex.

As for me, I felt…betrayed. Yes, that was the right word. I knew that that wasn't fair, but somewhere at the back of my mind I think I'd always imagined that my White Knight was contesting with the Demon King for my hand in marriage. Well, if not exactly in marriage…in bed, anyway. And that had turned out simply not to be true. Whatever desires he'd entertained, he'd never had the faintest intention of making good on the growing intimacy between us—all those comforting and tender embraces, all those thoughtful kindnesses. It had only ever been about his mission, to save the world from Azazel. And his rash declaration of love had been nothing more than the dregs of his emotions churned to the surface by fever.

As far as he was concerned it had never happened.

His stifled lust, or whatever he did feel for me, clearly didn't count for anything when weighed against his devotion and loyalty to the Church. Loss left a great hollow under my ribs, and emptied my head of any desire to talk, or think, or plan ahead.

We departed Africa on a troop carrier, afterthoughts lumped in amongst uniformed personnel who looked straight through us. No one asked for my passport, or frisked the new-bought clothing I wore, or quizzed me about the purpose of my trip. Not even when we touched down at USAF Minot in North Dakota. Whatever strings Egan was pulling, they were attached to some long levers.

But while we were crossing the Atlantic, I dreamed.

I'm in a white room. Clinically white, like a hospital, but round as an apple, and the core of that room is another round room with a wall of glass. Azazel and Penemuel are both inside that central chamber; Penemuel lies upon on her back so that the spill of her vast, darkly bronze wings fills the floor, and Azazel stoops over her, his raven plumage mantling them both like a thundercloud.

I slap my hands against the glass, but the sound is dead. My first thought is that he's kissing her, you see; his hands are on her breast and his mouth hovers over hers. I slap the glass and then hurry around the circle, looking in vain for a door. But the change of angle allows me to see more clearly.

He isn't kissing her, not exactly. Their eyes are open, locked in a mutual gaze, and between her parted lips and his a golden light is streaming. His hands aren't on her breasts, they are cupped in the center of her breastbone, with more of that light leaking from between his fingers and spilling downward over her bare skin, her beautiful body. They are absolutely motionless, like statues. I can't see even the rise and fall of a ribcage. It is as if they are frozen in a moment of absolute concentration. Only the air between them quivers, in a heat-haze of power.

And that look in Azazel's eyes—oh how well I know that look of hungry intent.

"Azazel!" I shout, banging a fist on the barrier between us. It doesn't even reverberate. And if Azazel hears me, he does not react.

Is this because of Egan? Is this my punishment?

"Where are you?" I scream. "Azazel, talk to me!"

There is a noise though—a deep thrumming, that grows louder with my shouts. It comes from behind me. In despair I turned and look—and then I see that the tiled outer walls and the curved roof over my head is covered in bees. Crusted curtains of wax honeycomb hang over my head. Transparent wings glint as they catch the light. Honey oozes and drips, spattering my upturned face. I feel its stickiness as I wipe at my skin.

And there is Roshana, wearing that tight yellow T-shirt. She holds a huge piece of broken comb in her hands, still crawling with bees, and as I watch she bites into it, chewing and swallowing in great greedy gulps, wax and all. She sees me staring at her and she laughs out loud, her teeth and chin smeared with honey and broken bees.

I shot awake in my flight seat. The thrumming of bees resolved itself into the throb of the plane engines. Egan, seated at a safe distance across the aisle from me, frowned.

"You okay?"

I nodded, ignoring him as I tried to recall every detail of my vision. Dreams with Azazel in them were not random, not to be discounted. I'd seen something significant, I was sure, if only I could work it out. Azazel was with Penemuel. Absolutely absorbed in Penemuel, it seemed.

But...Roshana? Was she still alive? Why was she part of my dream?

Because she's another signpost. I know where they are. I know.

୧୨

The lobby Egan led me through to in Dakota looked like an austere version of any provincial arrivals lounge. There was a scant row of uncomfortable chairs to wait on, a selection of vending machines and an ATM, and some booths for people who needed to book onward travel or accommodation, now mostly deserted. Egan left me with a twenty-dollar bill to buy snacks and drinks while he went and sorted out a hire car.

"I'll drive you home," he said wearily.

I selected a few bags of chips and a couple of sodas, then paced about the room with the change clenched in my hand. My attention kept sliding to the row of old-style payphones on one wall.

Eventually I couldn't hold back. This was my only chance at even semi-privacy until I bought myself a new cellphone. I fed coins in and pecked out the private number Roshana Veisi had given me when she recruited me to her plan for a family reunion. I remembered it because I'd happened to note that the letters on the pad spelled out her name.

Up herself, much? I'd thought at the time.

The dial tone thrummed in my ear like the sound of agitated wings and I held my breath.

"Hello. Who is this?"

That's her voice. It really is.

"Roshana—It's me! You're alive? Where's Azazel?"

There was a long pause, and then she said warmly, "Milja—We thought we'd lost you! Where are you, honey? Still in Ethiopia? I'll come and get you."

My lips parted, and I almost replied, but then instinct clawed at my belly. I stared into space, thinking of the burnt body in Uriel's arms. How had she survived that? How?

I clunked the phone back into its cradle, my stomach churning. When Egan rolled up outside the door twenty minutes later in a big black Toyota Hilux with tinted windows I was so preoccupied with my plans I hardly looked at him.

We went, at my suggestion, to a mall where a friendly ATM gave me a wodge of notes and I bought spare clothes and a nice comfortable pair of hiking boots and a prepaid cellphone. "I'll drive," I said when we returned to the parking lot. "You look all-in."

He nodded. "Long flight. I didn't get much sleep."

I drove him precisely five miles and stopped at a gas station near the interstate. "I want you to get out," I said.

"What?"

"You're not coming with me."

He looked shocked—I don't know why. Did he imagine we were still friends? "Where are you going?"

"None of your business. But I don't want you there. Thank you for getting me back, Egan. I'm grateful. Really. But we're through. I'll drop the hire off for you."

He didn't argue. He descended silently from the big SUV and stood watching as I pulled away. The sight of his pale face diminishing in the rearview mirror was, for a moment, like a stab in my heart. I wanted to stop and let him jump back and just *talk*, and maybe we could get back to the point where his every glance didn't hurt me. I wanted to have him at my back as I fought my way through hell. I wanted to see him smile again, warm and unfeigned.

But the fact was, no matter what our relationship, Egan was not on Azazel's side. He could not witness what I was going in search of.

I couldn't cry, so I bit the inside of my lip until the blood oozed into my mouth. Then I drove up onto the interstate and pointed the car at Minnesota.

&

The main gate to Roshana's ranch wasn't shut. I paused the car on the road outside, gathering my resolve. Through the autumnal rain, lines of red oaks were visible marching over the hills like a procession of burning torches. Mist patches rose like smoke.

Azazel was up there, I was sure. He had, of course, taken Penemuel back to the only place he was sure that they couldn't be overlooked or found by angels of the Host; that skep-shaped Watcher's tomb in the overgrown valley. If only I hadn't dynamited the cave behind my father's chapel, he might have gone there instead.

My hands felt sweaty against the steering wheel. I was strung out by driving and cheap motel rooms and solitude. I had no grand and devious plan.

I only knew one way in.

Easing the Hilux forward, I left the metaled road and sent the tires crunching and hissing over the private drive. I kept the pace slow and steady, trying to look like I had every right to be paying a visit. I'd wasted days trying to get out of Africa, but there was a good chance that Roshana hadn't made it back yet either. Maybe she was in Chicago, catching up on business matters. Or in some fancy hotel in Dubai, awaiting her transfer flight. Maybe there was no one home here except the housekeeper and the stable-hands.

My wishes were in vain this time. I'd been concentrating too hard on the road, I guess, to tip the scales of Chance. As I passed the house I saw a battered 4WD move out in my rear-view mirror to follow me. My heart jumped and I gave up on bluff and hit the gas, gripping the steering wheel as if I could pull it off its mount as I retraced our route through the fields of horses and up out of the valley. My pursuer sped up too, narrowing the gap between us. I slewed left around the corner onto the wooded track so hard that I nearly rolled into the roadside ditch, all in the hope that they would overshoot the junction, but that turned out to be wishful thinking too. As the track rose steeper and I ground down through the gears, I nearly bounced clear of my seat, but they were still there behind me. Yellow birch leaves plastered themselves to the windshield, defying the drizzle.

I nearly missed the dead tree with the bracket-fungi, in my desperation.

Dragging on the brake, I flung myself out of the open door. This time around I was wearing suitable boots and pants at least, but I still skidded on the leaf mulch and nearly went down in the mud as I made my dash for the slope.

An engine roared behind me. Then a single gunshot.

"Stop!"

I didn't. I couldn't. The slope was too steep. I slithered down on my heels, catching at the saplings to control my descent, and trying to fend off the branches aimed at my face. Someone was crashing in my wake.

"Azazel!" I shrieked, as the gradient flattened out at the bottom of the valley.

Someone slammed into me from behind and I went over, face-down, a solid mass on top of me. By the time I'd spat the leaves out of my mouth and blinked my eyes back into focus, there was a hot steel muzzle pressed to my temple.

"Stay down, bitch!" a man barked. "What the fuck?"

"Roshana," I coughed. "Roshana Veisi! She's my boss!"

A hand grabbed my shirt and hauled me to my feet. I looked into the ugly, panting face of a sinewy guy with an expression like thunder. Two more men were coming down between the trees.

"She invited me up here," I said. They all wore black, an understated uniform of some sort. I didn't recognize any of them, so I could only hope they were loyal employees. "Ask her. Roshana. Go on! My name is Milja Petak; I work for her at Ansha Engineering."

"That right?"

There was a growling conversation between them as they patted me down for weapons, more roughly than I'd have liked. I cast anxious glances about me, but there was no sign of an avenging Azazel burning toward us through the woods, and the guy holding me gave me a good shake to make sure I was still paying attention. The gun was eventually holstered though, much to my relief. "Get your ass back up there," they ordered.

So near to my goal, yet so far.

Why isn't Azazel answering me?

Weak with disappointment, I trudged and slipped and pulled my way back up the slope. Every so often one of my captors would put a hand on my ass to assist me with a shove. At the top, two of them took me into their SUV, while the third stayed to take care of my abandoned vehicle.

Slumped on the seat, I started to shake. I was all out of ideas for the moment.

Slowly we reversed down the slope to the main track, and then returned to the ranch house. I wondered if they were going to call the police, but it turned out they had different plans. They marched me around the back of the building and in through the kitchen—where several staff were bustling about—and down a long tiled corridor. The walls here were hung with, of all things, framed photographs of children, dozens and dozens of them, dating back to stiff Edwardian portraits. But I didn't have time to look, or to wonder. They hustled me through to a big conservatory covering a long swimming pool. The turquoise water was still and sterile under a glass roof that thrummed with rain.

For a moment, just as we passed through the door, I thought I saw a silvery shimmer over the water.

"Get up there," they told me. They steered me to the far end of the pool, where a young woman was working behind what looked like a mini-bar. She wore a white uniform like a spa attendant, and she glanced at me without interest. "Wait," the guy with the gun ordered, stomping off and leaving his companion to stand over both of us.

I looked cautiously around. There were two sun-lounger chairs nearby, though I was not invited to lounge and I suspected that they saw little sun up here this far north. The warm air smelled of chlorine from the pool. There was a mosaic tiled onto the house-side wall, which looked a lot older than the rest of the room, maybe antique. It depicted two classically-dressed men facing each other over a small pillar. One was holding out a bowl to the other, and the contents of that bowl seemed to be flaming.

Prometheus? I wondered. My brain had nothing else to work on.

The woman was blitzing ice and wheatgrass and fruit in a food blender. When she'd done that she poured the green, foul-looking concoction into a tall glass and left, all without saying a word.

"What are you going to do with me?" I asked quietly. "Are you contacting Ms. Veisi?"

"Shut up."

I couldn't think what else to do, so I filled in the silent minutes by picking wet leaves out of my hair. I didn't have the nerve to drop them on the polished tiles though.

A side-door banged shut. "Milja," said a familiar voice, and there was Roshana strolling up the poolside toward me. She wore spandex workout clothes, dampened across the breastbone by perspiration, and had a towel slung over one shoulder. "Fancy seeing you here."

I stared, too stupefied to answer. She looked fit and trim and absolutely unhurt, no mark of a burn upon her skin, her blue-blonde hair as long and glossy as ever. As if she'd never been through the fire. As if I'd never seen her broken, scorched body carried away in an archangel's arms.

My guard took a few steps back, standing against the wall.

"Well, honey," she said, reaching for the smoothie glass. "You made it back. To what do I owe the pleasure?"

Fifteen
SYMPATHY FOR THE DEVIL

"I thought you were dead," I said slowly, my thoughts trying to sift this new information. "In the fire."

She smiled tightly, easing herself back into one of the loungers. "I'm not as fragile as I look."

"How?"

"I woke up in a monk's cell. They tried to stop me getting away, but you can imagine how that went for them."

No. Liar. I saw Uriel take you. The words crowded into my mouth, but a deep foreboding stopped me blurting them out. If she was lying, then she wouldn't be pleased to be called out. If she was deliberately keeping quiet about Uriel…then maybe I shouldn't reveal what I knew.

"What about you, honey?" she asked, over the rim of her glass. She didn't care though, and she wasn't trying to hide it. She'd never shown much sense of curiosity about us lesser mortals, now that I came to think about it. With one exception.

"Yeah, similar," I muttered. *I'm not bringing Egan into*

this. Not if she's tried to kill him off already. "They let me go eventually."

"All's well that ends well, then." She hadn't invited me to sit down, or offered me a drink. I still stood before her like a naughty schoolgirl.

"I want to see Azazel. He's here, I know."

"The question is, why are you here? Can't you just call him?"

"He's…gone quiet."

"Well then, it doesn't sound like he wants to see you, does it?" She crossed her ankles elegantly as she set her smoothie aside. "Azazel has been ever so busy with Penny in the honeymoon suite since the moment they got back. Occasionally I pop over to find out if they want to come up for air, but they're engrossed in…well." She made, very delicately, an obscene gesture with thumb and fingers. "Non-stop. Oh, love's sweet enchantment… You know how it is. Well, you did."

Penny?

She was trying to upset me, but I was too wired to snap at her crude bait. Every nerve in my body was screaming at me that there was something wrong—that *everything* was wrong; every word that came out of her mouth, every inch of her smooth toned skin. She didn't just look like she'd recovered from all her exploits and injuries in Ethiopia, she looked like she'd lost ten years. I wasn't prepared to put that all down to Pilates and wheatgrass smoothies.

"Let me see him, Roshana." It was all I dared say.

"Now honey, don't be one of those sad, crazy exes. Men are just fickle bastards and it's up to us to keep our dignity. It's a bit of a shame you can't take him for alimony but hey, you knew it would end this way."

"End? It's not ended."

"I don't think that's your decision, sweetie. It's finished. He doesn't want to see you. And as his hostess I'm bound to respect his wish for privacy."

I would have melted her nasty plastic smile with my glare if I could have. "What are you getting out of this?"

"I'm getting my father back in my life." She tilted her head, flicking a glance at the waiting heavy. "You're getting to go home a little older and wiser. Isn't that how it always is in these stories?" Her next words were addressed to him, not me. "See her out."

A masculine hand closed firmly about my bicep.

"Don't bother going in to the office on Monday, Milja," she added as an afterthought. That was sprinkles on her cupcake, no doubt.

"I'll believe he's finished with me when I hear it from him!" I said as I was towed away.

"Sweetie, he's got better things to do than waste his breath on you. You were only ever his fuck-toy, remember. A convenient penis-shaped hole."

"Go to hell!"

She snorted. "Don't shoot the messenger, honey."

That was the last I saw of my erstwhile employer. Her payroll muscle marched me back to the front of the ranch house, where my hire car was waiting for me.

I got in and I drove away. What choice did I have? Should I have sat down and screamed and drummed my heels like a little kid who'd had a toy snatched from her grasp?

I drove out into the drizzling fall, my teeth clenched so hard that my jaw ached, my knuckles white on the steering wheel. I didn't believe a word she'd said. I couldn't believe Azazel had thrown me over for Penemuel. Not just like that, surely? He would have said something. Ghosting was just not his style; he was too unsophisticated.

And I'd had that dream. I'd seen him. Yes, he'd been rapt in Penemuel's gaze, but...

But something had been wrong. I was sure of it. If they'd just been rutting happily away my subconscious would have been able to picture that quite clearly. In fact, I was having a hard time not picturing it right here and now, after Roshana's poisonous words.

That wasn't what I'd seen.

Ferocious passion, yes. Concentration, yes. Not sex. Not as I knew it with Azazel.

Maybe it's different between angels?
No. No, that wasn't sex.
There was no joy in it.

Yes, that was what had felt wrong to me about my vision. Whatever the two of them were up to, there was nothing remotely joyous about it. And I knew what Azazel was like between the sheets—or on the rooftops, or on the back stairs. He loved sex with a wholehearted, simple, fierce delight. At his most tender or his most desperate, he still burned with joy in the act.

In my dream, the only delight had been in Roshana's hungry eyes. The atmosphere had been taut with something else entirely.

Despair.

༼༽

Two hours down the road, as I skirted yet another of those interminable Minnesotan lakes, headlights flashed in my rearview mirror. I looked up and recognized the ox-blood and chrome of Roshana's Nissan flatbed, the one she'd taken Azazel and me out for a spin in. It seemed a long time ago now.

What does she want now? Changed her mind, has she?

I pulled in obediently at the side of the road. The light was dim here under the canopy of the lake's wooded flanks. Roshana's headlamps stayed on as she drew onto the verge a few lengths behind me.

I slipped the engine into park and stretched my back, half nervous and half grateful. The windows I could see in my mirror were smoked and only reflected a strip of gray sky and the black, louring pines.

"Goddamnit," I muttered, unbuckling and sliding out onto the roadside. The air tasted fresh, and at least it had stopped raining. I walked around the back of my Hilux.

Both front doors in the other vehicle swung open and two figures stepped out. It took me a moment, in my confusion, to recognize two of the three guys from Roshana's ranch; the ugly sinewy one and the one who'd stood watch over me at the poolside. They sauntered forward.

The Nissan headlamps suddenly flared impossibly bright, filling my skull, enough to blind me. By the time I brought my arm down, blinking the blue lights from my retinas, there were not two but three figures in front of me. The two goons, standing quite still. And between them a tall man with silver hair and blue, perpetually disappointed eyes, rocking an unknotted tie and the most beautiful three-piece Italian suit known to humanity.

He looked so out of place.

"Hello, Milja," said the Archangel Uriel softly.

"What the hell do you want?" I stammered, as he closed on me. "You know what Azazel promised to do to you if you ever came near me again!"

"Yes. I remember." His smile was narrow-lipped and taut,

but his voice calm. "But there are exceptional circumstances that I'm sure even he'll forgive. I'm here to rescue you."

"From what?"

"From them." He waved both hands to indicate the guys behind him. They hadn't shifted an inch. In fact, now that I was paying attention, there was no movement anywhere in my field of vision. No leaf stirred, no drip of water fell from the long lank grasses. A lacewing fly hung motionless in the light from the headlamp, like a chip etched into the air's glassy surface. An absolute silence pressed down over us, the thousand tiny sounds of life sucked out of the world. We were the only agents capable of motion, here between the moments of time.

"These gentlemen are under orders," said Satan calmly, "to take you into the woods just there and put a bullet through your head. They've also been discussing, whilst driving along, the merits of getting you to—ahem—suck both their cocks before one of them pulls the trigger."

Cold water ran through my veins, and I backed hard against my rear fender. "Why..." I rasped, "why should I believe you?" I said this even though I could see the ugly one was poised with his hand reaching casually inside his quilted jacket. Their faces were expressionless, like masks.

"Have I ever lied to you?"

"Uh...you're the Father of Lies."

"Oh come on, now that's a libel I find *particularly* hurtful. That little weasel Paul—"

"Jesus. Jesus said that, actually."

Uriel sniffed like I'd slapped him. "Hh. He...had his reasons. But he was misinformed. Very well, Milja." He spread his hands. "As a demonstration of my sincerity and in the spirit of full disclosure, I will also tell you that your lover is less than ten minutes behind you on this road."

"My lover?" *Azazel?* I was completely confused now.

"The dirty priest. Oh, don't look at me like that, girl. The imprint of him is all over your soul. Do you think I can't see it?" He wrinkled his nose in contempt. "Honestly—you can't even stay loyal to a Son of Heaven? Huh. Just when I was beginning to respect you a little."

Oh crap.

"Well, I don't know how you found someone quite so messed up—he's got love and guilt more confused than you can imagine, I've listened in at the confessional and it is a *circus*—but he's been trailing you since you left him. Quite the stalker."

I think I managed to breathe, nothing more.

"Anyway, you have two choices at this point. One: I go away and let this all play out. There is, I am prepared to admit, a fairly good chance that the priest will get here and find you in time... Before they pull the trigger anyway. And also relatively good odds that he can kill them both without you coming to further harm." He smiled. "Choice two: you let me carry you away from this, all the way back to Chicago or wherever you like. You go free."

"In return for what?"

"So cynical! Alright, since you insist." He shrugged. "I do like a rational and equitable arrangement. In return for my saving you, I would only ask that you agree to give up on trying to approach the Scapegoat. Leave him be, unless he comes to find you."

"Azazel needs me."

"Not anymore, he doesn't. He has others. You know that. Besides, do you really want him to know about your bit-on-the-side? Do you think he'll take that well?"

That prospect made me feel sick with guilt, to be honest. Which was why I'd been studiously not thinking about it since the moment it happened. I ignored it now. "You think you can make me just forget about him, after everything that's happened?"

"I'm not asking you to. Think of him fondly all you like. Indulge your torrid dreams. Keep him topped up, if you must. Just stay away. I'd hate to see you hurt." He shot a glance back over his shoulder, a look of great distaste. "These thugs are not my doing, I assure you."

They're Roshana's. Good God, she really is that cold.

"That's thoughtful of you," I said weakly, stalling for time. *Keep him talking. C'mon Milja, work this out.*

"Yes, it is."

"You're not nearly as bad as they paint you."

Vanity was always Uriel's weakness. Well, that and controlling his physical reactions whilst in human form, including his expressions. He actually looked flattered. "I've been much maligned."

"It's got to be hard to be prosecuting council. No one appreciates your role."

"Well, I'm honored to be entrusted with the task."

"But it's got to be a lonely job, right? I don't see any of the other angels at your back when things get tough."

He narrowed his eyes. "It's enough to be right."

"I'm glad you think so."

For a moment he seemed on the verge of saying something, then he shook himself almost visibly. "So what's it to be, Milja—Home? Or fellatio and bullets?"

I tried to swallow. I could not bear the thought of abandoning Azazel, whatever was going on with him. But I was scared, yes, and worn down by bloodshed. The prospect of more violence made me feel like physical collapse.

"To be honest," Uriel mused, loosening his shoulders, "I'm not sure I understand all the fuss you people make about getting your penises sucked. Like it's some ultimate pleasure, better than any ecstasy imaginable, physical or spiritual. In all the universe: mouth-on-genitals. I mean, *really*?"

I didn't answer. I did not like the way this was going; Uriel embodied such a dangerously unpredictable mix of prudishness and prurience.

"Though I've never tried it myself of course—I have refused every offer." He took another half-step closer, and I shrank back. "Do tell me. Is it really so wonderful? Do you suck the Scapegoat's penis, Milja?"

"Yes," I said in a very small voice, my gaze sliding away from his as he brushed his hand across my cheek.

"Do you like doing it?" He was standing way too close now, all but pinning me against the back of the car. He smelled of frankincense, and his fingers felt cool on my burning face.

"Stop that." I *loved* doing it, but I wasn't telling Uriel that.

"Did you suck the priest's too?"

"Go jump in the lake, Uriel."

"What about me? Would you suck mine? I mean, you demonstrably don't confine your sexual favors to a single recipient. Why not me? I might even let you if you asked nicely enough. Do you think I could Fall for you, Milja?"

Oh this is bad. Panic made my heart kick. "You really hate Azazel, don't you?" I snarled.

Uriel went still.

"I mean, he's already been condemned and punished, but you'd disobey the Divine Command just to *hurt* him? Not to piss him off—you could do that by abusing me, any time. But to throw it in his face that I'd *voluntarily* gone with you—"

He took a step back. "Clever little monkey. Yes."

"Why do you hate him so much?"

Something flickered in his blue eyes, like a shark in the deep ocean. He spread his hands. "He just doesn't do what he's told." A huff escaped his lips as he shook his head. "Do you have any idea how frustrating that is? To see someone who knows for a certainty what they are supposed to do, lunge for exactly the opposite?"

"Really? Happens all the time, Uriel."

"Yes—that's precisely the problem with your kind! You're the only animal smart enough to be told what to do, and just what the consequences will be if you don't, and yet you won't obey! It's just...*irrational*." He said it like it was the ultimate condemnation.

"I can't argue with that."

"I mean, why is it so hard to do what you're told? *I* can do it! Why not you?" He gestured angrily at the cars, the road, and the men. "All this. So unnecessary and ugly and *pointless*."

"Yeah, I get it. You think humanity was a bit of a mistake."

His spine snapped straight. "There are no mistakes." For a moment his eyes glowed. Even under this overcast sky, his deep-set eyes looked a luminous swimming-pool blue. Then his shoulders slumped. "You are just...hard to like."

I almost felt sorry for him.

"So what do you like, Uriel? Out of all Creation, there must be something that doesn't offend you?"

He frowned. "Dragonflies," he said at last. "In all honesty I liked the Carboniferous best."

I found a wobbly smile on my lips, to my own surprise as

much as his. "Dragonflies. They're cool. Do you ever stop to think that we're the only two kinds of people to know about giant Carboniferous dragonflies?"

"What do you mean?"

"It's one thing we have in common. You angels remember them. We humans found fossils and can picture what they were like. Every single other species ever created in between is dead."

He rubbed distractedly at the back of his head, momentarily disrupting his perfect silver locks. He'd seemed so superior the first time I met him, but he had chinks in his armor just like anyone else. "Make your choice," he growled.

"I can't give up on Azazel."

He stared. "You see, I like that. Faithfulness. But if you are so devoted to the Scapegoat—tell me, Milja: why the priest?"

I wish I knew. "Irrational instinct," I whispered sadly. "Love."

"That's your excuse for everything, isn't it?" His lip curled. Then he lifted his hand dismissively, starting to turn away.

"Don't!" My voice was loud and the warning in it so clear even Uriel didn't miss it, though it must have been a novelty as far as he was concerned. "You don't want to make me do this, Uriel!"

He froze, one dark eyebrow arched. "What?"

"You've given me enough time to think. Thank you for that." I spoke with conviction, not allowing any hesitation or doubt into my words. "I know for a fact that as Azazel's witch I can use sex to heal people. Well, I don't see any reason it can't work the other way around. With ill-will, I'm sure I can maim and kill. What do they call malign witchcraft, Uriel—there's a word, isn't there?"

"Maleficium," he said grudgingly.

"So you're going to leave me alone with those guys? You're going to add that to the burden of my sins? Because I swear I'll do it if I have to."

He swung back to me, his shoulders as stiff as if he bore bristling wings. "Why do you have to make everything so difficult?" he complained. "I offered you a way out! You are just *deliberately* awkward."

"Oh, I know. If only I could be a nice obedient dragonfly just eating the head off her mate—"

"That's mantids! Oh for heaven's sake—" He snapped his fingers at each of the men in turn, and even from where I stood I saw their eyes glaze over white. "Get out."

It took a moment for me to realize what he meant, but even as motion came back into the world and my would-be-assassins gasped and pawed at their faces, I was on my way back to my car. As I gunned the engine and pulled away I heard one shot go off, but it didn't hit anything at all so far as I could tell. I looked into the rearview mirror and saw Uriel walk out onto the road, haloed in a silver shimmering light, watching me.

☙

I kept my speed high all the way to the town of Grand Rapids, and was lucky not to be pulled over. My driving was erratic, I'm sure, though I don't recall much of the journey. I knew I needed to think though, not just run. I had a lot to mull over regarding that encounter, and what Uriel had said. He'd genuinely tried to keep me alive, in his awkward, manipulative way. And that meant he had a use for me. He didn't want me dead, because that was no longer enough to cripple his enemy. Alive, I must still be—despite both his protestations and Roshana's—a lever he could use against Azazel. If not now, at some point in some possible future.

Unless he had some other motive.

His hard-on was real enough. Ah, I didn't want to think about that. Uriel's attitude to me seemed to be located somewhere on the line between weird and seriously unhealthy.

Just like every other man in your life then, hey Milja? "How do I keep finding them?" I asked out loud.

Roshana now, she was definitely at the hostile end of the spectrum. That was impossible to deny any longer. All the evidence was that she'd tried to eliminate me from the picture.

So I was a threat to her plans. Which meant, whatever was going on with Azazel and Penemuel, and whatever she thought she was getting out of the arrangement, I had the potential to change things.

That's good, isn't it? Hopeful? Maybe?

Roshana had got what she wanted, her long-lost daddy home again, and she meant to keep it that way.

Uriel had…got some sort of outcome that suited him for the moment, but he possibly didn't trust to last.

'*I do like a rational and equitable arrangement,*' he'd said to me.

'*I've refused every offer.*'

Roshana: '*I've sucked the cocks of tyrants.*'

"Oh God," I groaned, shooting a tree-lined junction without looking. "Oh God, how could you?"

☙

I waited it out in town, knowing that Egan would break sooner or later and come find me.

I really needed to talk to Egan now.

Grand Rapids, unlike its Michigan namesake, was a small town with a logging past and a tourist present. There were lots of cabins for rent and restaurants to hang out in. In happier times I might have liked the place. I was in a big cafe-bar one night, a near-empty refuge of raw wood and red padded leatherette booths, when it happened. I was reading *Lake Wobegon Days* because it seemed to be on sale in every tourist shop, and eating fries. A plain brown envelope flopped onto the table in front of me.

"I'd like to talk," said Egan, sliding onto the seat opposite me. He wore a sheepskin jacket and looked grim.

I felt like I was letting out a breath I'd held for three days. "Okay."

"You all right?"

"Been better."

"Still angry at me?"

"I was never angry at you."

"Yeah...yeah you were."

"Fine." I had to concede that one. "I'm not angry right now."

He nodded. "That's good enough."

The waitress came up and he ordered coffee for both of us. Once she'd gone he pulled out some scanned photographs from the envelope and flipped them over one at a time so I could see. "Roshana Veisi, your employer. You bolted to her place as soon as you threw me out, stayed less than hour, then came here. Vanda Veisi, her mother."

The photo looked like it had been taken sometime in the Eighties, judging by the big hair, but the face was identical to Roshana's own. Absolutely identical.

"Anoushak Veisi, her grandmother, taken back in Iran."

This one was very stylish, black and white. She looked like a Fifties movie starlet.

"Three generations of women, none of whom married, yet who all had a single daughter who fortuitously inherited everything. Amazing family resemblance, don't you think?"

I made a "Hmph" noise.

"I'm willing to bet that the pattern could go back maybe five hundred years or so, if I had time to chase it all up."

"Further than that."

My words took the wind out of his sails. He narrowed his eyes.

"She's one of the Nephilim—that's what you wanted to hear, isn't it? She's only half human. Yes. Well done. She's Azazel's daughter. One of the original ones. She's not a giant or anything, not anymore. But she is thousands of years old. You're going to tell me that's not possible, even for Nephilim, but it is."

He actually sat there with his mouth open; then the waitress arrived with her tray and coffee-pot. "No cream," he muttered. The interrupted conversation hung in the air over us until we were alone again.

"Do you remember the angel in the monastery?" I asked, spooning sugar because I felt like I was going to need it. "*Don't say his name.* The other angel."

"Oh yes. The Adversary." Egan's mouth went hard.

"He insists he's still on God's side, even if no one else believes him. Did you know that?"

"I gathered that was the case."

"Does the Church know it?"

"It is most certainly not part of official dogma." He spread his hands. "I'm not personally in any position to judge the facts."

Was there a patron saint of prevaricating? I narrowed my eyes at him.

"Well, he paid me a visit a couple of days ago. We had a talk—quite a long talk really." I took a cautious sip of my drink. "I think he doesn't have many people he can just, you know, have a chat with. He let some stuff slip."

"Like what?"

"I think—I'm pretty sure—that he's made a bargain with Roshana—which I don't really get, because he's one of the ones that hates the Watchers and is under instructions to kill all their offspring. I think he patched her up after Lalibela and bought her home—"

"Whoah. Back up. Veisi was in Lalibela?"

"Yes. She took a whole load of friendly fire, and the Adversary rescued her after Azazel took off. I saw that before I passed out. I think he's blackmailed her into trapping Azazel and Penemuel at her place. She's a narcissistic bitch but she loves her daddy, so I guess she thinks she's keeping him safe."

"They're trapped?"

"I think so. I've seen them." I passed my hand across my forehead. "In my dreams, you know. I keep trying, but I can't get Azazel to snap out of…whatever it is he's doing. He can't hear me. Or he doesn't want to. I think he's keeping Penemuel alive. She was really badly wounded, and I think he's sustaining her."

Egan stirred. "Her?"

"Angels are pretty flexible on the whole body thing. You should have guessed that."

"Ah, grand."

"Anyway. I get the feeling… Have you heard of those monkey-traps where they put nuts in a pot with a narrow neck, and the monkey can't pull its hand out because it refuses to drop the nuts? I think Azazel's the monkey. If he lets go of Penemuel she'll die, so he's trapped there." *Which is why he didn't come back for me*, I wanted to add. *He hadn't forgotten me; he just can't do two things at once. It's not his fault!* "And

Roshana's standing guard now. She won't let me near."

"Jealous of you?"

"Territorial enough to set armed men on me."

"Oh, this is not good."

"Really? I thought you'd be doing the bloody Riverdance right now. Azazel's trapped. That's what you wanted all along, wasn't it?"

Egan's lips were drawn back from his teeth. "Are you sure Veisi is thousands of years old?"

"Yes. Azazel recognized her from way back."

He pressed the tips of his fingers together, frowning at them. "Do you know why the Israelites were forbidden to consume the blood of any animal, in Leviticus?"

I wet my lips. "No."

"The further back you go, the stronger the Watcher... strain is. Their contribution to the human animal. It's much weakened after the first generation, the real Nephilim as it were...though you get the odd throwback of course, giants like Goliath of Gath. Maybe, just like there's four percent Neanderthal in non-Africans or whatever it is, there's a bit of angel in all of us. Maybe it's what makes us the way we are. But it doesn't seem to be exactly a DNA thing. Maybe it's not a properly biological thing at all, but it is carried in the bloodline. Like Original Sin."

"I'm Orthodox, remember. We don't do Original Sin."

He blinked. "Really? You lot don't believe in the Fall then?"

"That we are subject to death, yes. Just not that we have any innate tendency to evil."

"I see. There's optimism." He looked into his coffee cup. "The point I was making is that blood has powerful spiritual connotations, always has. It can cleanse. It is shed deliberately to pay for guilt. But other contact with it makes people ritually unclean. It's too powerful to be used casually."

It carries intent between the spheres.

"Okay," I said cautiously, not sure where he was going.

"There's Watcher blood in animals too, or there was for a long time. The Bull of Knossos, the Horses of Achilles, the Roc, the boar Twrch Trwyth, the Glas Gaibhnenn cow back in Ireland…"

"Oh," I said. "Eww."

"You're not the only one to think that way. The strongest, the best, the most flawless of beasts…they were the ones that had to be sacrificed. Firstborns too, though we aren't sure whether that was just superstition or whether there really is a connection. Anyway, it's no longer really relevant. We seem to have mopped up the animal strain. The thing is…it was considered important, vitally important, not to let people drink any blood that the Watchers might have tainted."

"Why not?"

"It prolongs life. Not for everyone you understand. I doubt it'd do you or me any good. But for one of the Nephilim to drink the blood of another—or generational relatives—would allow them to carry on indefinitely. Power adds to power. We're told they were incredibly violent, and they fought each other as well as killed humans. *And when men could no longer sustain them, the giants turned against them and devoured mankind. And they began to sin against birds, and beasts, and reptiles, and fish, and to devour one another's flesh, and drink the blood*, says the *Book of Enoch*. So if Roshana Veisi is as old as you say…" He trailed off, his silence as loaded as his words.

I shook my head. "She's been drinking blood? What, like a vampire?"

"I guess these stories have to come from somewhere."

"And whose? If there were loads of Nephilim kicking about still, wouldn't we know?"

Egan looked pained. "Well there's one obvious solution to the lack of tainted blood."

"What?"

"You breed your own."

"What? You mean—her chil—" I shut myself off and bounced up from my seat, too horrified to sit still. "No, no way—no woman would do that!" But as I paced in a small, desperate circle I couldn't help picturing all those children's portraits in the back hall. *If she did it, if she memorialized them, for God's sake...then she is totally fucked in the head.*

I sat down again, gracelessly. Egan was watching me, his face pulled into lines of concern. The question that had been gestating under my breastbone clawed its way up into my throat.

Honeycomb.

"What would happen if one of the Nephilim drank actual angel blood?" I asked.

He chewed his lip and drummed his fingers on the tabletop. "I've never heard of such a thing happening," he said with great precision. "Do you believe that's what Veisi is planning?"

That was what he thought, quite clearly.

"Penemuel's wounded. But I can't believe Ur— that the Adversary would allow that," I muttered, more to myself than to my companion. "I can't. He doesn't think much of the Christian Church but he follows his orders, that's what he says. The Divine Plan. If he's enabling her to… Oh, that really is a marriage made in Hell."

"It's not good. Now what I really want to know, Milja, is

why you're telling me this."

"What?"

"As you say, what you've just described is a situation largely to my advantage. Your man is trapped—or at least gone to ground, and not currently presenting a danger to humanity—and that's exactly what my people have been trying for all along. Veisi is a wild card, but that's a separate issue. You're far from stupid. Why would you tell me all this? Why would you tell me where he is?"

I pressed my damp palms against the laminate. "Because you're going to help me save him."

Sixteen
COLORS OF THE FALL

Egan sat back, holding his cup like he was about to raise a toast. "Right so. This is going to be interesting."

"Azazel is trapped, sort of, but he can break out anytime he chooses to ditch Penemuel. Or if she dies. I think he's keeping her alive, but that's all—if he could have healed her, he'd have done it by now for certain. He's keeping her going, and me and Roshana are keeping *him* going by paying him attention. Just about, anyway."

"Okay."

"The moment that balance slips and she dies, he's going to come back and he is going to be *pissed*. You think he's been vengeful up till now? You have no idea! Christians killed his angel BFF?—he will set out to teach them a lesson with *extreme* prejudice. Do you get it? Azazel has been restrained so far, believe it or not."

Egan blinked slowly.

"Right now you're thinking about calling in a Vatican SWAT team and taking him out while he's at his weakest, aren't you?" I picked up a fry and jabbed it in his direction. "Two Watchers for the price of one, as well? Thing is, you don't know where he is. That's a whole big forest out there. And Roshana is not going to let you guys waltz across her land and take her daddy away from her. She is way more dangerous than she looks, I can tell you."

Egan's eyebrows rose and he inhaled through his nose, but he waited.

"But the real reason you're going to help me is that you need Penemuel alive and onside. You can leave Azazel to me. *If* you weren't just bullshitting me about a negotiated solution, then she's the one you have to save."

"Really."

"*Really*. She's smarter than he is—even he'll admit that. She thinks stuff through more than he does, and she's more cautious, and she worries about long-term consequences. She's interested in books and the betterment of humanity. She's the one you can negotiate with."

I shut up, holding my breath.

For a while Egan just looked into my face, as if trying to weigh my soul. "But will your man listen to her? Especially if I'm in on this?"

"He doesn't know your full involvement back at the monastery. I never told him. He thinks you were just bait."

"Well that explains why I'm still alive, I guess." His voice was low and unnaturally calm. "But that's not the incident I was thinking of."

I blushed, to my own surprise. I'd thought I was all on top of that memory. "He's not jealous, not like a normal guy," I mumbled. And that was true enough as far as it went. I knew Azazel felt a wicked proprietary pleasure when others were turned on, whenever he put me on sexual display. He'd even indulged Egan in a cruel threesome (kinda-sorta-only-that-once-and-we-will-*never*-mention-it-again), of course. I didn't suppose he could even picture ordinary human men as rivals. Quite how far his kinky tolerance would stretch if his ego was genuinely threatened, and it wasn't just a dream but real life sex, I didn't know. "He's complic— No, not 'complicated,' no. Just *different*. And if we save Penemuel, he'll be grateful. He knows what gratitude is."

"I have to say that from my perspective he comes across as a selfish, sociopathic dick—"

"He saved your life, remember? When you got shot."

"Yeah. But, to continue, I do trust your judgment, Milja. If you see something in him—other than the *obvious*,"—Egan pulled the face of a straight man trying to grudgingly acknowledge another guy's penis without actually picturing it —"then I have to accept that he may have his finer qualities."

"Wow." I smiled weakly. "Breakthrough."

"I said '*may*'."

"Thank you."

"Don't break out the balloons and the streamers just yet. What exactly is it that you want me to do?"

"Get me to their physical location. I've got the best maps I could buy, but it'll mean going across country, and there's no way I can do that on my own. Plus, Roshana's got armed security, and you know what Americans are like about trespassers."

"Sounds like my skillset, sure."

"We need to save Penemuel. Angels, even fallen ones, need care or attention or love, however you want to put it, and I think if they haven't got God they need humans instead. We're the ones with the divine spark. Even the Adversary keeps his icons in churches, under his archangel name. So we need to need her to get better." I thrust out my lip. "I wish I'd thought of a better way to say that. But you get the idea, right?"

"Yeah."

"Then when she's okay, we can talk. Are you in?"

"I'll think about it." He pulled his wallet out and shed some bills onto the table.

"What?"

"Milja, you've just proposed me setting *two* Watchers free on the world."

"But it could fix everything."

"It could. Though I can't see we'd be negotiating with her from a position of strength. Which makes me nervous."

"You've got hostages. Worst case scenario, you can kill them."

He looked at me, not blinking.

"Come on, the various religions have to be holding on to nearly two hundred hostages across the world. Don't tell me you hadn't thought of that, Egan, because I just won't believe you."

He sighed. "I'm a little surprised you did, that's all."

"Yeah well, hang around with ruthless people long enough and some of it rubs off on you."

"Am I that ruthless?"

I don't know. "I meant Roshana," I said, breaking eye contact.

He rubbed his forehead. "Okay…as I said, I'll think about it. It's late. Shall I walk you to your car?"

"My cabin's actually just across the road there. Thank you."

We walked in silence out across the parking lot, not too close to each other. He'd held the restaurant door open for me, but been really careful not to brush against me. The stars overhead were partly occluded by wispy cloud, and I could hear pines sighing in the night breeze, but this spot seemed sheltered. It wasn't that cold, not as a mountain-bred girl like me thought of cold, but Egan jammed his hands into his sheepskin pockets like he was scared of what they might do unfettered.

We crossed the road into the cabin complex. My desire to bury my face against his chest was so fierce it made me dizzy, and I knew I really wasn't mad at him anymore. I took a gulp of night.

"Egan... Will you forgive me for what happened in the hotel? Please?"

He stopped, but it took a moment before he could turn to face me. "Forgive you? Are you sorry it happened?"

"I'm sorry I hurt you. I'm sorry I betrayed your trust." That was as far as I could go. I couldn't lie to him.

He sighed. "Milja, you're not the one that needs forgiveness."

"You think *you* do? Oh come on, no."

"I wasn't honest or open with you since the start. I led you astray. And I put you under...pressure."

"Egan..." It was hard to keep the frustration from crackling through the pain in my words. "Stop doing that, please."

"Doing what?"

"Acting like I'm the victim every time; that it's never my decision, it's always Azazel or you making a fool out of me. Like I've got no idea what I want, or what I like."

His face, in the glow of the distant security light, was a mask.

"Yeah, you could have been more honest. But I did what I

did because I wanted it, and I'm really sorry that I got it wrong but you didn't make me. I enjoyed doing it."

"That's no guide to what's right," he said hoarsely. "Just the opposite."

He's got love and guilt more confused than you can imagine.

"You know I love you, don't you?" It must have been the least romantic confession in the history of the world. I said it in despair, because it was the only way I could think of to get through to him. *When all else fails, girl, try the truth.*

"Milja… Oh, that's not good for you, or for me." The mask was rigid, unchanged, but in the weird light I could see the gleam of a wet line down his taut cheek. "And it's not an excuse."

I felt my lungs crumple inside me. Somehow, despite all that I'd been through, I'd held on to a girlish faith that love solved everything. That all it took was the magic words and the world would flip around and *ta da* everything would be fixed.

It had fixed nothing.

He saw me back to my door and left without another word.

I lay on my bed and stared at the varnished planks of the ceiling, and dared for the first time to try and get my head around the fact that I loved, craved, cared and lusted for Azazel—and that I felt all those things for Egan too.

It made no sense to me. Love was all-consuming and all-excluding. Wasn't it? That's what I'd been told all my life. You knew that you loved someone because they made you feel complete. Two people making one whole. One flesh.

That didn't leave room for a third.

How was it that I could be aching for them both?

༄

Egan took me to a big sports outfitters to buy outdoor gear fit for a few days in the wild. Rations, packs, fishing line, a pup tent he could carry, sleeping bags, warm and waterproof clothes in autumnal camouflage colors, mosquito repellent; the whole shebang. He also stocked up on ammunition for a pistol which he apparently already owned, and chose a hunting slingshot that looked to my jaundiced eye to be made of equal parts NASA engineering and machismo.

He tried to pay using his card, but it was declined by the machine so I bought the whole lot with cash. I didn't even feel guilty anymore.

"What's up?" I asked as we wheeled our trolley out of the store and he slipped his credit card wallet back into his ass pocket, grimly.

"That's the office pulling on my leash. They want me to report in right now."

"Are you going to? Yes-or-no answer, please."

He sighed. "No."

"Good."

"Not yet."

"Oh for goodness sake…"

"Look, I'll need to get back in contact at some point. They're my superiors, and I don't have any choice. But I'll wait until we have a result with Penemuel. Will that do you?"

"I suppose."

"Fine. We're going to be on our own out there, you realize. No backup. No cavalry."

"We won't need it once we've got Azazel."

"Yeah, feel free to imagine how that fills me with enormous joy and anticipation."

The wilderness landscape of the Minnesotan Great Woods meant that we couldn't get anywhere close to our goal by road, not without coming at Roshana's ranch head-on. We drove up to a village a few lakes over, using Egan's vehicle since I was worried mine might be recognizable. I didn't know what the two hitmen had reported back, or how long Uriel had condemned them to blindness, but I had to work with the assumption that Roshana knew I was still alive.

There was a long-distance walking trail that started from behind a diner where we left the car, and before we set off we made sure to give the impression of just another hiking couple out to spend a few days enjoying the colors of the fall in all their glory. Three hours up the trail we struck off southward across country, disappearing amongst the trees.

We didn't talk much for the next three days and two nights. Egan wanted us to move as quietly as possible and pass unnoticed. Truth be told, it was hard enough work just walking with all our gear that I didn't have much breath to waste, so I put my head into neutral while travelling and just followed the big rucksack in front of me, letting my hindbrain take care of my footing through rock and bog and undergrowth.

The weather had turned again and we were getting the full fall show now; brilliantly sunny days and crisp nights that flirted with frost. If it hadn't been for where we were heading, our little expedition would have been pleasurable. I'd grown up in the mountains of Montenegro and a big part of me missed the wilderness now that I'd moved to the city. The trees here seemed to be in competition to flaunt their fiery colors against the cerulean sky, so that we walked across drifts of copper and under showers of gold. Sometimes it was so beautiful that I couldn't help stopping to gape in amazement, or to snatch at a leaf as it flickered past me like a gilded sprite. Then Egan would turn and stare at me and I would muffle my brief impulse of delight, embarrassed.

But all the time Azazel lurked at the back of my thoughts, a great black thundercloud. I walked in brilliant sunlight, but my heart yearned for the darkness.

By the time we'd pitched camp at the end of each day I was too tired to want to talk. We'd eat and then I'd crawl into my sleeping bag, aching all over and with most of my clothes still on, and pass out so soundly that I didn't even hear Egan follow me in. I was far too tired to have inappropriate impulses concerning the big warm body pressed up against mine in sleep.

I can't vouch for his thoughts, but they were his business. We had reached a state of truce which we both seemed able to cope with. We needed each other and we had feelings for each other that we could do absolutely nothing about, and those were the facts of the matter. For the moment we were companions, and for me at least it was a melancholy comfort to just be in his presence.

And I appreciated him anew, seeing him in action. Quiet and methodical and patient, his version of masculinity was everything that Azazel's wasn't. He read maps and landscapes easily, he could light a fire, and he fed us with fish he caught at dusk and dawn at the lake margins and with squirrels he brought down with the slingshot. The latter tasted much like rabbit.

"Good against Goliath too I hope," I joked as he scored a serendipitous squirrel meal for us from where we sat by the fire.

He smiled. "Want to try?" So I spent a half-hour whizzing ball-bearings at a tree trunk while he gutted and skinned and set dinner on to roast.

I'm not saying I was morally purified now that I'd made my confession. On the first morning I was brushing my teeth behind a bush when I glimpsed Egan walking back up from the lake, bare from the waist up, carrying his shirt and still damp from his splash-wash. The misty dawn sunlight cast a sheen on his muscles, and that sight made me nearly inhale my toothpaste, I admit.

It was a good job I had the walking to keep my energies focused elsewhere.

On the second night I woke up in near-total darkness needing to pee. I could feel Egan's solid back against mine through the separate sleeping bags that cocooned us, and hear the slow, deep draws of his sleeping breath. I didn't want to get up. I liked it lying there close to him, and I could feel the nip on my exposed nose that warned it was going to be chilly out there.

But there was no way I could drift back to sleep, my bladder told me.

Trying not to disturb Egan, I wriggled with painstaking slowness out of my bag and slid out into the night. The stars were hard points like silver nail heads beyond the thinning canopy of the trees, but the moon was nearly down. I thought of the Nails of the True Cross that had so nearly pinned Azazel, and I shivered.

He was out there, only a few miles away now. I'd dreamed about the cave again, just as I had done every night since the flight. I was dreaming deliberately, trying to make some sort of contact, but the details never changed. That stark white domed room, sticky with honeycomb; the two winged figures motionless behind the wall. I couldn't reach them no matter how hard I pounded on the glass. The only detail missing was that I didn't see Roshana anymore. But I tasted her gleeful presence, like a perfume lingering in the air.

I'm coming for you, Azazel.

IN BONDS OF THE EARTH

Feeling my way into my boots, I went off to take care of business.

Just as I got back to the tent, I paused at the flap, feeling the hair rise on the back of my neck. I hadn't heard a thing, but I was seized by the conviction that there was *something* out there watching me. I turned and stared into night. Without a direct, full moon, it was hard to make out anything but layers of shadow.

I went as still as I could, all motion leaching out of me into the earth. And as I stood, my pupils widened, and the cool gray light of the night bloomed on every surface until I could see trunks and branches and even individual leaves, the whole forest opening up as if someone had lifted a shadowy curtain.

There: under the trees, across the banked fire pit from the tent—a paler shadow, moving so slowly and fluidly that it seemed to flow into the open. For a moment I thought *Ghost*, but then the starlight caught on moist eyes with a hint of a green glow. It was a wolf—a big pale timber wolf, watching me. I could see its shaggy pelt and the tips of its teeth, exposed by the curl of its lip.

We had wolves in the Durmitor Mountains, back home. They sometimes killed sheep and the village shepherds hated them, but as a girl I'd had more sympathy for the wolves than the men, and less fear of them too.

Silently, Egan slid his arm around my waist from behind. I'd sunk so far into my stillness that I didn't jump, just trembled against him. His right arm extended over my shoulder, and the steel of the gun in that hand caught the night's ambient glow with a cold shine.

I heard a faint growl from the beast.

"No," I breathed, laying my hand on Egan's forearm. I

could feel his ridged muscles.

If I am a witch now, then I am of the night too, and witches have power over wolves. I focused on the animal's lambent eyes. *Go away, brother wolf. Do not come near us. Leave us be, and we will not harm you.*

The pale shadow flipped and vanished into the deeper darkness. I watched it run away among the trees.

"Wow," said Egan softly.

"Beautiful."

"Let's hope it doesn't come back, though."

"It won't." His arm was heavy on my shoulder and I twisted out from beneath it, turning to face him. I didn't know how good his night vision was—pretty good, I guess, since he'd spotted the wolf—but I could see every detail of his face down to the individual blond hairs of his stubbled jaw.

"Milja, what the hell's wrong with your eyes?"

"What?" I put my hand on his cheek, caught up in the marvelous clarity of my vision, and how handsome he was all tousle-haired from sleep.

"They've gone black. I mean, *all* black," he whispered.

"All the better to see you with," I laughed, but it was a nervous giggle and I dropped my gaze, self-conscious.

His left arm tightened forcefully around me, and I didn't resist. Though the night was cold, he felt blazing hot—and very strong. He was holding me terribly close, as close as a lover, but I was also conscious of the gun in his other hand.

The Church takes a very hostile stance toward witches, of course.

I could feel his heartbeat against my own breast. I could feel…

"Christ give me strength. Milja." He dropped me abruptly and turned away. "You should go back to sleep. I'll…sit up for a while. Get the fire going. We don't want the wolf to come back."

"Yes," I whispered. Falling to my knees, I crawled in under the tent flap. "The wolf," I whispered to the lining of my sleeping bag. The blood was racing in my veins, waking parts of me that exertion had quelled until now.

I stuffed my hand down the inside of my thermal leggings to comfort myself.

This is not fair. Goddamn, it hurts.

I pictured Egan coming into the tent behind me and seeing me lying like this with the curve of my ass up, my thighs apart. The fantasy warmed me further. I could see his expression in my mind's eye; that look of surrender as he gave in at last to his base instincts. He wouldn't say anything, I thought; there'd be no point in speaking. He'd just pull down my tight grey leggings to reveal my two bare cheeks and everything he needed in the whole world right there in between them, and then he'd take hold of my hips and pull my ass up and back to sit in his lap. I was so juicy already that he'd slip inside me with no trouble at all, giving me exactly what I so desperately craved. My fantasy was so intense that I could almost feel the physicality of his bulk inside me. He'd hunch over me under the ridge of the tiny tent and thrust until he'd filled me to every last inch, and then flood my own wetness with his spill.

Or no—that was more Azazel's way. Egan… Egan would flip me over so that he could look into my face as he pushed up between my open thighs. His hands would touch my skin like he was afraid he'd break me, and I'd writhe with impatience until the wet suck of my sex on his fingers drove away all doubts and made him lurch into action. He'd kiss me, his mouth oddly tentative even as he drove home into my depths, his eyes wide with helpless guilt, pleading mutely for absolution. I'd twine my arms and legs about him, pulling him closer, and he'd groan my name. I'd meet his mouth with mine and find him suddenly hot and ravenous, his kisses wild arrhythmic things through which we would both gasp for breath as his cock powered into me. And I'd forgive him everything—every hesitation, every betrayal—for the sake of those kisses and that beautiful, big, achingly-hard length thrusting, thrusting—

I came, alone, my hand trapped between my body and the tent floor. Fire flooded through my whole body. My whimper was a long-drawn-out sob of need and despair.

And then, even in the backwash of flames, I froze. Had he heard me? It was only a tent, and offered no sound insulation. Was he outside right now, listening?

I heard only an autumnal owl, screeching as if in mockery.

☙

The next morning I saw the first ghost. It was an old man in a blanket, sitting before a fire and singing nasally. Egan walked right past him without seeing or hearing a thing. I glanced down into the man's face as I walked past, and saw a cluster of pox lumps at the corner of his mouth.

He didn't stop singing, but he frowned a little and his eyes tracked me.

Why do I see them? I wondered. *There must be a million dead people in Chicago, but I never saw anything. Just my father back home, and that girl in the tower in Montenegro—but I didn't see the Turks chasing her. I suppose I might have been related to her somehow. But not to these people here. Why am I seeing them?*

The ghosts were more and more numerous as we pressed on that day. We came down into that little valley of Roshana's from the far end, following the map and going nowhere near the track from the ranch. Our pace dropped as we took more caution, moving through cover wherever possible. There wasn't much of that; the trees here were almost bare.

"I think it might be that there," I whispered to Egan, pointing at a massive lump of rock jutting from the valley-side. It looked too different from this angle for me to be sure.

"Wait there behind that trunk," he told me, offloading the rucksack.

"I want to come."

"If there are guards..." He didn't need to finish the grim sentence. He checked he had gun and knife and slingshot, then set off at an angle.

I waited for what felt like far too long in the dappled sunlight, feeling my stomach churn, watching the slow fall of leaves and the last of the year's mosquitoes landing on my arms. I'd given up slapping at them since I found that I could quell the itch and inflammation of a bite with a touch and a focused thought. Now I only waved my hands to keep them from tickling my nose and ears.

It was better than looking at the scarred and suffering ghosts.

Why's he been so long?

Is he coming back for me? Or is he going in to find Azazel on his own?

Is he going to betray me again?

At last my anxiety grew too much and I jumped to my feet—only to see Egan coming back toward me. He held his finger to his lips so I knelt again until he crouched next to me.

I eyed the strange walkie-talkie in his hand. "Where's that from?"

"She has set a guard. I could only see the one but there

may be others. Come on. Leave the pack here." He dropped the radio.

We sneaked back down toward the rock. Ghosts lurked in every direction I looked. Just as I grew sure that yes, this was the right place, we passed a motionless body stuffed under a bush—and this one was real; that black uniform was too dark and too modern to be part of the phantasmagoria. For a moment I cringed, thinking the guard was dead, until I realized that he was hogtied with his own bootlaces. It was the guy who'd put a gun to my head once and come unnervingly close to it a second time. There was blood in his hair.

It might be mean, but I couldn't help hoping that whatever Egan had done to him, it had hurt.

Egan had his pistol out as he took the lead into the rock passage. We waited in the shadows, breath held, straining for any noise from within the cave itself as our eyes adjusted to the gloom. But we heard nothing. Then Egan ducked his head around the doorway briefly before pulling back.

"Arse," he whispered. "There's a camera set up in there—I can see the LED. We've got to assume we've been spotted. Let's do this quick."

I nodded, and we scurried into the round belly of the tomb. Egan gave it a once over and remained by the door on watch, but I peeled wide my inner eyes so that I could see everything clear as day, and walked right in.

The static charge in the atmosphere made my hair rise and crackle. All of a sudden it was hard to breathe.

We were the only humans in here; that was a good start, I thought. The ghosts still hovered over the pile of bones, shifting restlessly, but they were no more than a distraction right now. In the center of the chamber, just as I'd dreamt it, Penemuel lay supine on the stone slab that covered the pit, and Azazel knelt over her with his hands on her breast. Neither was winged of course—I only really saw them winged in my dreams. They were naked and gray, like stone. For a moment I thought it an artefact of my enhanced vision, but as I approached I realized that they really were horribly bleached.

The tiny camera mounted on the wall died with a sharp crack as Egan put a steel ball-bearing through its lens.

I reached across Penemuel to put my hand on Azazel's shoulder and a static spark flitted from my finger, making me jump. What should have been muscle felt far too cold and hard for flesh, more like boiled rawhide. Even his unkempt hair was stiff, like horsehair soaked in plaster. His eyes were opaque and sightless.

I'd never seen anything quite like this, even when he was starved and weak, and it creeped the hell out of me. "Azazel," I whispered. "I'm here."

No flicker of recognition or even life rewarded me. I couldn't see either of them breathing.

Penemuel was dead-eyed and gray too, except for the wound in her chest, which was black and sticky like tar. The gag still stretched her mouth and the Roman spear was still lodged firmly in her sternum. Azazel's hands were clasped around the iron head and the wound as if trying to staunch the blood that had welled up and congealed all over his fingers. The spear shaft was black with dried blood all the way up.

I circled the scene with horror. They looked more like some vile art installation than living beings. Then my foot kicked over something that sounded like glass as it fell. I looked down. Bottles. Empty Jack Daniels bottles.

Something else.

I'd come far enough around now to see Azazel's back. He'd been wounded by the spear too, of course, and it hadn't healed. A ragged hole remained, and from that hole protruded a plastic tube which drooped down to one of the bottles.

The bottle was half-full of bright crimson blood. As I picked up the loose end of the tube, a single drop slipped out and spun into the dust like a tiny autumnal leaf.

Seventeen
ONLY BLOOD IS FOREVER

You know, I think I'd assumed that even if Roshana was cruel and crazy enough to *take* blood instead of, say, asking for a donation, that she'd have taken it from Penemuel. Not her own father.

"Egan," I said, "Oh *fuck*. She's been bleeding him!"

"What?"

I wrapped my hand around the tube and pulled it from the wound. I didn't stop to think if this was safe, or wise; I just wanted the horrible thing out of him. It was tipped with valve and a wide-bore cannula needle. I thought I was going to throw up. "Look," I gasped.

"Ah shite."

The wound dribbled a little more blood, then stopped.

"Egan, you have to come over—"

From outside came a faint shout. A man's voice. We weren't alone anymore. Maybe we'd missed other cameras hidden in the trees.

"Stay," said Egan grimly, gun up and heading for the

arch. He slipped out into the passage while my mouth still hung open.

"No," I whispered, "I should go—" but it was already too late. "Crap," I hissed. I was alone and holding a bloody transfusion tube—but my entire plan entailed Egan being in here. I needed him to be the one to rouse Penemuel.

And yes, I hadn't explained that bit to him as fully as I might have. Here was a beautiful naked woman, badly injured and in dire need. Egan might not like the news, but he was tailor-made for this situation—how could he help but want to save her? Whereas I… I'd had a plan, yes, and I wanted it to work, but all my feelings right now as far as angels were concerned began and ended with Azazel. I had nothing over to spare for Penemuel.

I dithered hopelessly as my plans fell apart, running first to the door to hiss, "Come back!"—but the light was blinding in my sensitized eyes and Egan had already moved out of range—and then back into the shadows to grab at Azazel, as if I could wake him by slapping my hands on his leather-hard skin. "Azazel—please!"

A fusillade of shots peppered the silence out there and I felt my own blood run cold.

Oh no, Egan. I dropped the tubing—probably on to Penemuel, I frankly didn't care—and seized Azazel's unyielding face between my palms. "Help me, please! I'm here, Azazel! Help me!" Then I kissed his lips. "Azazel! I love you!"

It had worked in the monastery in Montenegro. It had given him the strength he needed. It didn't work this time.

Now he might as well have been a mummified corpse. For all I could tell, he was.

Milja, do what you came here for, I told myself. I flopped to my knees and for the first time laid hands on Penemuel—

on her belly, and her shoulder. For all her feminine beauty she was no softer to the touch than he was, and with the open doorway at my back my skin was crawling, but I tried to compose myself.

"Penemuel, I'm here for you." I muttered the words out loud just to save myself from hearing what was happening outside. "We came hundreds of miles and walked three days to be here for you. We went thousands of miles to Lalibela to bring you up out of the darkness, we fought, we bled, we suffered through captivity—all for you. You are precious to us, to Azazel, to the world. You are the key to peace. We need you. Come back to us."

I meant it all. Maybe not for the right reasons, maybe not unselfishly, but I meant every word. Penemuel could save Azazel and Egan. That was enough for me.

Beneath my hands I felt the kick of a pulse, like a single knock against the wood of her hide.

I kept repeating, "We need you. Come back to us."

"Honey," said Roshana bitterly behind me, "I should have known."

I turned on my knee.

Roshana stood with the seep of the outdoor light framing her, setting her hair alight in a cold blond halo. She was accompanied by Egan—in as much as she was holding his prone body up by the scruff of his jacket, without any apparent effort. His head hung limply toward the floor. As she took a step into the chamber, dragging him, I could make out the cluster of round red bruises on her otherwise beautiful face.

Well damn, at least Egan had the chutzpah to shoot her in the head, I thought bleakly. What a shame she had her father's immunity to weapons, now that she'd drunk his blood.

"You just had to interfere didn't you?" Roshana complained, though God knows that given our relative positions her resentment didn't seem justifiable, not from where I crouched. "You couldn't leave us alone? He's my father, but oh no, you couldn't let me just have him and be happy. You selfish bitch."

"But you're killing him," I squeaked.

Roshana let Egan fall, and to my relief he grunted and twitched as his face smacked the rock. At least he wasn't dead yet.

"He left me," she snarled. "He burnt me and then he left me for dead—*Again*. He left my mother to die. I wait all these centuries for him to find me and then he dumps me for some cunt he just wants to fuck." Her voice shook a little. "He's supposed to be my *father*."

Oh God, Roshana.

She thrust her hand at the gory diorama. "He deserves this. He fucking deserves it all. Anyone can see that. Even you, surely?"

My jaw sagged. I couldn't argue with the six-year-old child trapped in this woman's immortal body. I wasn't even sure she was wrong. All I could say was, "*They* don't."

"What?"

"*They* don't deserve this. Penemuel doesn't. Egan doesn't. Let them go."

She glanced down at him. He'd managed to roll groggily onto one side. "He shot me."

"He was just trying to protect me."

"Like you matter." Her mouth twisted, like the butterfly's wing beating at the heart of a hurricane. I saw the impulse surge through her limbs; she seized and lifted his ankle high in one hand and shoved down on the side of his knee with the other. The pressure exerted was precise, almost neat. I heard the bone snap a split second before I heard Egan scream, and then my voice joined the cacophony too.

Well, that brought him back to consciousness. He flailed around, trying to grab her perhaps, so she took a half-step away and simply stamped on his other leg. I felt the blow through the rock beneath me, as if she'd struck him with a sledgehammer. I screamed and covered my ears, screwing my eyes shut.

When I opened them Egan had collapsed into retching, his open mouth pressed to the rock and his lower legs at insane angles. His fingers clawed at the stone beneath him.

"You fucking psycho," I gasped.

She laughed.

"If you were my kid I'd have cut your throat, never mind disowned you." I was grasping for words that would hurt, and those at least wiped the smile off her face. She strode across the chamber, grabbed the front of my camo clothing in one hand and hefted me to my feet.

"Going to put your eyes out," she told me flatly as she raised her other hand, middle finger pointed. "Going to smash your teeth in and pull out your hamstrings and keep you alive so you can feed him for years and years and years. You could have fucked off and lived happily ever after, but that wasn't enough, was it? You couldn't stay out of my hair. Well—"

Something dark sheered along her temple and bounced off into the shadows, only just missing my face. Bright blood spurted from the cut.

She forgot me for the moment, throwing me down as she whirled. I saw Egan—thank God for him, my white knight. He was up on one elbow, the slingshot in one shaking hand as he groped about him on the floor for another stone.

I knew she was going to kill him then. I saw each pace she took as if in slow motion.

I grabbed for the only weapon within reach, the spear of Saint George, heaving it out of Penemuel's chest; and I ran at her back as she loomed over Egan and kicked the slingshot from his hand. She broke a few more of his bones then, but who was counting?

At the last moment she heard me, or felt me, or knew from the look in Egan's eyes that I was behind her. Maybe it was just her father's warrior instincts in her. She turned, contemptuously, which is why I got to see her expression as the spear-point bit under her chin and punched clean out of the top of her skull.

Blood counts.

The holy relic was covered tip to toe in Azazel's blood, and what will hurt an angel will hurt their child. She died, I think, almost instantly.

I let go as the spear became too heavy for me to hold up. I staggered back and kept going, all the way to the wall of the chamber.

Then I threw up everything I'd eaten that day.

When I lifted my head it was because Egan gasped my name. I looked across, my heart thudding so hard in my breast that I could hear it in my ears. He was alive, and I was so grateful that for a moment I mistook it for joy.

He was alive. He was pushing off Roshana's limp corpse, which had collapsed upon him, and the shakes had really taken hold of his frame. As I staggered in his direction he looked up at me again and groaned, "You angel," then let out a horrid barking gasp. I think it was supposed to be a laugh.

"Egan!"

He grabbed the spear shaft in one hand and the crook of

his elbow, and hauled it sideways. It wrenched free from her as he roared with pain and fell flat.

The ghosts at the other side of the chamber hissed and rose up.

Out of Roshana's body flowed something black, lying like an oil slick on the prickling air, gathering form. It was so dark, so utterly devoid of light, that in this shadowy place it looked more solid than rock or flesh or angel. It pulled itself up and I recognized its outline. Her outline. All curves, and delicacy, and wild tendrils of hair.

"Roshana, no!" I said as her demonic spirit turned and poured itself down onto Egan's face.

I screamed.

It *bounced*. There's no other word for the way it recoiled from him, and then hung for a moment as if stunned. I could actually see it shake its head.

Oh, I thought, panting. *He's consecrated ground. A priest, even a dirty sinning priest, belongs to Someone Else.*

"What?" Confusion tinted Egan's barely-contained agony.

I pointed, though it was obvious that he couldn't see it. Only I could do that.

Ghosts and demons. Some gift.

Roshana turned toward me just as I realized that, unlike Egan, I wasn't under the aegis of the Church in any way.

I ran. I ran for the passageway, and I felt her at my back like a blast of cold foul air. I had some confused idea that maybe she couldn't survive in sunlight, but as I staggered out onto the carpet of leaves I felt chilly hands claw at my back, numbing where they touched. Ghosts turned and stared. I tripped on a rock and somersaulted down the slight slope, and as I tried to climb to hands and knees again she was on my back, her long throttling fingers around my neck, more in my hair, pulling my throat taut, her voice a poisonous hiss in my head.

Jealousjealousbitchyouwerealwaysjealousofmeeee

My wide eyes saw her impossible black silhouette above me against the bare branches and the sky, like a gateway into some infinite night beyond reality.

Mineheismineminemineforever

Around us the gray figures of the long-dead clustered closer, distracted from their ancient suffering.

NowIwillhaveyouandhavehimboth

"Help me," I begged through gritted teeth. My throat was so numb with the cold of her touch that I could hardly breathe. "She's the one that moved your bones."

Openwidewhorebitchcunt

One of the gray figures fell upon her from behind and embraced her, and where they met they melded into one. From my twisted angle below it looked like Roshana was absorbing the ghost—except that it left her dark silhouette a little grayer and a little ragged at the edges. She hissed, jerking her head from side to side as if trying to look behind her. More ghosts closed in, arms outstretched. I tried to prize her hand from my throat but my fingers couldn't even find her, and the cold chokehold seemed to be inside my flesh. The light was fading at the corners of my vision—was it lack of oxygen to my brain, or the massing figures of the dead pressing around us?

I will not let you in, was my only coherent thought. I carried it like a stone as the world around me shrank.

Suddenly, Roshana let me go. I pitched forward onto the thick mulch of damp leaves, sucked a breath full of woodland detritus, and then rolled to the side. The demon was writhing and flailing, trying to push the ghosts away, but they homed in on her like moths to a black flame, and every time one of them burnt up in her nimbus it ate away a little at her outline. She looked ragged now, and no longer as dark as the void but just dirty, like vapor.

Finally, she launched herself into the air, trying to break away by rising above them. They clawed at her from below, shredding her, and as the sun dazzled my eyes I wasn't sure whether that last tire-fire wisp of smoke escaped or simply dispersed.

&

I'm not sure how long I was out of it. Not so very long, because the light hadn't changed much by the time I swam back to consciousness, but long enough for the sweat to have cooled beneath my clothes to a horrible clamminess.

I was dog-tired. All I wanted to do was sleep. Every muscle ached and the inside of my throat felt raw. But I couldn't just lie here. I forced myself to my knees and then my feet.

There were no ghosts in sight. Just the bare trees, and the split in the rock. No sound from within. A stranger's body lay a little way off, face down and dressed like one of Roshana's men, but I didn't go over and look. I assumed he'd been shot.

Egan—are you okay?

My head filled with the memory of him, broken and bleeding, reaching out in his agony and wrestling the spear from Roshana's corpse. *Oh God—the spear. Egan—No!*

That short distance to the tomb half-convinced me that I was drunk, as the world dipped and spun about me. The rock felt solid under my outstretched hand, but the cave-mouth dilated and then shrank. I forced my eyes to adapt to the shadows.

Nothing had changed. The two angels were still locked in

their closed-circuit *pieta*. Roshana's corpse sprawled by itself in a wide and sticky pool of blood.

No, I was wrong—something had changed. Egan had moved over to the Watchers. He had crawled there, I realized as my breath caught in my chest; crawled there dragging his broken legs. I couldn't see the spear though, not anywhere. If he had intended to use it on Azazel, something had changed; something had stopped him. He lay now with his head pillowed on Penemuel's stomach. His boot-knife lay next to him, discarded, alongside a nasty twist of leather that I took to be her gag. As I got close enough I could hear his slow, labored breathing, each exhalation an ugly whistle as if there was something terrible going on in his lungs. His eyes were half-open, white slits of sclera.

He'd found the transfusion tube, I worked out. My brain seemed to be struggling to parse the scene before it. He'd stuck the cannula needle into his neck. And fed the open end into the spear-hole in Penemuel's chest. The plastic tube was a thin red line from him to her.

No, Egan, I thought, stooping to touch his face. *Oh no, that's far too dangerous!*

But that was the point, wasn't it? He'd done exactly what I'd asked of him in giving her love, and of course he understood sacrificial devotion way better than I did.

Penemuel was breathing. I could trace the rise and fall of her breasts.

I thought my heart might stop. This was too much to bear, that the world required such things.

I didn't touch Egan. I was scared he might die under my hand. Instead I went around and embraced Azazel. "You can stop now," I whispered, closing my eyes and pressing my face to his shoulder. I felt like I was dreaming even as I stood there.

"Egan's got her. You can let go."

My mind, heavy with exhaustion, was unable to resist the gravity of his.

☙

I am standing on an open hillside, in a blizzard. The snow howls around me, all but obscuring the mountain peaks. I can feel the cold, but it is faint and untroubling. They are his memories, not mine.

There's an elk. It is vast, prehistoric; sable-black and shaggy, the spread of its antlers like dead branches. It's pacing a circle, bellowing with rage, and the mist of its hot breath is pink with exhaled droplets of blood. It has been wounded just behind the ribs, but the wound has frozen.

There, in the center of the circle; another elk. But this one crownless and fallen, a doe, snow heaped up against her bronze flanks, her neck arched to brace her twisted head against the earth.

He is not angry at her, as I first thought. He is raging against the storm. Where he paces, the wind and the snow withdraw for a moment; ice melts, thin green grass shivers from the earth and flowers bloom. She is sheltered within a tiny pocket of spring. But he cannot keep the circle intact, no matter how fast he marches, and as soon as he passes the storm presses in again at his heels, scouring at the collapsed doe.

His sides are heaving with exhaustion, and icicles are hanging from the frozen foam on his pelt. His nostrils are crimson.

"Azazel!" I step up to the circle he's tracing, and he doesn't see me because his eyes are crusted shut with blown ice. "Azazel, stop! Stop now!"

The wind blows my words away.

I have to block his path to get him to notice me. He's

huge and stinking and primal, and his hooves shake the earth with every step. He will trample me down and never even know, I think as I lift my arms. His sweeping antlers are like the spread of an oak tree falling around me, wide enough that they miss, wide enough that I can step inside and grab his broad head.

He knocks the breath out of me. The shock of our collision runs through the mountain, launching avalanches. I cling to the greasy, shaggy pelt, digging my fingers under the elk's great jaw, searching out the body-warmth hidden beneath the hardened rime.

"Azazel!" I shout, and suddenly he has stopped bugling, the wind is silent, there is a vast and awful silence. "Stop! You have to stop! It's over! You've done as much as you can!"

He starts to shake.

"Let her go, my love! Let her go! It's finished!"

Now it isn't the deer's head, but Azazel's chest that I am embracing. He stands against me, trembling and taut. I can feel the hardness of his ribs, his spine, his long muscles. I can feel his skin slick with perspiration.

I look down at the doe, and she is nothing but a mound of snow.

Then the mound blows away into nothing.

Azazel roars in despair. I feel his hands knot in my hair, and as he drags my head back I look up into a face raw with fury and pain, tracked with tears, filthy and wild and savage. He can barely see me.

"Azazel—I love you."

His hands are biting and suddenly heavy. He's pushing me to my knees. He has defied the storm and lost, and he is dying, and this is the last bit of him left alive—this tangled knot of hurt and rage and passion—and I understand this even as he forces himself on me.

I understand, so I open my mouth and take him willingly even though he's desperate and unrestrained and his cock is too big and too hard, even though he's so forceful it hurts. But it's only pain, and I'm used to that. I like that, truth be told. I like that he is too much for me, too strong, on the very edge of unbearable. I have always liked this. His overwhelming need excites me, and his panic is so strong it catches me up with it and spins me into his hurricane. Roshana called me nothing but a convenient-shaped hole and there is a bit of my secret soul—as well as my body—that blossoms hot and wet at that thought, that wants nothing more than to be fucked, to be used, to be *his*.

My pain flashes like diamonds, infinitely precious. Just as he promised.

His thighs are stone hard under my hands. I'm choking. His ball-sack is a clenched fist. His cock is a spear thrusting for the back of my skull.

But this is my dream as well as his, and in that dream I can take it all the way. No matter how big he is, no matter how he batters my throat, no matter how hard his hands or cruel his urgency. His heat is my heat, his thrusts my pulse. I open to him without reservation, holding nothing back. If he tore me apart right now I wouldn't resist, nor feel any fear. There is some part of all of us that wants to surrender to God, I think.

And he is my god.

Then he is fire in my mouth, in my throat, in my core, and he howls above me and lets go and falls away, flat on his back in the glorious clean sweep of the snow, staring up wide-eyed into the brilliant blue sky.

The light bursts around us, tearing the breath from my

lungs.

※

When the hillside blew apart, we were at the epicenter.

I came back to my waking body coughing and gasping out grit, clinging to Azazel for support. The last aftershocks of my orgasm racked me as my eyes found focus. He stretched slowly and groaned in pain. Standing upright seemed to be the limit of his ability.

A pall of dust hung over the valley, blanking out the sun. Small chunks of rock—nothing bigger than a fist—were still thunking back to earth. The cave was gone, completely. Pulverized. We were exposed in the open. But when I looked for the trees I saw none standing, not within a hundred yards. We stood on the flat circle that had once been the tomb floor, and though that was untouched, beyond it a huge raw gouge had been taken out of the hillside. There were still roots and stones clinging precariously up there in the distance, or clattering down as they lost the fight with gravity.

Azazel lifted his head to the glow of the invisible sun and blinked hard. Color was running back into his skin.

"You okay?" I coughed. My hair was so thick with dirt that it felt like I'd been flour-bombed.

He nodded, flexing his fingers, every movement clearly costing him. Slowly he groped at the entry wound in his stomach, wincing a little. His attention drifted from his hands to my face and back again like a ghost, not latching on to anything. His eyes were mirror-silver again, deflecting my gaze. But he was alive, and that was half of what we'd come here for.

Egan. Oh God.

I looked around our feet. Egan lay further away than I'd been expecting, curled like a leftover bit of cookie dough on a floured board. I nearly fell over in my hurry to reach him.

"Egan?" The thump of falling stones had ceased, but a susurrus of lighter grit still encompassed us.

He smiled weakly up at me through the dirt. Blood had made a black crust around his lips. "Don't worry. She took the hurt away. I'm fine."

I looked at his mashed and ruined legs. They were so *not* fine, and they should still have been hurting. A whole lot. "Where's Penemuel?" I asked, wanting to demand her aid. "What happened?"

"She just got up and walked outside. Before…"

Okay, that sort of made sense—the first thing on Azazel's mind too, when I freed him from centuries underground, had been to get out into the light. She must be desperate with claustrophobia. Given the explosion, I hoped she'd got a long way off. I grabbed Egan's hand and he curled his ice-cold fingers in mine.

"It's all right," I muttered. "Just hold on." I was starting to shake. *Can I get Azazel to fix him? Will he—*

"Avansha." Azazel's voice wasn't loud, but it made my blood run cold. My fingers tightened on Egan's.

Roshana. I killed her. His little girl.

"Oh God," I whispered. I didn't dare look. I fixed on Egan's face, stroking his filthy hair back from his forehead.

Azazel's voice was stone and darkness. "What happened to her? Did *he* do this?"

That made me turn, because he meant Egan. Azazel was kneeling over Roshana's body.

"No," I said, my heart so cold that it could barely squeeze out a beat. I left Egan and stood. Every footfall I took across the waste ground between us rasped loudly in the still air. "Not him." I watched his shoulders tense as I stood at his side.

"Oh shit, I'm so sorry, Azazel."

"Who then?" The dust hissed and slithered in circles across the rock.

There was no way out. He knew already. I could feel the air around me turning cold.

"It was me."

Azazel's arm shot up and his hand closed around my throat. Tight. "My daughter," he said through bared teeth. "My only child."

I. Can't. Breathe.

"Let her go!" came Egan's weak shout.

My jaw was held so fiercely and at such an angle that I couldn't see Azazel's face, just the hillside above and the trunks of fallen, blasted trees through the thinning pall of dust. I blinked and pawed at his wrist.

"She was the last I had left—"

"Veisi was killing you," Egan yelled. "She was going to drink all your blood and make herself immortal, you stupid fecking gobshite! Put her DOWN!"

Azazel heard him that time. He sprang to his feet, dragging me closer, staring into my face.

I saw it. I saw him...*understand*. A scent, a stain, an imprint on my soul—I don't know how his vision works or what it is he sees, but he saw then, and I watched the realization dawn in his eyes like ink pouring into water. He looked from me to Egan and back again.

"You *hypocrite*," he breathed incredulously.

Please, I mouthed, my heart breaking.

He dropped me like I was a turd. In three strides he was standing over Egan and had hauled him off his feet, both fists bunched in his jacket. He might have been wounded and weakened, but he made Egan look like a broken toy as he shook him. "I've had enough of you now," he said simply.

"Azazel!"

"NO!" The command was like the crack of a whip.

The two of us who were capable of turning our heads did so, and stared.

Through the haze, from the ramparts of broken trees, Penemuel came striding, an autumnal goddess. She still looked frail, but she had rallied; she had drawn around her a cloak woven of myriad fall leaves, red and ochre and orange; a robe of fire. She was beautiful beyond words and her eyes blazed gold.

"Do not hurt him, Azazel!" she ordered. "He is mine!"

Azazel gaped.

"And we must leave now," she added urgently, as gilding touched her lashes and her skin. "Michael is coming."

"Michael is already here," said the warrior-saint, stepping out of the air with his rigger boots and his shining crystal sword. At his side appeared the Archangel Raphael; I recognized him from my vision at Burning Man even though he wore his hair a lot shorter these days, only down to his jawline.

Raphael carried a sword of sapphire ice.

"Are you ready to fight this time, Azazel?" Michael demanded. "Or is Penemuel to be your champion?"

I think that, in that first moment, Azazel just went blank in the face of all these conflicting demands. The shock was all just too much for him. Penemuel, thinking faster, took a swift sidestep that put her a little behind the other Watcher. And I don't blame her; she'd only just tasted freedom. The look of terror and loathing she fixed on Michael and Raphael would have melted glass.

"We must go," she muttered, laying a hand on Azazel's

arm.

"Come on, Scapegoat!" said Michael. "Have you forgotten all your courage?"

Azazel, to my profound surprise, ignored them both. He swung his attention to Egan, suspended in his fist. "Do you love her?"

"Yes," he croaked. No hesitation.

Oh Egan, you poor sweet fool. The little unclenching of my heart only made the blow that came next worse.

"Well I cannot, so take her." Azazel bared his teeth in a snarl more animal than human. "Do what you like with her—I give her to you."

No. No...

He lobbed Egan in my direction, overarm. I even tried to catch him, but only just managed to break his fall before he crashed onto the stone, and I went down too under his weight, cracking my elbow on the hard ground. Egan's head thudded bruisingly on my breast.

"Azazel!" I shrieked, but the sound that came from my dry throat was an empty whistle. And they were gone by then anyway, blinking out of the world in a flurry of dead leaves. "Azazel! Please!"

You can't, you can't, please no—don't leave me!

Only the two loyal angels remained.

"Hnh," Michael said, disappointed. He shot me a long dark glance, then bent and picked up Roshana's limp body in one hand, before tucking her under his arm and turning away.

"Wait," I gasped hoarsely. I didn't have time to worry about Roshana. I gestured down at Egan, who looked gray as slush and really wasn't moving now. I couldn't even be sure he was breathing. "He's one of your warriors. For God's sake, save him!"

Michael snorted. "I've given up saving your kind."

"You came to help him before!" I rasped at his back. "Years back—and he dedicated his life to you!"

"Michael," said Raphael reprovingly, the smallest of frowns tucking his brows.

His brother stopped midstride, then swung around and glared at us all. "Alright." Stomping across to where he sprawled, he put his heavy boot on Egan's chest. "For the Nephilim you've killed."

Egan coughed and took a sudden wheezing breath.

"Is that it?" I asked. Egan's legs were still at impossible angles.

"I stopped the bleeding," Michael said flatly, and vanished with his prize in a clap of gritty air. Raphael shook his head once and followed his example.

But that's not enough, I wanted to wail—only it was already too late.

I pulled Egan up into my lap, checking his pulse at his throat. When I was sure that it was working, if weak—and that, incidentally, the little puncture wound had healed over—I took some deep breaths and tried to get a grip on my fractured mind.

There was a lot to think about. Too much. A mountain's weight of guilt. A tsunami of panic and hurt. My battered body clamored for care as well. But I could perform miracles too; I could hold all those things off while I focused on what had to be done *right now*.

"Please, Egan, hold on in there."

His eyes stayed shut. If he was conscious of my voice, he didn't show it.

I kissed his bloody lips and looked up the slope. It was possible—in fact likely—that there was a vehicle up there, one or more belonging to Roshana and her men. But there was no way I could drag Egan up that far. And he couldn't walk. Even if he woke up, he couldn't walk on those legs.

Maybe he'll never walk again.

I could, in theory, try to heal him. What was the point of being a witch if you couldn't heal the ones you loved? But even if I was prepared to ride roughshod over his consent, I doubted very much that I was capable of getting any response out of him in this condition.

I could ring the emergency services, but it wasn't likely that Roshana's people would co-operate with intruders. In fact I was expecting more of them to turn up sometime. I'd need to find the gun and the spare ammo. We needed to hide.

I fumbled in his breast pocket and extracted his phone. Thankfully, the device was secured with his thumbprint and not a passcode. I pressed his limp hand into service.

Good. Bars. Frantically I scrolled down through his contacts list. *Please, please.*

He hadn't listed anything blatantly indiscreet and I didn't know the names of any of his military friends. But, stifling my despair, I found a Mr. Glassmaker. A long time ago, Azazel had told me that *vidimus* was a technical term used by the makers of stained glass.

I hit the green phone icon and listened to the dial tone.

"Hello, brother," said a man's voice. Not an American accent.

"Hello, Vidimus." I cleared my throat. "I have Father Egan Kansky here. He's really badly hurt, and we're on Nephilim territory." I looked down into his face, cradled in my lap. "You had better come and get us, straight away."

END

IN BONDS OF THE EARTH

To be continued in
The Prison of the Angels

JANINE ASHBLESS

ABOUT THE AUTHOR

Janine has been seeing her books in print ever since 2000. She's also had numerous short stories published by Black Lace, Nexus, Cleis Press, Ravenous Romance, Harlequin Spice, Storm Moon, Xcite, Mischief Books, and Ellora's Cave among others. She is co-editor of the nerd erotica anthology 'Geek Love'.

Born in Wales, Janine now lives in the North of England with her husband and two rescued greyhounds. She has worked as a cleaner, library assistant, computer programmer, local government tree officer, and - for five years of muddy feet and shouting - as a full-time costumed Viking. Janine loves goatee beards, ancient ruins, minotaurs, trees, mummies, having her cake and eating it, and holidaying in countries with really bad public sewerage.

Her work has been described as:

"Hardcore and literate" (Madeline Moore) and "Vivid and tempestuous and dangerous, and bursting with sacrifice, death and love." (Portia Da Costa)